A Huge, Dirty Pile of Money

Jerrell Deaver

This is a work of fiction. Names, characters, businesses, places, events, and incidents are either the products of the author's imagination or used in a fictitious manner. Any resemblance to actual persons, living or dead, or actual events is purely coincidental.

A HUGE, DIRTY PILE OF MONEY

ISBN-13: 978-0692980040

Edited by Kari Perlewitz
Cover art by Victor Guiza

First Edition: December 2017

www.facebook.com/ahugedirtypileofmoney/

Dedicated to my family.
I am grateful for your love and support.

A Quiet Jog

Stephanie Kenseth had just finished her second pass through the residence. She was both concerned and agitated. She took a deep breath and asked the house manager a question she feared she already knew the answer to.

"Where is the Vice President?"

"I don't know ma'am. I know he was here but I have not seen him in a while."

She could tell by the tone of his voice he was thinking the same thing she was. He's where he usually is when he's unaccounted for.

"Would you like me to find out who his driver is and find his location?"

"No, that isn't necessary."

∎∎∎∎∎∎∎∎∎∎∎∎∎∎∎∎∎∎∎∎∎∎∎∎∎∎∎∎∎∎∎∎∎∎∎∎∎∎

The text was received by Vice President Kenseth at 8:37pm on September 10, 2012. It read:

COME SEE ME TONIGHT. NOT TOMORROW. TRAVEL PLANS CHANGED. NEW GATE CODE IS 281904.

William Kenseth responded immediately.

He immediately placed a call to the Security Desk at Number One Observatory Circle, where he lived with his wife.

"Good evening Mr. Vice President. How may I assist you?"

"John, is that you?"

"Yes, sir. Is everything good?

"Oh, yes. Hey, I have decided to play cards tonight. Have a detail meet me in front of the house in 30 minutes."

"Yes sir."

John knew that 'play cards' was the Vice President's code language for take a jog. As a veteran of both the United States Military and the Secret Service, John found it amusing that the Vice President felt compelled to communicate in code. Everyone knew it was strictly forbidden for the Vice President to leave the Naval Observatory grounds without a full security escort. However, everyone also knew that he commonly did so in order to jog, usually under the cover of darkness. And almost everyone knew that his clandestine off-campus activities involved more than just running.

At 9:15pm the Vice President exited the residence onto the porch to find the two navy personnel who would serve as his escorts. Including himself, all three individuals, two men and one woman, were dressed identically in jogging suits common to personnel assigned to the Naval Observatory. The only way to distinguish the Vice President from the others were the cap he wore, his thick black framed faux glasses, and his faux mustache. Adorned with these items, and with his

2

hood up over this head, he believed he was no longer recognizable as the Vice President of the United States.

All three joggers were armed. Under their hoodies, each wore a shoulder holster containing a pistol. The security detail carried military issue 9mm side arms. The Vice President also carried a 9mm handgun, though it was his personal weapon: a Glock model 26. He preferred to carry his personal weapon instead of the larger military-issued pistols. The size of his weapon allowed him to frequently carry it concealed. He wasn't a paranoid person, but the concept of *enemies foreign and domestic* was never far from his mind.

The three joggers stepped off the porch of the one-hundred-year-old house to begin their run. Two SUVs exited the gate through which the joggers would soon follow. The drivers and passengers wore civilian clothes, but they were armed with two M4 carbines located at their feet. The SUVs would station themselves several hundred yards apart on the specified route, and as discreetly as possible, leap frog each other as the joggers advanced. The goal was to draw zero attention to themselves and the joggers.

As they ran, the joggers would each be separated by approximately ten yards, with the Vice President always staying in the middle. Everyone except the Vice President would be connected via ear wigs and microphones. The Vice President's late-night jogs were not uncommon, particularly when his wife was away, so the drill was well known by everyone involved. There was, however, one difference on this night that added an element of risk to the evening. The Vice President's wife was not travelling. In fact, she was expected back home by 11:00pm.

As was his custom, just as the joggers commenced stride, the Vice President indicated the route. "I need to visit the Japanese Consulate tonight" were his simple instructions.

They neared the familiar turn that would lead them to the Japanese Consulate, the lead jogger quickly took her position ahead of the Vice President. She then spoke into her microphone in a hushed voice. "We have a conjugal visit at 2529 Massachusetts Avenue." She turned right and increased her kick as she left the back entrance of the Naval Observatory.

The Japanese Consulate was located less than a mile from the Naval Observatory, a straight shot down Massachusetts Avenue. When the first jogger reached the driveway, her role was to stop running, and continue forward at a walking pace, as if resting. When the Vice President reached the driveway, the third jogger would also gear down to a walk, keeping the Vice President protected as he entered the access code into the keypad to the left of the driveway.

Once he was safely behind the gate, the escorts would continue to jog around the compound in a staggered fashion until the Vice President re-emerged. Typically, he re-emerged after about 30 minutes, however he has been known to "visit" for up to two hours. Everyone involved was hoping this would be a quick night, so they could return him home well before his wife Stephanie arrived and avoid an uncomfortable confrontation.

The Vice President entered the final digit from the new access code he had received from Aimi

Yamoto's phone, and the white gate swung open. Before entering, William looked over his shoulder at the third jogger and nodded once. This was all part of the routine. This nod meant that tonight would be brief. The escort felt a wave of relief wash over him as he slowed to a walk and continued down the dark, empty street. In a signal to the lead jogger, the rear jogger held up his right hand with his thumb and index finger close together, indicating a short visit. The lead jogger replied with a smile and a thumbs up.

William Kenseth began walking the 150 feet separating the gate and the front door to the Japanese Consulate. He always used this walk to help reduce his heart rate as he prepared to meet Aimi. Still feeling a little too warm, he unzipped his hoodie, revealing the shoulder holster underneath. He also removed the glasses and mustache and placed them in his hoodie pocket. He ran his left fingers through his hair, attempting to hide the effect of the hoodie on his thick mane.

As he walked closer, he noticed the house was darker than usual tonight. There were no interior lights on, and the external front door lights were also switched off. Did Aimi have a surprise in store for him?

He ascended the three small steps to the front door. As was always the case when he made his visits, he found the door unlocked. He was quite expectant as he closed the door behind him.

Neither the joggers outside, nor the drivers of the SUVs, saw the two muzzle flashes from within the consulate, even though the absence of light in the house caused the flashes to be quite intense. They also failed to hear two loud, staccato reports from the

Japanese Ambassador's pistol. This was likely due to the fact the Japanese Ambassador had attached a sound suppressor, an item legal in the United States but illegal in Japan, to the pistol he used to kill the Vice President.

The first person to know of the Vice President's fate, other than the Japanese Ambassador, was Stephanie Kenseth, the Vice President's wife.

Misdirection

Stephanie Kenseth's phone rang as she continued to search her home for her husband or any clues about where he might have gone. She grabbed her phone. It was William. Though she still did not know where he was, she felt a sense of relief, assuming he must be OK (and not in the arms of some other woman) if he were calling her.

"William. Where are you? I've been worried." She sat to remove her shoes, eager to see which excuse he was going to amuse her with this time.

An unfamiliar voice answered her. The male voice was terse and direct. "Mrs. Kenseth, you need to come fetch your husband immediately."

She reflexively stood to address this unknown threat. She tried to muster the strength to match the firmness of the caller's tone, but there was fear in her voice. "Who is this? Who is this, and where is William?"

"This is Katsu Yamoto, the Ambassador to the United States from the country of Japan. Your husband is dead. He is lying on the floor in front of me, inside the Japanese Consulate. He was shot as an armed intruder entering this residence under the cover of darkness. You may retrieve his body should you choose. If you are not here in ten minutes to do so, I will call the police to remove this piece of shit from my home."

The shock of the message she had just heard quickly overshadowed any worry or anger she previously had. One of Stephanie Kenseth's greatest skills was clear thinking in a time of crisis. She needed that now more than ever.

Before she could ask any questions, the Japanese Ambassador had hung up. She immediately dialed the Security Desk downstairs. "I need a car and a driver in front of the residence immediately." Technically, as the spouse of the Vice President, she did not have access to motorcade support. She knew this full well, and depending on who was on the other end of the call, she knew she might get pushback. She punctuated her command. "We have a situation. I expect a car and driver out front before I get outside."

Still wearing the blue suit she'd worn to deliver a speech earlier in the evening, she was outside before one of the two SUVs that had been shadowing the Vice President entered through the back entrance. Not noticing it, she began quickly walking in the direction of the motorcade building. The SUV sped in front of her from the direction of the back entrance. She was startled by the vehicle, which came to an abrupt stop in front of her. Seeing two individuals in the front seats, she opened the back passenger door and jumped in.

The driver, who she knew, turned to look at her over his right shoulder as she got in. Before he could speak, she was giving orders. "Take me to the Japanese Consulate as quickly as you can." The driver and passenger exchanged worried looks as the driver turned his body back toward the steering wheel and hit the accelerator hard.

As the SUV sped in the direction of the Japanese Consulate, Stephanie Kenseth had a moment to think. She hoped, then anticipated, the Japanese Ambassador had been bluffing about William's death. She assumed by his tone, and the late hour, and William's past marital indiscretions, this situation had to do with a woman. Presumably his wife. This theory was only further solidified by the obvious unspoken communication she had just witnessed between the passenger and the driver. She often wondered how people could think she was so stupid not to know what her husband was up to. The wife always knows.

It seemed like only seconds had passed when the SUV pulled into the Japanese Consulate's driveway. There were two unarmed guards standing behind the gate, which was opened immediately upon their arrival. The guards remained in place as the SUV hurried up the circular drive. They closed the gate after the vehicle entered, and did not allow access to the second SUV, which arrived seconds too late to follow the first vehicle in, and which Stephanie hadn't realized had been parked across the street.

Stephanie marched resolutely up the three steps leading to the front door, still holding onto the hope that the temerity of the Japanese Ambassador's message was a ruse; an effort to get her to come and find out what he had undoubtedly found out that night for himself. All the lights were on and the door was ajar. She could see the house lights through the crack between the door and the frame. The force of her body in motion caused the door to fly open wildly as she entered the consulate.

Only two steps into the residence, her anger turned to horror as she saw the contorted body of her husband on the floor, lying on top of the spilled contents of two planters. His right foot was up in the air, resting on one of the planters, likely upended from the concussion of his fall. His eyes were open, as was his mouth. The expression on his face was one of tragic surprise. His hoodie was unzipped, and revealed two baseball size blood stains on his white t-shirt. These stains were almost directly positioned over his now still heart.

"Oh, William!" It was all she could say as she slowly lowered to her knees beside her husband's corpse, gently placing her right hand on his left cheek.

Entering the building only seconds behind Mrs. Kenseth, Security Detail captain John Quinn saw what Mrs. Kenseth had not; the Japanese Ambassador sitting on one of the white couches just a few feet away. He was wearing a dark business suit. His legs were crossed, and he was smoking a cigarette. He looked as if he was expecting them. John's eyes darted between the two men, one living, one not. The Japanese Ambassador rose to his feet.

John remained where he was on the elevated foyer, and pointing toward the Vice President's body, he addressed the ambassador with a firm voice. "You want to explain what happened here?"

The Ambassador calmly and resolutely took two steps toward Mr. Quinn, then began speaking directly at him. "The individual you see on the floor began an affair with my wife, who was placed on a plane back to Japan several hours ago. I suspect, sir, you knew something about his indiscretions. Not only that, I suspect you helped this well-known philanderer enable his *activity*."

The Ambassador now took two steps to his right, allowing for a more unobstructed view of the Vice President's body. "Furthermore, this individual entered the Japanese Consulate tonight under the cover of darkness, unannounced and armed. He was shot as an armed intruder. I of course had no idea that the cat burglar I shot was actually the Vice President of the United States until I examined his body."

Mrs. Kenseth was now standing and looking directly at the Ambassador. He returned her eye contact as he continued to speak. "You were called here as a matter of diplomatic courtesy. I am certain that your government, and your family, would prefer to deal with this matter discreetly, in a manner that allows for continued cordial relations between our countries, as well as management of the public's perception of your Vice President's passing."

John Quinn's focus remained on the Ambassador. He did not know what to say. He knew the Ambassador's assessment of the events of the evening, and those preceding, were accurate. He was also fully aware the Ambassador was protected by diplomatic immunity.

Mrs. Kenseth's initial shock at the sight of her dead husband had given way to resignation. Through all the years of her marriage to William, through the countless affairs she knew he had engaged in, in the back of her mind she had always feared that death at the hands of a jealous husband would be William's fate. William didn't just cheat with random women. He sought out wives. The conquest of another man's wife was as thrilling to him as the conquest itself. She never suspected the end would be on a stage quite like this though, with national and international implications. As much as she wanted to kill the

Japanese Ambassador herself right now, the pragmatist inside of her appreciated the fact he had given her a chance to manage the situation.

Without looking away from the Ambassador she said, "John, we need to get William's body in the vehicle."

"Are you sure?" John replied tepidly, looking away from the Ambassador for the first time.

"Just get his body in the truck."

The man from the passenger's seat of the SUV had been standing in the doorway during this exchange. He now entered to help his colleague lift William's body. As they were doing this, Stephanie Kenseth walked over to the wall and with one swift motion, extinguished all the exterior lights.

William Kenseth was six feet three inches tall. With one man carrying him by the arms and the other by the legs, his lower back was just barely lifted off the ground. Stephanie commanded the men, "Whatever you do, do not get his blood on your clothes or on the truck. Put him down gently." She'd seen pictures of crime scenes before in which copious amounts of blood had exited the body of a person struck by gunfire. Based on the limited amount of blood on William's shirt, it was obvious he had bled out internally. She hoped he had lost consciousness quickly, and had not suffered as he died.

Still standing in the foyer she watched in the faint light as the two men placed her husband's body on the ground, opened the back of the SUV, then lifted his body into the back of the vehicle. As they struggled to raise his body to the height of the cargo area, William's head hung unceremoniously down toward the earth. After the vehicle's back door was closed, she gathered herself, turned and took several steps in the direction of the Ambassador. "Give me his phone. You called me on his phone. Give it to me."

The Ambassador reached into the right-hand pocket of his suit jacket and produced the phone. He took several steps toward her and handed it to her. As he did he said, "I am willing to forgive your husband's transgression against my family. I trust you understand my aggression toward your husband was necessary as a matter of honor." There was no remorse in his tone.

As he spoke, he remained on ground level. Standing on the raised foyer, Stephanie was several inches taller than the Ambassador. The feeling of looking down on her husband's killer gave her an irresistible sense of power. This, coupled with the anger and the sorrow she was feeling created an urge in her that she could not suppress.

As she took her husband's phone from the Ambassador with her left hand, she drew her right shoulder back as if she were turning to leave. Instead, she coiled her right arm and drew her clinched fist up to shoulder level. With all her strength, she launched her fist toward the Ambassador's face, and struck him squarely in the nose. The veracity of the punch combined with her elevated height caused the Ambassador to crumble backwards and strike his head on the floor. He was immediately knocked unconscious.

She remained in position and stared at him for several seconds. Though she closed her eyes as tightly as she could, several tears escaped before she regained her composure. She exhaled noticeably, and allowed several sobs to leave her body before regaining control. She then scanned the room before turning to leave. She noticed a cell phone on the couch, next to the spot where the Ambassador had been seated. She assumed it belonged to him. She also felt the Ambassador may have been despicable enough to have taken a picture of his victim before she arrived. She walked over to the couch and placed the cell phone in her jacket pocket before walking out the front door.

When Stephanie took her seat in the SUV, she put her chin on her chest and exhaled heavily. Had she been breathing in there? It didn't feel like she had. The SUV began moving toward the gate, which was opened as they approached. John stopped the vehicle as the driveway met Massachusetts Avenue. He turned to her and asked, "Where shall we take your husband's body Mrs. Kenseth?"

She did not immediately answer. She transitioned her view from the darkness of the floor in front of her, to the road in front of them. As she did, she finally noticed the second SUV. She stared at it for several seconds before turning her face toward John to answer his question.

"You will take the Vice President's body to Columbia Heights. Specifically, to Meridian Hill Park. Without being noticed, you are to place his body on the sidewalk. The Vice President was shot tonight while on a secret jog in Columbia Heights without his security detail." She paused before continuing. "The Vice President was shot tonight while attempting to prevent a mugging in Columbia Heights. As soon as you place his body, you are to re-enter the vehicle and call me on my cell phone. You will tell me that you have found the Vice President, and that you are sending a driver for me immediately." She looked directly at John. "Do you understand?"

John nodded his head once. "Yes, ma'am."

Mrs. Kenseth exited the vehicle and walked over to the second SUV, which was idling behind them. From the backseat, she gave instructions to the security detail to take her back to the Naval Observatory. She began scrolling through the contact list on her phone.

"Mrs. Kenseth, what happened in there?" Anthony, the driver, asked.

Without looking up from her phone she simply said, "No questions, please." She found, and called the number she was looking for.

"Hello?"

"Hello Louisa? This is Stephanie Kenseth. I'm sorry to bother you at this hour but I need to ask you, do you still live in Columbia Heights?"

"Yes ma'am. Why do you ask?"

"Louisa I need your help with something very important. Please listen carefully and do as I say."

∎∎∎

On September 17, 2012, William Kenseth's body was laid to rest in a very public ceremony in his hometown of Jacksonville, Florida. He was hailed as a fallen hero, having been tragically killed while coming to the rescue of Louisa Jenkins, a White House maid whom he recognized as being assaulted while he jogged at night in one of the most dangerous neighborhoods of Washington DC.

PTL

At exactly 7:59am Jeffrey Saint entered the conference room. His slender six-foot frame was characteristically adorned keenly with a razor-sharp crease in his tan khakis and a blue and pink plaid shirt that looked like it was being worn for the very first time. He marched to the front of the room smiling, without making eye contact with any of the PTL committee members. The low murmur from multiple conversations which had existed when he entered the room quickly died away as everyone now made their way to an open seat. Jeffrey had a well-earned reputation for starting his meetings on time and in a flash. Today was no exception. As soon as he reached the front of the room he addressed the group.

"Good morning ladies and gentlemen!" he said with a broad smile and with his sharp eyes now directed at the center of the room. He did not pause to receive a response.

"Thank you for your commitment to serve on the 2014 PTL Committee. The work we will do here is important, vital, and will have a profound influence on the 2016 presidential election. You are here because you are special."

He now paused and took a moment to make eye contact with each of the twenty attendees. "You were chosen to be here because of your commitment to two things: the Democrat Party, and winning. We are here to further the interest of the first, and ensure achievement of the second."

"For those of you who I have not yet had the pleasure of meeting in person, my name is Jeffrey Saint. I am Stephanie Kenseth's Executive Campaign Manager, as well as acting chair and founding member of the PTL Committee. To date, we have not yet branded nor have we put PTL on any of our material. Yet, you have been invited to be a part of this elite group. So, without any branding, you might be asking, 'what the hell is PTL?'"

With this Jeffrey stared blankly at the back wall, tilted his chin slightly to the left, raised his right hand in a cupped position and put it behind his right ear.

Silence filled the room. Without changing his body position, he repeated himself, "So right about now you might be asking yourself, 'what the hell is PTL?'" Jeffrey brought his chin back to a centered position, and now placed both hands in a cupped position behind each ear.

A few voices, nowhere in unison, took the bait. Mumbled but audible, they replied "What the hell is PTL?" A few chuckles followed.

Jeffrey's face now took on a look of bewilderment, fused with a smirk. Looking across the room he asked, "Is that all you've got people?" More chuckles. "Hey, I realize its 8:00am on a Saturday, but I need you to ramp up and ramp up quick! We've got a lot we must accomplish in a very short amount of time. And it all starts today!" he said while smiling, lightly pounding his right index finger on the podium in front of him.

The attendees were now sitting a little

straighter in their seats. Jeffrey smiled again and resumed "Now, take another shot of your latte or your tea or whatever it is that causes you to be coherent and repeat after me: I feel good!"

An enthusiastic "I feel good!" returned to him from the room, but not to his satisfaction.

"Now like you mean it: I feel good!"

"I feel good!" with enthusiasm reverberated beyond the walls and the closed door.

Jeffrey continued, "I feel fine!"

"I feel fine!" was returned to him with equal fervor.

Jeffrey finished, "I feel this way ALL the time!"

His audience, now fully engaged, responded in kind. Jeffrey smiled more broadly, leaned in and said, "You're a bunch of liars because nobody feels good and fine at 8:00am on a Saturday! But I love you and I appreciate you and together we are going to accomplish great things. Now let's get it going."

Jeffrey's face and tone became more serious. "Our job, on this committee, is to know our political opponents and their relationship with their base and the general population, better than they know any of these things themselves. PTL, by the way, stands for Pick the Loser. No one typically likes picking a loser, right? Well, just like the Vegas bookies who make a living picking losers, our job is to identify and promote the losing candidate, from the opposition's field of candidates."

"This strategy was effective in the 2012 Presidential election, when PTL identified and promoted the Republican candidate we felt now President Ingle had the best chance of beating. The idea then, and now, is to pick someone good enough to win the Republican nomination, but too weak to win against our candidate in the general."

"In 2012 when President Ingle was seeking his second term, he was vulnerable on a number of issues. We successfully identified the Republican candidate who was vulnerable on those same issues. We helped that candidate rise to the top of the Republican field. We helped install the candidate we wanted Ingle to run against. It was unprecedented, and it worked."

"This may sound easy on the surface, but it's not. That's why you're here. This strategy worked in 2012 and it can work again in 2016. In 2012, we were much less structured. Our committee, if you can call it that, was more free form. In this presidential election cycle, we are putting more structure and resources behind this PTL effort. Because Stephanie Kenseth is the front runner and presumed nominee, it is her campaign's privilege to recommend the PTL candidate to the National Committee. You were chosen to be here because of your historical, ideological and financial commitment to Stephanie's message. Congratulations on being chosen. I mean that sincerely."

"Our task is more difficult this election cycle. President Ingle's approval ratings are low and trending lower. There is genuine Democrat fatigue in the country. This will be a head wind for our candidate. Hundreds of Democrat seats have been lost in county, state, and federal elections during President Ingle's tenure. In addition, in certain circles Stephanie has likability issues. In short, people, getting the Democrat candidate elected, getting Stephanie Kenseth elected, is going to be hard as shit. But we're going to succeed, and we're going to do so because of the hard work and dedication of people like you, across this great county." Jeffrey paused momentarily. A smile now came over his face. "And there is nowhere I'd rather be, and no one I'd rather be with, than you great Democrats, right here, right now."

Jeffrey now turned and pointed his clicker at a laptop which had been set up before he entered the room. Immediately pictures of the faces of the four individuals expected to compete for the Democrat nomination popped up on the large screen behind him.

"In order to actually have a horse race, you must have more than one horse. As you know, Stephanie has been the presumed front runner for the nomination since Ingle selected her to replace her late husband as VP. Before taking on this role, she had a long history of being in the public eye, and is no stranger to the spotlight. Many people believe she was the brains behind William Kenseth's political career all along. When she becomes the nominee, she will be the first female candidate for President of the United States to represent a major political party. These gentlemen on the screen, bless their souls, are simply players on the stage owned in this presidential cycle by Stephanie."

Jeffrey now turned his body away from the screen to face his audience. "Let's examine the field of candidates she is expected to run up against."

He pointed his clicker at his laptop and 20 potential Republican candidates popped on the large screen behind him. A chorus of boos rose from the committee.

After a brief pause Jeffrey spoke. "So, which one of these reprobates do we want to run against?"

"It doesn't matter, they all suck!" shouted a woman seated near the front of the room. Mild laughter followed the outburst.

"You are both right *and* wrong" came Jeffrey's quick response. "You are right, they all suck. But you are wrong to think we can just pick any old one to focus our efforts on. It's not going be that easy!"

A hand went up in the back of the room. It was attached to John Wesson, a highly successful and influential blogger for various Democrat causes. This was his first exposure to this level of organized Democrat strategic planning.

Jeffrey addressed him directly, "Good morning, John. Welcome to the group."

"Thank you, Jeffrey, it's good to be here. You mentioned the strategy worked in 2012. For my benefit and potentially that of others, can you give some backstory as to what that looked like?"

"Certainly," Jeffrey responded. "Quick history lesson, people. What was the big issue in 2012 and leading up to 2012 that had the opposition organized and energized?"

"Healthcare!" came the response from several in the room.

"Exactly" responded Jeffrey. "The president's signature healthcare law put into place in 2010 with zero Republican support. President Ingle was vulnerable on this issue. This issue was the rocket fuel for the opposition's base. Our desire in 2012, our hope in 2012, was that the Republicans would nominate a candidate who was equally as vulnerable on this topic, thereby diluting the rocket fuel."

Several heads in the room began nodding.

"We succeeded in helping get Mike Russell to the top of their ticket. He was governor of New York when that state implemented a state-wide health care plan that had very similar characteristics to what the President and his team instituted nationally. Russell was uniquely disqualified to attack the President's healthcare law. We neutered their opponent on our champion's most vulnerable issue."

"Damn fine job!" rang out from the back of the room. Jeffrey acknowledged with a wink.

John nodded. "OK, I get that. I get how you identified a desired opponent. What I'm less clear on is how you influenced the Republicans to nominate him. I mean, I guess you could do that by rigging the polling machines during the primary election. But short of that, and I'm assuming we don't do that, how did you fulfill the strategy?"

Smiling, Jeffrey feigned incredulity in his response. "John, of course we don't rig the voting machines in the primaries. I mean, c'mon." He paused while laughter traveled through the room, then continued, "We only do that during the general election." Several more in the room laughed. Jeffrey did not.

"Seriously though, to answer your question. For all the money that is spent on political advertising, the single greatest influence on most people's decision making is the message put forth by the major media outlets. Note how I phrased that: put forth by. If the media does not latch onto a candidate, or help perpetuate the message the candidate wants out there, he or she will be doomed."

"Generally speaking, the people who comprise major media are our ideological kinsmen. We think alike, we value the same things, and we certainly share the opinion that the Republican Party and its ideas are very bad for this country."

Jeffrey continued, "So, to answer your question succinctly John, our candidate and the leadership of the Democrat Party can and do influence the amount and type of press coverage the reprobates receive. In 2012 we asked, excuse me, we encouraged, our major media friends to give Mr. Russell the lion's share of their Republican coverage, which acted as free advertising for their campaign and helped them win the nomination. Make sense?"

John nodded again. "Got it."

Jeffrey returned to addressing the group as he continued his speech. "This is a complex equation people. Our committee must identify the individual who is appealing enough to Republican primary voters to win the nomination, but is so unappealing to a majority of the general electorate that Stephanie wins. A classic *win the battle but lose the war* scenario."

Jeffrey again turned his attention to the faces and names on the screen behind him. Each of these individuals were considered to have the potential to win the Republican nomination for president. One at a time, he presented a short briefing of each candidate to the PTL committee. He went over their political background, any offices they've held, their strengths, weaknesses, personal baggage, potential scandals, and more. It was a lot of information packed into a few short minutes per candidate. Everyone followed along in the dossier they had been given upon their arrival to the meeting. It was a grueling, precise process... and it had to be.

After the presentation, the committee began debating the merits of the potential candidates. It was a delicate balance identifying the traits in a candidate who could appeal to the Republican base strongly enough to win the primaries and the nomination, but at the same time be weak enough against the Democrat candidate in the general election. As the group sharpened its discussion and focus, two names began to emerge as the preferred candidates to run against: Colton Tedie and Bob Steele.

Now that it was narrowed down to just two candidates, each was examined in a more in-depth fashion by the committee.

"Colton J. Tedie is an ex-major league baseball star. He parlayed a professional sports career into owning a national chain of fast food restaurants, which he later sold. He converted the proceeds into hotel and entertainment properties across the country, and later internationally. In seemingly all his professional endeavors, he has experienced marked success."

"Tedie grew up in Brooklyn, New York. His father managed several hotels, and his mother was a lifelong public educator. Colton Tedie was an outstanding high school baseball pitcher, and realized a childhood dream of being drafted by the Dodgers, whose original home before moving west was Brooklyn. He played his entire professional career, 12 seasons, with the Dodgers and was on two teams which won the World Series. His playing career was cut short by a shoulder injury."

"While in southern California, he met John Martinez. At the time, Martinez owned and operated a single taco truck near Dodger Stadium. They became fast friends. With his baseball earnings, Tedie financed more taco trucks, then a stand-alone store, then multiple stores, which later grew into a highly successful regional chain operating in multiple states."

"After his baseball career was over, Tedie sold his interest in the restaurant business and moved back to New York. Figures were not made public, but it is believed his share netted him $100 million. With these earnings, he leveraged up with debt, and invested in multiple hotel properties in the United States and abroad. He has built a successful brand, and continues to add new hotel properties across the globe."

"His latest business expansion is the creation of Tedie Media Group, which is producing multiple cable and premium sports news shows. He makes occasional appearances on these shows, and the episodes he appears in garner the highest ratings."

"He is a man that loves the spotlight. Though he has hinted at running for political office many times, he has no experience in politics. He is a frequent and outspoken critic of public policies which he believes hurt his businesses or the US economy in general. He is an outspoken critic Ingle, which is why many are speculating that he will make his run during this next election cycle. He is blunt, brutally honest, and doesn't play by the same rules as career politicians. If he doesn't like someone, he'll come right out and say it. At times, he can be seen as brash. At other times, he's just a plain old asshole. He is the opposite of politically correct, and is not shy about leveraging media to publicly attack his opponents. He has created many enemies as well as supporters through the years, because of his tactics."

"In summary, he is a mixture of political ignorance and New York arrogance, with the good looks and long hair of a man at home on a southern California beach. He is equally comfortable in a board room or street fight. To illustrate this, consider that for many years during his professional baseball career, he led the league in hit batsmen."

"Based on his public statements and positions, I believe he would appeal wildly to the populists in the Republican Party, which would propel him in the primaries. But the same lack of political experience which will appeal to the public will also likely cause him to fall short of his goal of becoming the next president. He doesn't know how to organize a campaign, perform well in a debate, or set down his business dealings to put enough energy into running for office. He's charismatic, but he falls short of being a serious contender for Stephanie. He could be the very opponent we need to propel our candidate straight into the White House."

Jeffery stopped to take a sip of water. He scanned the room to make sure his audience was still with him before continuing. "Bob Steele is also a newcomer to politics. He has not had nearly the exciting public life that Colton Tedie has had, though most would say he's made much more of an impact. Bob Steele, Dr. Bob Steele, had a spectacular career as a professor of neuroscience, rising to the top of his profession and gaining national notoriety, though in a small circle, for doing so."

"His claim to fame publicly and politically is his outspoken opposition to President Ingle's healthcare initiative. Without this platform, he would be unknown. Like Tedie, he is mostly a blank slate politically, so he does not have a legislative track record to attack. Due to his ethnicity as an African American, I believe the Republican Party will promote him to show how all-inclusive and racially sensitive they can be."

"Steele is also appealing to us because he is

significantly weak when it comes to foreign policy. If foreign policy is a weak point for our candidate, and I believe it is, then running against Steele negates that weakness."

"Finally, his national fundraising capacity is highly limited. I believe he can win the Republican nomination in a grinding contest. But it will require an inordinate amount of his resources to do so. He will be a wounded candidate in the general, due to a lack of resources and an appeal based on a single issue."

Jeffrey now closed his laptop and looked up. "Ladies and gentlemen, the floor is now open for discussion and debate on these two gentlemen."

Jeremy Lamb, a senior editor for the New York Times was the first to speak. "Tedie is our guy." Lamb was known for being judicious with his words, therefore when he spoke people turned an ear.

"I've known this pompous asshole for years. He is a shit storm waiting to happen. He can be goaded in to inflammatory rhetoric, I've seen it. Put him in front of an audience in the South talking about guns and the dangers of a federal government and he will fill every hickville high school stadium down there. And while he is working up their base in to a frenzy, every word he says will drive a wedge between him and people of intellect and conscience in this country."

The group was nodding and buying into Jeremy's reasoning. "Does the Times have historical material to create hit pieces on him after he wins the Republican nomination?" Jeffery asked.

"I can't tell you that for sure, Jeffrey. But with as many years as he has been in the spotlight, I'm sure they exist. I am certain we can find something."

"His carbon footprint has to be enormous, doesn't it?" asked Adilah Daher of The Weekly Standard. "He does not go anywhere unless he's on his jet. I am certain we could find stories of his buildings—his very large buildings, built for rich people by the way—and uncover how they were built with energy consumption and not energy conservation in mind. I feel good about our ability to cast him as an enemy to the environment."

Amy Patterson asked, "What is his view on immigration and Hispanics?" No one answered.

Jeffrey broke the silence. "Great question, Amy. The answer will be important. It is very possible, likely even, that he's employed some illegal immigrants throughout his career to get ahead financially. Exposing that would be great for us."

Leslie Lawrence asked, "Do we know his views on women?" Leslie was the West Coast President for the National Teacher's Union.

Lamb again inserted himself into the discussion, "Yes, we do. He's written a couple of books, and he's been interviewed a hundred times. Over the years he's made dozens of comments about women characterizing them in negative, sexist, and superficial ways. Most of those comments did not receive national attention because he did not really have national appeal at the time."

"If he were to make a serious run at the Republican nomination, two things would happen. First, we would resurface those past comments to the blogging and media community. For many people in the country, his comments would be new to them. Most people will be disgusted. There will be a genuine shock factor. And we would wait until he won the nomination to surface those stories. Second, the guy's mouth would be one of our greatest assets. He cannot help himself. In planned interviews and in public speeches we would only have to slightly broach the topic of feminism, and he would rush in and create carnage like a bull in a china shop."

Silent nods followed Jeremy's words. Jeffrey let the silence and contemplative process work through the room. He scanned every face for clues before continuing the discussion. "So, are we in agreement that Tedie is our primary guy?"

"Hang on, Jeffrey" interjected Laroy Fishburne. Laroy was the national director of Now Get Offended, a college outreach organization. Laroy's tone was skeptical. His backing and the involvement of his organization was critical. Everyone took note. "I need to ask a question. Tedie sounds like our guy. In fact, he sounds perfect. Even if we are unsuccessful in helping him win the nomination, we can paint this guy as the face of the Republican Party and that will be huge for us from a fundraising and public perception standpoint. But do we really think he will run? I mean, why is he going to want to run?"

Silence again. Everyone in the room began scanning faces, looking for someone to answer the question. Finally, a response came from Anthony Ianucci. Anthony was the President of the New York Construction Workers Union. He and his organization had had dealings with Tedie for many years.

"He will run because he has a maniac's ego. Running for the nomination, running with a chance to be President of the United States, will give him a rush unequaled in his entire life." Wry smiles began appearing on faces. "The man craves media attention the way a junkie craves the narcotic. He'll probably say no at first. I mean, I'm assuming someone is going to have to put the thought of seriously running in his head. He'll say no at first because it's not his idea. But if he warms up to the idea and makes it his own, he will run, and run with abandon."

"Great. Thank you, Anthony. Keep in mind everyone, Tedie has in the past hinted at running for public office. He may need a little push to throw his hat in the ring. I'm confident we can help engineer that, with or without his knowledge."

Jeffrey paused for objections. There were none. Perfect. "So, we are in agreement?" He paused again. "All right, we have our guy. Job well done, people!"

AWM

Two days later, Jeffrey was again in a conference room, but this time as a participant with a role, not as a leader. His Tampa flight had run late, his Uber driver had gotten a ticket last week and refused to speed, and Jeffrey arrived at the meeting just as the presenter was taking the podium in front of the two dozen attendees. Jeffrey took the last seat at the large conference table. His chair was next to Stephanie Kenseth, and he flashed her an apologetic smile for his nearly late arrival.

Debra Wassultz, current leader of the Democrat National Committee, opened the meeting and spoke without notes. "Good afternoon everyone. I want to personally thank each of you for making the trip to Tampa. Everyone knows, or should know, that Tampa is the unofficial second headquarters for the DNC. I'm not quite sure how that tradition started, but I'm guessing sunshine, beautiful beaches, and great food had something to do with it."

Wassultz's face now took on a more serious tone. "Something everyone here definitely needs to know; is this is an unofficial DNC meeting. Highly important, but off the books. There are no minutes being taken, there will be no recordings of our conversations, and there will be no coverage in the media."

"Everyone here," she now slowly looked

around the room with her bright blue eyes, "was selected to be here. Our work is very important for our Party. Our purpose today is to bring more structure to our presidential strategy for the upcoming 2016 election. The decisions we make here will affect media coverage, advertising, and the commitment of human as well as financial resources for the duration of the campaign. Everyone needs to be on their A-game."

"I'm going to turn the meeting over now to DNC staffer Todd Prozan, who will provide summary detail on our expected field of candidates. Each of these individuals, some privately and some publicly, have indicated their desire to run for the nomination. After Todd speaks, Jeffrey Saint will speak briefly on behalf of the Kenseth campaign. Todd, the floor is yours."

Wassultz retook her seat next to Stephanie, and Todd took the podium. Before he began speaking, Stephanie leaned over and whispered something into Debra's ear, which she acknowledged with a smile and nod of the head.

Todd began. "Good afternoon everyone. I'm going to share briefly some information on the Democrats who we believe will formally seek the nomination. Currently there are three, and we are comfortable with this number."

Todd turned his body slightly to the screen positioned behind him to his left, pointed, and began again. "This is Ron Littleton, the current senior Senator from Florida. Ron is perceived as a centrist and a uniter. Ron is a longshot at best, but he will energize Florida, which is a critical state for us to carry."

"Next up, we have David Miller, former

House Representative from Iowa. As you may recall, Miller cast the deciding vote which passed President Ingle's healthcare bill into law. He unfortunately lost his re-election bid in the next cycle. David is running with our blessing as a reward for his solidarity. The matching campaign funds he will receive as a candidate will help offset the debts he created in his re-election campaign."

"Not that that has anything to do with anything!" Debra interjected loudly into Todd's marginally enthusiastic presentation. Laughter filled the room, and Todd seemed to lighten up a bit.

Smiling and nodding, Todd continued. "Not that that has anything to do with anything. It is fortuitous that David is from Iowa. We believe his presence in the race will help draw away some attention from the Republican primary there in February.

Todd pointed at the screen one last time. "Finally, we have Vice President Stephanie Kenseth. The assumption that she would run for president has been in the public realm for many years, and most significantly since the close of the last presidential election. Everyone, I think, is familiar with her background." Todd now looked over in Mrs. Kenseth's direction. "And, oh look, she's even here with us in Tampa!" Todd beamed at Stephanie amid the polite chuckles in the room. Stephanie acknowledged Todd's attempt at humor with a cordial smile.

Todd set his notes aside and addressed the group. "This is our expected field. We want you to have this information as you return to your state organizations. If you hear someone bring up one of these candidate's names, we discourage you from sharing anything you've learned about them. Instead, listen intently, and share the valuable information you learn from the 'world at large' with us. That information is critical."

Satisfied that everyone understood his request, he clasped his hands in front of his body and said, "Before I turn the meeting over to Jeffrey, are there any questions?" He paused. "OK. With no questions, I will turn it over to Jeffrey Saint, a man who requires no introduction."

Jeffrey's job was to present the recommendation of the PTL. Because of his relationship with Stephanie, and because of the success of the same effort in 2012, it was a fait accompli that whoever Jeffrey recommended as the target for promotion on the Republican side, Stephanie and the group would endorse.

Jeffrey began by going over the credentials of all the PTL committee members. In addition to simply being informative, this was a tactic to reinforce the soundness of the committee's decision and to minimize opposition.

After sharing the make-up and credentials of the committee, Jeffrey finally got to the message that everyone was eager to hear. "We think we have an outstanding candidate to target. He is a non-obvious candidate. Your first reaction may be to think 'WTF?' Some of the committee members reacted that way initially. But as we talked it through and developed a strategy, the value of this candidate grew exponentially."

"Interesting. Tell us more." Stephanie was doing her best to act as though she did not already know who the chosen candidate was.

"This candidate is the mirror image of Barry

Ingle, but with one significant difference. Oh, and please note I said mirror image, not carbon copy. A mirror image is the same, but opposite. When you look in a mirror, left is right and right is left. It's the same person, but opposite." He took a deep breath.

"The Pick the Loser Committee is recommending Colton Tedie as the Republican candidate that we will help promote and ultimately triumph over in the upcoming election."

At this point, Jeffrey paused and looked around the table, and then at the staffers along the wall of the conference room. He had anticipated push back at this point since the pick was an outlier. Faces in the room were not yet communicating disagreement, so he continued.

"We believe Tedie will have great appeal to the Republican base, to those voters most disenfranchised by current Ingle policies. He is bombastic. He is charismatic. He can be counted on to deliver shock value almost anytime he speaks. He should prove to be an easy mark for baited, demographically focused questions which will reveal him as diplomatically inexperienced, naïve, even sexist. As we promote him in the press and in the polls, his ascension will also reflect on the Republican party as a whole. He alone will help drive a wedge between the Republican base and the rest of the country. Regardless of whether he wins the nomination, and we believe he can win the nomination with our help, his presence and prominence in the primaries alone will help paint a picture of the Republican party as clueless, out of touch, and potentially dangerous for the country."

Larry Trudeau, DNC Director from Washington State seized this moment to interject.

"Thanks to you and your committee, Jeffrey. I like where you are going, but I am still stuck on your mirror image comment. Why would you say Colton Tedie is the mirror image of Barry Ingle?"

Jeffrey had expected this query and was prepared for it. "Think about Barry Ingle in 2007 and 2008. He was a blank slate at the national level. He did not have a voting record to assassinate and run against. He appealed wildly to a large swath of our liberal and progressives base. He was charismatic like few others from behind the microphone. He was hip, cool, you wanted to be like him, or sleep with his hot wife, or both."

"Conservatives were dumbfounded by his candidacy and his success. They could not understand how someone with almost no political experience, someone with no industry experience, no history of achievement, could both run for president, and have tremendous success."

"Now consider Colton Tedie. He too is a blank slate politically. He will, we believe, appeal wildly to conservatives, the Tea Party, Preppers, and others who are at odds with the policies of this administration and direction of this country. He can fire up a crowd from the microphone. He is a pop culture icon, he's unafraid, and perceived to be very rich. Those qualities will appeal to a large number of Republicans. Those qualities will also be easy for our candidate to run against, and for our bundlers to fundraise against. Oh! Did I mention he has a really hot wife? Certainly no one in this room would be dazzled by this fact, but a large number of Americans want to be him, be like him, have his bank account, and/or sleep with his hot wife."

He continued after a brief pause for laughter. "And,

just like with Ingle and the conservatives, our base will be dumbfounded by any polling and electorate success Tedie will have. They will not understand how someone so polarizing, with views so contrary to their own, will be taken seriously."

Jeffrey intentionally stopped at that point to allow the others to process his theory.

Another question came, this one from Linda Macintosh from California. "When you began this mirror image analysis you mentioned one significant difference between the two. What is that?"

"Thank you for reminding me, Linda. The difference is simple actually." Jeffrey paused here and repositioned himself to emphasize the point. "We, own the media. Without a media which was favorably disposed toward our good looking, young, hip candidate in 2008 and 2012, all those experiential and political gaps our candidate presented would have been easily exploitable. A friendly media looked past those holes in our man's game. The media will not, will not, will not look past those same gaps with a Republican candidate, particularly one as loud and proud as Colton Tedie."

"How do you know the media will go along with it?" This was not a question Jeffrey was expecting, and especially not from the source he was getting it from. The question came from Loren Black, a very wet behind the ears staffer from DNC headquarters in Washington. In these strategy meetings, when staffers are against the wall and decision makers are around the table, staffers are expected to remain quiet except when they're spoken to.

Jeffrey's initial facial expression communicated incredulity. When he realized it was coming from Loren, his expression changed and his attitude mellowed a bit. He knew Loren, who was fresh out of graduate school and unaware of proper protocols. His question, Jeffrey thought, was more a negative reflection on his boss for not sharing the acceptable code of behavior with him than on Loren.

Loren had interviewed with Jeffrey for a job on Stephanie's team a few weeks prior. They had gone out for drinks afterward. If Loren had handled the situation a little differently, he might be on their team now. Jeffrey had chalked Loren's behavior up to a lack of understanding of what is required in order to be on the A-team. Jeffrey's compassion for the fact Loren was uninitiated helped temper and shape his response to the question.

In a very matter of fact and pleasant tone, Jeffrey responded. "The media will go along for many reasons, not the least of which is we are kindred souls. Members of the media, members of the Democrat party, have a shared ideology. We see the world through the same lens, and want the same things. We share the same sense of right and wrong. The media votes and promotes Democrat candidates not because we tell them to, but because they want what the Democrat candidate is saying to be true."

"They will also go along because we give them access. They know their readers want to know what Stephanie Kenseth thinks, what she eats, and what she wears when she lets her hair down. The public wants that times 1,000 elected and government officials. Because the public wants it, the media wants it. Because we know the media wants it, we grant them access for favorable coverage. It is a quid pro quo, and it is a timeless formula for success."

"Finally, and potentially most importantly,

they will go along because candidate Colton Tedie is going to sell a shit load of advertising. Candidate Colton Tedie is going to say things that cause people across the entire political spectrum to cheer and swear in the same breath. Once we talk to them about this strategy, there is no one, I mean no one, the media would rather promote than Colton Tedie. I mean, you tell me... you want to sell papers and get viewership on cable talk shows. You can promote some guy who goes to church, has been married once, and got into politics because he wanted to make a difference. Boring! Or, you can promote this billionaire with the volcano for a mouth and the hot wife... not to mention the ex-wives. The billionaire that is bound to say something stupid, to screw up, and to run a completely off-the-wall campaign? You tell me."

"I see your point" was Loren's quick, simple response.

"Can we count on him to run?" Another question from another source Jeffrey was not expecting. This time it came from Jeryl Burnette, also seated along the wall. Jeryl was an DNC staffer from California. Jeffrey had long thought that if she was not sleeping her way in to these high-level meetings, she was missing a hell of an opportunity.

Jeffrey paused, and now appeared agitated. Again, in a matter of fact tone, but much more direct, he responded. "Jeryl, if we freaking want him to run, I can convince him to run. Leave that to the professionals." Besides there being a difference in Jeryl's and Loren's gender, Jeryl had been in this game longer than the newbie. Jeffrey was certain she should know when not to speak up or question him, and his response reflected this.

Jeffrey held eye contact with Jeryl for several

seconds after finishing his remark. He then turned his head to address the entire room. "Does everyone get that?" His voice was now louder. "This is not about 'can we' with a question mark. It's about 'we will' with five damn exclamation points! Every one of us benefits from having another Democrat in the White House. The paycheck and livelihood of everyone in this room is directly tied to our success in the presidential election. You like the fancy clothes and fine dining? You like having lobbyists spend money on you and kiss your ass? Hell yes, you do. And I do too. So this is not about 'can we?' Regardless of the candidate's name or your specific job title, our job here, in this committee, is to promote and protect the Democrat brand and our Democrat candidates by any and all means necessary. Our job is to win the next election. And it will not be easy. There has never been a president with lower approval ratings than our guy has right now. That's not propaganda. Those are our polling results. We must overcome that. We *will* overcome that!"

Jeffrey re-took his seat at the table.

Debra stood back up. "Are there any comments or concerns about Colton Tedie as our chosen opponent?" She looked each person at the table in the eye quickly. One by one, each person visibly or audibly indicated concurrence.

She continued, "OK, very good." She now turned toward the Vice President. "Stephanie, I understand you and Jeffrey have pressing business elsewhere. We're going to continue our meeting, and I appreciate you making time to be here."

Debra now turned toward Jeffrey. "Before you go though… Jeffrey, you have a well-earned reputation for applying unique nicknames and acronyms to projects you work on. I'm curious if you have one of those yet for Tedie?"

Jeffrey smiled as he was rising from his chair. "But of course, Debra. In our communications, Tedie will be known as AWM."

Loren quickly piped up. "Angry White Male!"

Jeffrey looked at Loren and winked. "That's the one."

Once they were outside of the room Stephanie asked in a low tone, "So how *are* you going to make sure he runs?"

Jeffrey paused and looked up as he waited for the elevator door to open. "Damn if I know. You know the man. That's your job!"

Jeffrey continued walking. Stephanie stopped temporarily, looked at the back of Jeffrey's head and responded "Ha!" before following him onto the elevator.

Setting the Stage

Immediately after the PTL Committee picked Tedie, and before that choice had been endorsed by the DNC, Jeffrey had hired a private investigation firm to follow Tedie and collect information on as many of his public and private dealings as possible. Jeffrey was certain the DNC would agree with his choice, and he wanted as much intelligence as possible on the man he was going to stealthily promote as the next nominee for president representing the Republican Party.

Jeffrey received several emails weekly on the activity of Mr. Tedie. The information was interesting but none of it was very useful. On April 1, however, he received information he *could* use. The email simply said "AWM seen entering 310 First Street SE DC."

The address of Tedie's visit is what made the message compelling. Every political pundit who has ever spent any time in Washington knows that 310 First Street SE DC is the address for the Republican National Committee's headquarters. The building located at 310 First Street SE DC is also a multi-tenant facility. So, it was possible, perhaps even likely, that Tedie's visit was to some organization other than the RNC. But for Jeffrey's purposes, that did not matter. In his business of influencing reality, perception, speculation and narrative were far more valuable than truth. He had what he needed.

Jeffrey immediately called his close friend and CNN reporter Trina Banks. Trina was one of the many resources Jeffrey had at his disposal for strategically delivering messages. Trina and Jeffrey knew each other from many years together working different sides of the same political street: Trina in reporting, Jeffrey in strategy and intelligence. Their careers had paralleled each other, and there was a strong mutual respect.

Trina saw Jeffrey's name and photo on her phone and she instantly felt a rush of excitement. When Jeffrey Saint was calling, it usually meant she was about to receive some juicy information she could use.

"Hello Jeffrey, how are you?"

"I am wonderful, Trina. I trust you are the same."

"I am great, thank you. I was just thinking about you the other day."

"Oh yeah? Well, why was that?"

"I was thinking I had not heard from you recently, and that made me sad. Now I am hearing from you, and that makes me happy."

Jeffrey had a few minutes to kill so he played along. "Tell me Trina, what is it about hearing from me that makes you happy? Is it my wit? My intellect? The knowledge there is a handsome man on the other end of the line? What, exactly, is it?"

"Oh, yes, Jeffrey it is all those things. All those things and more actually. You make me happy because you help me make my boss happy. And when boss lady is happy, everyone is happy."

They both laughed and Jeffrey agreed, "Word to that."

Trina continued, "So tell me Jeffrey, what's on your mind today?"

Jeffrey knew his response to that question would set in motion a chain of events he had carefully engineered, but ultimately, once he spoke, he had no control over what happened next. This was the part of his job he enjoyed the most. He did not gamble with money. But he assumed the rush he received from playing puppet master was similar to a gambler's rush when they make a calculated bet and won. There was a tingle up the back of his spine and a slight shudder in his body as he began to answer Trina's innocuous question.

"Funny you should ask. I was wondering if there was anything to the rumor that Colton Tedie might run for president?"

"Colton Tedie? Are you serious? I hadn't heard that one. I think there are a dozen or more people who are going to run on the Republican side. He might as well be one of them. Where did you hear this?"

"One of my sources told me he was seen leaving the RNC headquarters recently."

"Really?" Trina was quickly checking the CNN internal database for Tedie's recent movements. Tedie was one of several celebrities in their up-to-the-minute database.

"I know he was recently in Washington for a fundraiser for one of his wife's charities..." Her voice trailed off as she continued looking.

"Which one?" Jeffrey wanted to fact check his background information against CNN's database, which he knew Trina was scouring in that very moment.

"I think Women's World Hope. Its headquarters are in DC… at 310 First Street SE.

That's where the RNC is headquartered." said Trina, thinking out loud.

Jeffrey tried to kindle the thought in Trina's head. "Which makes Women's World Hope a perfect cover for visiting the RNC, doesn't it?"

"Yes," replied Trina. "But Tedie does not need to come to DC to meet with RNC officials to contemplate a presidential run."

"You are right, he does not. But it would make for one helluva story, wouldn't it?"

Trina thought for a moment, then spoke. "See Jeffrey, this is why I love it when you call. You just make me happy."

"You make me happy too, love. Later today, on the screen?"

"Blink and you might miss it! Talk to you later, Jeffrey."

The call ended and Jeffrey checked his phone. 9:41am. He turned 90 degrees in his office chair to do something he often did; take in the view from his Arlington office. It was a beautiful sunny day and the Marine Corp memorial, the Potomac, and all the memorials on the east side of the river were gloriously bathed in sunlight. This scene was in stark contrast to the view from his office when he arrived daily at 5:00am.

Jeffrey then turned his chair back to his desk and impulsively checked the time again. It was 9:43. He looked up to the middle television on the wall. As always, it was muted and tuned to CNN News. He began reading the scrolling headlines at the bottom of the screen. Another minute passed. Jeffrey's phone rang. Caller ID indicated it was Stephanie. He let it go to voicemail and continued watching the screen.

Another minute passed and the scroll stopped. "Breaking News" flashed across the bottom of the screen, followed by new scroll. Jeffrey leaned forward with his elbows on the desk. The scroll now read, "Colton Tedie speculated to be considering run for president." Jeffrey smiled.

"Atta girl, Trina." came out of his mouth from down deep. He was now in the midst of a well-deserved feeling of satisfaction. Win, lose, or draw, he had pulled the first lever in a series of events which he believed would heavily influence the news cycle for many months, as well as influence the choice of presidential nominee for the opposition party. Gambler's rush had given way to utter exhilaration. He was pleased with himself.

He stood and noticed the phone indicating a voicemail message from Stephanie. He needed to walk off some of this high before attending to the message. A quick visit to the Marine Corp memorial seemed a fitting reward for having initiated his AWM strategy.

Over the next 24 hours, several other news organizations picked up the storyline of Tedie considering a presidential run. Having given the story sufficient time to marinade, the next day Jeffrey called one of his closest friends, Kimberly Thompson. Kimberly was an accomplished journalist working for Rolling Stone magazine. She had recently done an expose on Tedie, focusing on the recent successes of several entertainment ventures he was involved in.

Jeffrey knew this because of their friendship. The story was set to run in the next issue.

"Hello Jeffrey!"

"Hello, Kimmy. How the hell are you?"

"I are the hell fine. How the hell are you Jeffrey?

"Finer than a frog's hair here."

"Outstanding. So, what's going on?"

"Another day in political paradise. Working hard to feed the poor children, protect grandma, and right the social wrongs of a greedy society... all before lunchtime. How about you?"

"I'm just washing my dog. He doesn't care about any of that shit." They both laughed. Jeffrey responded, "Sometimes I wish I didn't care about any of that shit!" Again, they laughed. It was funny primarily because they both knew it was not true. Jeffrey Saint was one hundred percent in the element he was meant for.

Jeffrey now subtly turned to business. "Hey, I just saw a headline that made me think of you and your Tedie piece."

"Oh really, what was that?"

"Did you know he is considering running for president?"

"What?!"

"I take it he did not mention that in your interview with him?"

"No, he didn't. But that *was* several weeks ago. Maybe he was still in the decision-making stage at that point. Where did you hear this?"

"It's all over cable news. Story broke yesterday. And you may be right. He might not have had his mind made up when you interviewed him. But if it's true, I'm sure he would appreciate the coverage." He paused. "You might think about calling him back, before the article runs. You've still got time I bet."

"Yeah, I've still got time."

Jeffrey continued, "If the story is true, you'd have the first national article on it! How cool would that be?"

"Wow, yeah. That'd be fucking cool alright." Kimberly now had fully transitioned her attention away from the dog to Jeffrey. "Tell me again where you heard this?"

"The story broke on CNN yesterday morning. Several more are reporting it now. I'm sure Tedie has seen it. It was probably his team that leaked it to CNN. No word from Tedie on Twitter yet."

"Hey Jeffrey, thanks for the heads up. Let me run and see what I can find."

"No problem Kimberly. I'm just doing what friends do. Hey, let me know what you find out if you can. I'd like to keep Stephanie informed."

"I can and I will. Give Stephanie my best. Ciao!"

"Toodles, love." Jeffrey put the phone down and allowed himself a brief moment of satisfaction before heading to his lunch appointment. For the second time in two days, he had successfully and stealthily caused movement on the national political scene.

■■■■■■■■■■■■■■■■■■■■■■■■■■■■■■■■■■■■■■

Jeffrey arrived at the restaurant first. He always wanted to be seated before his guest arrived.

He did not like surprises. He preferred to choose his seat, preferably the one that allowed him to have his back to the wall, and he liked to review the menu alone (he did not trust website menus, too often they are not updated). He wanted to meet the server first and get his water before his guest arrived. These were all ways he minimized the opportunity for surprise, and made the environment his own.

What was not a surprise, was that his guest David was late. David Flouphe was considered the best campaign manager in the country not currently committed to a candidate or campaign. He was in Washington working as a consultant for several different industries. His past campaign successes allowed him great access to many influential decision makers. He was well-connected and very well paid. Everyone with any knowledge of David and his skills assumed he would manage a high-profile campaign in the upcoming 2016 season. That is what Jeffrey wanted to talk to him about. Jeffrey had made this appointment with David the day after PTL targeted Tedie.

Ten minutes after their scheduled start time, David was delivered to the table where Jeffrey was seated, sending emails. Because of how he was positioned, Jeffrey noticed David coming and rose from his high back chair to shake the tall man's hand as he approached. David was impeccably dressed in dark suit, white shirt and yellow tie, as if he was coming from or heading to a meeting with the President himself. His smile revealed nearly perfect teeth as he extended his hand to meet Jeffrey's.

"David, my friend! How are you?"

"I am great Jeffrey, thank you. How are you and team Stephanie doing?"

"We are doing great. Ramping up as you would expect. Trying to cram thirty-six hours of work into every twenty-four-hour day. You know how it is." They both chuckled as they sat.

"Yes, I do. And I can honestly say I don't miss it." Jeffrey knew David was lying, and that David had just tipped his hand. David thrived in a competitive, political environment as much as Jeffrey did. He was a brilliant political strategist, which is why Jeffrey was there in the first place. The only reason for David to say he did not miss the action was to play hard to get. In the world's greatest market for dishonest buyers, Jeffrey now knew David was a dishonest buyer for what he was dishonestly selling.

"Don't give me that crap, David. Remember me? I'm Jeffrey, your friend who knows all and sees all. I know you miss it." Jeffrey said with an acknowledging smile.

David returned his smile. "Well, maybe I miss it just a little."

Good, thought Jeffrey. He is not going to play too hard to get.

After some idle chat and placing their orders, Jeffrey continued the pursuit.

"David, I'm glad we could get together. It's always good to stay connected. I was thinking of you the other day and wondered, have you heard from Tedie's camp yet?"

"Colton Tedie? No, why would I?" David knew why Jeffrey was asking, but wanted to see what information he would share.

"You've not heard?" Jeffrey asked. He suspected David was being coy.

"Heard what?"

"There is a story floating around that Tedie is considering a presidential run. If it is true, I'm assuming he would have reached out to you."

"Nothing on this end," responded David. "Do you think it's true?"

"Don't know. But it makes sense to me. I think he would be a powerful Republican candidate."

"I agree," said David, though he had never considered Tedie in a political sense. "Tell me your perspective on him."

"Well he'd be a disaster as a president," Jeffrey began.

"Because he's a Republican," interrupted David smiling.

"Partly because he's a Republican. Partly because he's from New York." David was originally from New York, which Jeffrey knew.

David quickly responded "Hey now Jeffrey, watch it! The Empire State is where it's at and you know it!" They both laughed.

Jeffrey continued, "Seriously, he is on our radar. We think he would be a very powerful opponent. Obviously, we believe we would beat him. But we think he would have tremendous appeal to large portion of the Republican base."

Jeffrey's comments about beating Tedie and about being a disaster as a president were meant to fan a flame inside of David. He knew David was very competitive, and at heart he was a Republican. Most professional campaign consultants had to be ambidextrous regarding which party their candidate belonged to, and David had this skill. But from an ideological standpoint Jeffrey believed David trended with the Republicans.

Their meals arrived, creating a short break in the conversation. David used these seconds to contemplate this new idea Jeffrey had planted in his brain. He was intrigued. Not wanting to appear over-eager, he waited for an appropriate amount of time to pass before he began to probe Jeffrey again. "So, tell me more about why you think Tedie would make a great candidate."

"It's simple really," Jeffrey began. "He will be a great candidate because he will be the opposite of Barry Ingle. He is a business man. Business men make money because they sell what people want. He will sell what the people want."

"And you believe the American people want the opposite of Barry Ingle?"

"I'm afraid they do." Jeffrey was lying. He did not believe the American people wanted the opposite of the sitting president. But he did believe the Republican base lusted for this. "I believe Tedie will seize on this phenomenon more than any of the other political class candidates. Tedie will analyze Ingle's positions on key issues and blaze a jet stream one hundred eighty degrees in the opposite direction. He will recognize opportunity that is laying on the ground begging to be picked up. Opportunity which I believe most of the career politicians seeking the nomination will miss. And when he does, he will be wildly popular."

"Interesting," was David's only response as he put his fork down to take a swallow of water. Jeffrey knew this was a tactic for David to analyze the bread crumbs he was laying down. He waited a few seconds before continuing toward the close.

"David, we live on this crazy planet known as Washington DC. Most people do not. Colton Tedie does not. Do you know how many down ballot seats Democrats have lost and Republicans have won since Ingle became president in 2008?"

"Tell me." Again, David knew the answer, but wanted to test Jeffrey's information and conviction. David knew Jeffrey was a Democrat ideologue at heart. He wanted to see if that affinity would cause him to mellow out the facts, which were carnage from a political power standpoint.

Jeffrey put his fork down on his plate for emphasis. "Democrats have lost over 900 state legislature seats since Ingle took office. That is unprecedented. And that is on top off losing twelve governorships, sixty-nine House seats, and thirteen Senate seats."

David was nodding his head, pretending he had just been told something he did not already know. He was mildly surprised that Jeffrey had given him unedited and accurate information. David knew that most political pundits on planet Washington tended to allow their ideological convictions to cloud their view of reality. That he had told him the truth caused his respect for Jeffrey's professionalism to grow.

As Jeffrey gave his answer, he knew the question was a test. He was certain David was aware of the damage that had been done to state as well as national level elected Democrats since the election of Ingle. It was David's job (as well as his passion) to know these things. As painful as it was for a fully sold out Democrat like Jeffrey to speak these words out loud, he knew his credibility was on the line with the answer. He was fully aware that his credibility was the number one asset he had for use in encouraging David to reach out to Tedie's team, to help influence Tedie to run, and to keep his allies close.

Jeffrey thought the time was right to sum it up. "The bottom line, David, is the president and most everyone else in this town live in an 'alternative reality' bubble." David nodded signaling acknowledgment. "The reality of the situation is this Democrat president and his policies are significantly disliked by a large number of people in this country. If a Republican candidate seizes on this and runs a halfway decent campaign, that candidate stands a great chance of winning the nomination, and quite possibly the presidency. The logical candidate to pull that off is not currently serving in DC. And I don't think any of the governors who are expected to run are capable of separating themselves from policy dialogue, to communicate effectively enough to connect with the angst that exists within the public. In my mind, the potential candidate, the one most capable of seizing the opportunity and pulling off a most improbable but successful bid for the nomination, is Colton Tedie."

David had another probe to make. "You mentioned governors. You don't think Chris Landon can connect with the mood of the country? He seemed to do so effectively in New Jersey."

"Colton Tedie is a thousand times better at the game Landon played to get elected. Landon is loud, Tedie is louder. Landon is savvy, Tedie wrote the book. In a national race, no one outside the state of New Jersey will care that Landon is governor of New Jersey. Landon is viable in a race that does not include Tedie. The second Tedie enters, Landon is toast. Buttered toast. Which he will be resigned to eating once Tedie enters the race."

David was buying into Jeffrey's theories, but he had just never taken Tedie seriously as a candidate. He knew Tedie had boasted in the past about entering politics. And it was clear the man's ego would only allow him to run for one office, the highest office in the land. But he just wasn't quite convinced yet.

"Jeffrey, I hear what you are saying, and I agree with a lot of it. I just don't know about Tedie. He has zero political experience."

"He has exactly one ounce less political experience than Barry Ingle did in 2008. And he has a list of accomplishments a thousand times longer than Ingle did. If the country can elect someone with Ingle's resume in 2008, it can elect someone with Tedie's resume in 2016. Bank on it."

"You just might be right," were David's last meaningful words on the subject. From that point on, the conversation was aimless small talk as the meeting wound down. David offered to pay for lunch but Jeffrey insisted.

David made the short trip back to his office and immediately sent an email to Joyce Berkowitz, Chris Landon's chief of staff. The email read "Something has come up. Sorry, need to cancel our teleconference later today. Will be back in touch for a good time to reschedule." In that moment, he had no intentions of rescheduling.

■■

Kimberly spent the early afternoon reviewing all her notes from the Colton Tedie interview. She wanted to see if Tedie had dropped a clue about running for president that she had overlooked. After slowly reviewing the notes, she was pleased to not find anything. She would have been highly disappointed in herself if she had missed something that important.

Her story on Tedie was the cover article in the next issue of Rolling Stone. Her editor had loved it, and it was ready to go. The article would be her first to grace the cover. She knew she had done great work on it, but there was no way she could not follow up on the rumor that Tedie might run for president. After convincing herself she had no other choice, she picked up her phone.

"Hello, Kimberly."

"Hello, Veronica. How have you been?" Veronica Juarez was Colton Tedie's primary assistant and schedule coordinator. Kimberly and Veronica had worked closely as the interview for Tedie was arranged. They had only conversed a few times, so Kimberly was flattered that Veronica had added her cell phone number to her database.

"I am excellent, thank you. How are you? Is Mr. Tedie's interview ready for press?"

"It's almost ready to go. There is one final item I need to speak with Mr. Tedie about, a clarifying matter, actually. I know he is always very busy. Is there a time I may speak with him? We don't want to miss this month's deadlines."

"Certainly. You may be in luck now. He is in route between appointments and may have a minute to speak with you. Hold just a moment and I will see if he is available."

Colton Tedie was accustomed to attention. His face had been on the front cover of dozens of national magazines before. Even still, Kimberly expected

Tedie to take her call. It was apparent in their time together that his ego was insatiable. Her Rolling Stone story was wood for the fire.

The silence on the phone was broken by Colton Tedie's distinctive voice. "How are you, Kimberly?" Before she could answer, he followed with, "How is the story coming? Are we on the racks yet?"

Kimberly suspected Tedie knew the answer to the last question already. She had been very specific with him on the press date for the article. In their time together interviewing, she quickly noticed that one of his frequently used tactics was to alternate between complimenting people strategically, followed by putting them in a defensive position, as he had just done with her.

"Mr. Tedie, we will be on the racks in just a few days. I think you will like the piece."

"I'm sure I will Kimberly. It was apparent to me in our time together that you are an excellent writer. Now tell me what's on your mind."

"Well Mr. Tedie, I wanted to follow up on a news story I saw yesterday on CNN. The story indicated you might be running for president. For the benefit of the upcoming Rolling Stone article, I wanted to ask you if the story is true?"

"You know Kimberly, you are about the one hundredth person to ask me that question in the last twenty-four hours. I had no idea CNN had that many viewers."

Kimberly could not tell if the jab at CNN was a joke or not. But she sensed a change in his tone that made it seem like he was at least intrigued by her question.

Tedie continued, "Who else told you about this idea?"

"No one else. I just saw the story appear on the news, both on CNN and on some other news outlets. I was wondering if there is any truth behind it?"

Uncharacteristically, Tedie paused before responding. "No truth whatsoever, Kimberly. I don't know where CNN or anyone else got that story. They probably made it up because they *want* me to be president. I'm sure I would be a great president, probably the greatest ever. I would return opportunity to the American dream. I would get this country back on track and we would have prosperity again. But no, Kimberly, I am not running for president. I'm very busy, and besides I could not afford to take the pay cut."

Again, Kimberly could not tell if he was making a joke or not.

"Promise me you'll leave this president rumor out of the Rolling Stone article. I don't want your great article being diluted with unsubstantiated drivel. Can we agree to that, Kimberly?"

"Certainly Mr. Tedie. The article is excellent as is and it will hit the press as it is currently written."

"Thank you, Kimberly. I look forward to seeing your good work." And with that Tedie abruptly ended the call.

Tedie immediately sent a text message to Katy, the woman at the head of his marketing team.

GET IN FRONT OF THIS PRESIDENT RUMOR NOW. I EXPECT A TWEET TO GO OUT IMMEDIATELY FROM MY ACCOUNT.

In less than a minute, his phone buzzed.

WE'RE ON IT.

Later that afternoon Jeffrey's phone rang. Kimberly was on the other end of the line.

"Miss Kimberly, how are you today?"

"Great, but I'm frustrated."

"Sounds like a personal problem. One that I personally cannot help you with, darling."

Kimberly replied, "Well then, it's a good thing I don't mean that kind of frustrated, now isn't it?" Kimberly fought the urge to punctuate her sentence with 'smartass.' She assumed her tone was sufficient to get her point across.

She continued, "Tedie says there is no truth to the story about running for president."

Jeffrey sat a little straighter in his seat. "So he talked to you about it?"

"Well not exactly. I asked him about it; he denied it. Said he was too busy and made too much money to be president."

"Well I suppose both of those are true." Jeffrey chuckled. "Well that is weird. CNN and others ran the story and he denies it. I wonder how that happened?"

"No clue. It was a short conversation. I told you I would let you know, so there you have it."

"Kimberly, you are a woman of your word and a dear friend. Thank you for letting me know. I'm sure I'll be talking to you again soon."

It had been twenty-four hours since his meeting with Jeffrey Saint, and David could not get their conversation out of his mind. Jeffrey's analysis of the impact of Colton Tedie running for president seemed absolutely spot on. The more he thought about it, the more excited he got about the uniqueness of the candidate, and the political environment in which the candidate would exist. It was a perfect combination he thought, and he wanted badly to be a part of it. David had assumed he would be a part of a presidential campaign in the upcoming cycle. He just did not know which candidate. In the past twenty-four hours, he had made his choice.

David had had minor interactions with Colton Tedie on projects before, both as a business consultant in Washington, and as a political advisor to candidates Tedie was backing financially. He had Veronica Juarez's phone number in his cell phone, which was as close as anyone not directly associated with Mr. Tedie got to him.

Nothing David was currently working on had any ties or association to Colton Tedie. That would have made his initial outreach to Tedie easier. But in the absence of an easy entre, David did as he always did. He took the direct route and dialed the number.

"Good afternoon Mr. Flouphe. This is Veronica Juarez, how may I help you?"

David was momentarily speechless. He had not expected Colton Tedie's assistant to have his contact information in her database. But she obviously did.

"I am well, Veronica. I hope you are the same."

"Yes sir, never better. How may I help you?"

"I would like to speak to Mr. Tedie about an important matter. Would it be possible for me to get 10 minutes on his busy calendar sometime in the next few days?"

"What shall I tell Mr. Tedie you wish to speak with him about?"

"Please tell him I would like to discuss the cost and value of real estate at 1600 Pennsylvania."

"I will give Mr. Tedie the message, Mr. Flouphe."

■■■

Jeffrey thought twenty-four hours was a sufficient amount of time to see if David Flouphe had taken the bait after their previous day's lunch. But he did not want Flouphe to know of his interest. Jeffrey reached out to longtime friend and political activist Marvin Brown. Their professional and social paths had crossed many times through the years, resulting in a strong friendship. Marvin was currently working for the Landon presidential campaign.

"Jeffrey, how are you?" came Marvin's voice through the phone.

"Marvelous Marvin, I am marvelous, thank you! I trust you are the same."

"Living the dream my friend, living the dream. How are things on planet Washington today?"

"The same as yesterday, the same as tomorrow: one bad bill, one bad piece of legislation, one bad decision away from society being out of control and in the hands of an angry mob of lunatics."

"Which is why you are there," replied Marvin.

"Which is why I am here Marvelous Marvin, it's why I am here! Protecting the unprotected against the evils of a capitalist society. And speaking of capitalists, how is your boss doing today?"

"He is scrambling as usual. I think today's emergency is the person we had targeted to be our campaign manager blew off a meeting yesterday. Everyone's in a panic that we're not getting our guy, and we're running out of time."

Jeffrey responded, "That was Flouphe, right? That's too bad because he's good."

"Yes, Flouphe."

"Yeah, you mentioned you guys were in discussions with him before. He is on my radar. All of us at the Stephanie campaign have been wondering which horse he will lead."

"What does the smart money say?" asked Marvin.

"Smart money says Tedie," responded Jeffrey.

"Tedie? For president? Seriously? I saw that, what, yesterday on the television. You think that is for real?"

"A long shot at this point. But if Tedie and Flouphe get together, watch out. That is a winning team."

"Hey speaking of winning teams, when are you going to get me a gig with Team Stephanie? You know my allegiance is not with *these* people."

"I didn't know you wanted out. I thought your love affair with Landon's personality combined with your New Jersey roots created the perfect environment for you."

"Screw you, asshole," Marvin said through a smile. "You know I'm only here because my kids are nearby and I needed a job."

"Whatever," came Jeffrey's sarcastic reply. "But seriously, I will see what I can do. Depending on how things evolve though, you may be more of a benefit to us where you are. And there is value which would accrue to you if that happens. Hang in there."

"Hanging low. Hey, I gotta go… later man."

"Marvelous, it's been marvelous. Talk to you soon."

Much to David's pleasant surprise his phone rang two hours later. It was Veronica Juarez calling. "Hello, Veronica."

"Please hold for Mr. Tedie." It was customary for Colton Tedie to have his assistant call ahead, just to make sure the person he was calling for was available.

"Hello David, this is Colton Tedie. How have you been?"

"Excellent Mr. Tedie, never better. I very much appreciate you returning my call."

"Veronica said you had something to talk to me about so I thought I better call you back. Something about real estate at 1600 Pennsylvania. I assume that reference has something to do with politics. A man of your talents warrants quick attention. Now tell me what is it you wish to discuss? Clarify this mysterious tease you left me with. I'm very busy and only have a few minutes."

Quintessential Colton Tedie, thought David. Seduction through compliments, then a demand to action.

"I'm calling to initiate discussion on my fee and terms of service as your campaign manager for your upcoming quest for the Republican nomination for President of the United States. Based on my analysis of the players, you are the most uniquely qualified Republican candidate in the field. The time is ideal for a Colton Tedie presidential run and I am the most qualified campaign manager to ensure your quest to the White House ends in victory. I am ready to travel to New York and meet with you at your convenience to begin the discussions in person."

Tedie was uncharacteristically silent for a moment. David could hear a long exhale. Then he spoke. "David, I am honored by your offer. Certainly, and I know, you are one of the best if not *the* best campaign manager out there. The work you have done for some of my friends and colleagues has been first rate, highly commendable."

As Tedie took a breath, David interrupted, "Thank you Mr. Tedie for your kind words. When should I... "

Tedie now continued, "But let me make two things clear, David. You used the word quest in your overture. We don't do quests at Tedie Inc. Quests are what Jacques Cousteau did on The Wild World of Sports or whatever that show was with the Indian head as the logo. Quests are what other people do. What we do here is we win. Do you understand where I am coming from? We win. Period. So, in the event you ever come to work for me you need to understand that. Because you are highly qualified and would do an excellent job, I know this. You just need to understand my expectations."

"Second, and I'm being honest with you here, I don't know where this whole presidential run thing came from. It was not from me and not from my people. I'm perfectly happy, perfectly content with my life. The country is indeed a mess, but someone else is going to have to fix it. I have no current plans to run for president."

Now it was David's turn to be temporarily silent. He had proceeded forth from a false assumption. He assumed the possibility of a Tedie run had been leaked by the Tedie team as a trial balloon to gauge public opinion. Either he had been wrong, or the trial balloon had produced unfavorable results. He latched on to something Tedie said and changed his pitch.

"Yes, sir the country is indeed in a mess. When I survey the landscape of potential candidates in 2016, and juxtapose that against the challenges faced by the country, I see no one other than Colton Tedie whose life experiences and business successes are better suited to lead the country to a better place."

"Well, you certainly are wise in these matters David and I suspect your assessment is one hundred percent accurate. However, as you know, successfully running for president requires a national network of operatives and volunteers and we have not even considered establishing this yet."

"Which is entirely why you need me, Mr. Tedie. A national network is one of the things I deliver to the team."

"Indeed, David, indeed." Tedie hesitated briefly, breathed deeply, and began again. "As I said, at this point I have no plans to run for president. But if I do, you have my word you and I will have another conversation before I make any decisions about a campaign manager. That is the best I can do. Is that fair? Is that fair enough, David?"

"That is fair enough, Mr. Tedie. Thank you for your time."

"And thank you, David. And I mean that sincerely."

In one motion Colton Tedie ended the call with David and immediately dialed Katy.

"Hello, Mr. Tedie."

"Katy, you *did* put that message out on Twitter about the presidential run like I asked you to, yes?"

"Yes, sir I did. And I've been trolling Twitter the past twenty-four hours for reaction."

"Well what have you got?"

"The overwhelming response has been negative."

"Negative that I might run for president?"

"No," Katy replied. "Negative that you are *not* running for president. Thousands of negative replies to my tweet clarifying the news story. The hashtag #tedieforpresident has been trending near the top for the past twenty-four hours."

"No shit."

"Yes sir. No shit."

"Thank you, Katy."

Later that afternoon, Jeffrey received a text from Marvelous Marvin. It read, "We got a call back from Flouphe. He is interested in us again. You said he was on your radar. Thought you would want to know."

"Damn." he said to no one in the room. "Why won't Tedie bite?"

Progression

The next morning, Jeffrey was on the phone with Stephanie for their daily debrief. Today's topic was more critical than most. Jeffrey initiated.

"We've set the stage for you to have a conversation with Tedie. We believe his interest in running has been kindled, but so far, he is not ready to make the move. I think you can leverage what we've done and lure him in."

Stephanie responded, "I think you are right. He will respond to me. The man's got an ego that rivals any I've ever encountered on any continent. If he thinks he has a chance of successfully being elected to the highest political office in the world, he'll jump. Keep working your end, but I'll take lead with AWM."

Stephanie Kenseth and Colton Tedie were well known to each other. The social circles of the Vice President and the national real estate mogul frequently intersected. Tedie had contributed to her husband's campaigns, as well as to her charitable causes through the years. Their social relationship went back over twenty years.

Immediately upon ending the conversation with Jeffrey, Stephanie called Colton Tedie directly. He took the call.

"Madam Vice President, it is good as always to hear from you. How are you today?"

"I am great Colton, thank you for asking. I'm going to be in New York tomorrow and would like to speak with you about something very important. Do you have a few minutes we might chat?"

"Stephanie, you know I always have time for you. Tell me what works for you and I will make it happen."

"Thanks Colton. I'll see you at 10:00am in your office."

"Stephanie, let's make it 11:30. 10:00am is no good. 11:30 is ideal. And I look forward to seeing you then at my office."

Stephanie immediately followed the call with Tedie with a call to her scheduler. "Clear my calendar tomorrow until 2:00pm. I am going to New York." She also sent a text to Jeffrey.

I'M IN WITH AWM TOMORROW MORNING.

■ ■

When they met, they greeted each other with a light embrace.

"Welcome back to New York, Stephanie. It is good to see you."

"Thank you, Colton. It is always good to be in New York."

They sat down at the small conference table inside Tedie's large Manhattan office overlooking Central Park. Stephanie had been here before and was therefore not awed by the view or the Tedie memorabilia which adorned seemingly every vertical and horizontal flat space in the room.

Upon seating people at his conference table, Tedie was accustomed to his guests pausing to take in the view. It was a very expensive view, and he tended to interpret a lack of appreciation for it as almost an affront to his hospitality. He took note of how easily Stephanie dismissed the view while maintaining nearly constant eye contact with him. He was beginning to understand this was not a social visit. He offered her water or soda, which she declined, further confirming his assessment. He saw no reason to delay.

"So, tell me Stephanie, to what do I owe this impromptu visit by the Vice President of the United Sates? Twenty-four hours' notice is not much time to rearrange schedules, but for you I did it and was happy to do it. Tell me what is on your mind."

"Thank you, Colton for being so accommodative, and yes we are all so very busy. Up until yesterday my schedule for today was full as well. But this is a matter of great importance." Stephanie repositioned in her chair. She moved forward, placing her clasped hands in front of her on the round table.

"There is a very important matter I want to discuss with you, and as hard as it may be to believe, it involves politics."

Tedie responded quickly with a slight smirk. "Whoa, wait right there. I had no idea you would come here to discuss politics. I am shocked. I wish I had known, I would have read the papers today."

They both laughed, then Stephanie continued. "I am very concerned about our country, Colton. And specifically, I am concerned about the political discourse in Washington."

"Well that makes two of us, Stephanie. Welcome to the party. I hate to say it, but you are a little late my friend to be concerned with this."

Stephanie continued, "And that is precisely what I want to talk to you about. With a presidential election less than two years away, there is someone in this country who has the ability to significantly and positively impact the direction of the country, and I need your help recruiting that person to the cause."

"Tell me what I can do Stephanie. Tell me how I can help you and our beloved country. You know I will do whatever I can. Tell me how I can help."

"Run for president."

Tedie was temporarily silent. He was sure he had misunderstood the statement. He was sure he had missed the first, or last, or both the first and last parts of the statement. It was disarming to him though how often he was hearing his name recently in the same sentence as the word 'president.'

After a pause, he said, "Yes, Stehpanie, I know you are running for president. How can I help you..."

Stephanie interrupted him and clasped his left wrist with her right hand. "Colton I want you to run for president!"

Colton Tedie was dumbfounded. He could understand others asking him to run, or asking him if he was running. But not someone who would be his opponent. Not someone who, in his opinion, needed his help, not his opposition. He was trying to form words, but his brain temporarily found none to supply. After a long pause, he replied with the only word that made sense to speak at that moment. "What?"

Stephanie Kenseth had never seen Colton Tedie in a state of bewilderment. It took all the diplomatic discipline she had acquired during her forty-year long public and political career to not laugh at the sight she assumed she would never see again. She'd made men look and feel like fools through her words before, but that was almost always by design. This meeting had been put together so quickly she had not taken time to consider the potential effect of her ask on Tedie. She did her best to hide her amusement at his temporary stupor.

"Colton, let me explain." She repositioned again in her seat, again further forward. "The Republican Party is in disarray. That party, your party, represents almost half of the registered voters in this country, and it is in disarray. Let that sink in."

"There are fifty or so of those buffoons planning to run for president. Their ideas are divisive and dangerous. Regardless of the fact none of them will beat me, during the campaign they will move the country in a negative direction. At a time when the world needs leadership from the United States of America, this presidential election cycle has the potential to further diminish our standing in the world community, because of the ideas and morals of the opposition party."

She continued, "You have the power to influence that. You have the power to do that by leading it. I know you are a good American, someone who wants what is best for this country. I know we don't always agree Colton, and we would be running on opposite tickets, but I know you want what is best for this country."

Tedie was not shocked by the message, but he was certainly shocked by the person delivering the message. Why in the hell would the presumed Democrat nominee recruit him to run against her on the Republican ticket? Why would she want to make a victory for herself and her party more difficult to achieve? Did she not believe in his ability to win if he decided in fact, to run for office? Was she as big a fool as he sometimes thought she was? Either way, a man of his power never lets his emotions show, especially not in front of a potential opponent.

After holding eye contact through several seconds of awkward silence, he responded, "Of course I love my country. Every red-blooded American should love their country. But why would the person who is going to run for president on the Democrat ballot ask someone to run on the Republican ballot? If you were not in the race yourself, it would make more sense for you to be here. But this is highly peculiar Stephanie, you have to admit. Highly peculiar."

"Yes, it is highly peculiar Colton, but that is because of my highly peculiar love for my country. Of all the potential candidates in the field, quite frankly, you have the best chance of beating me. So, I am taking a huge risk here. But let me tell you why, and I'll draw on American history to do so. Do you know why Dwight Eisenhower ran for president?

"No, tell me," was Tedie's quick reply.

"He ran for president because he believed the Republican party was in disarray, and in danger of becoming irrelevant as a political force. He believed America was best served by there being two dominant, healthy political parties. The Republican party was far from healthy when he entered the 1952 presidential race as a Republican. He helped save his party, and in doing so, helped his country immensely."

Tedie was still incredibly skeptical of her true motives, and he had no trouble sharing that skepticism with her. He leaned back in his chair and looked at the table as he began speaking. "Stephanie, your whole career, your whole life, has been pointed toward this moment in time. Some might still question your path to getting where you are today. That's neither here nor there. You are certainly a strong contender to become the next president of this country. The first woman president. And yet you are sitting here asking me to run against you. My mind is blown. Why would you encourage and recruit the person who would certainly beat you and end your political career?"

Stephanie realized at last she had touched a competitive chord in Tedie's soul. The conversation and his thought processes were moving in the direction she wanted them to.

Coyly, she responded, "Who knows Colton, you *might* win. President Colton Tedie. Has a ring to it, doesn't it?"

"Might win? *Might* win? Win is what we do here, Stephanie. If I were to enter the race, it would be with the expectation of winning. No other reason."

Stephanie went for the presumptive close. "You are making the right decision, Colton. There's no one else I'd rather square off against."

Colton wasn't ready to let her have that satisfaction. He did not become one of the wealthiest real estate holders in the United States by letting people back him into corners. "Hang on, Stephanie. No decision has been made. I don't get talked into anything, let alone something like running for president. I will give it some thought, you have my word. I am intrigued by the idea, and I am certainly flattered by the fact you are so confident you would beat me," he said with sarcasm.

Stephanie hid her disappointment at the near miss. "In all seriousness, Colton I do believe I would beat you. I would beat any of the losers running on the Republican ticket. Not one of them has a single good idea to move the country forward. We need someone new, someone that hasn't spent their life in politics. Someone who's unpredictable, who has earned their success through hard work and intelligent risk-taking. That's you Colton. Maybe I *am* making a mistake by encouraging you to run. Time will tell. But my allegiance is to my country, and I believe the country is better off with you running for the Republican nomination."

Stephanie rose from her chair to signal the meeting was over. She extended her right hand, which Tedie quickly grasped in a firm handshake after rising to his feet.

"Think about it, Colton. If I can be a resource for what running and enduring a campaign is like, I will be happy to offer you and Michelle my perspective."

"Stephanie, you are a great American, and an even greater person. It took balls for you to invite me into the race, and I respect you for it. I will give the matter its due consideration, and I will let you know when I make a decision."

After making sure the elevator door had closed behind Stephanie Kenseth, Tedie picked up the phone to call his wife, Michelle. Tedie almost never called his wife during the business day.

"You remember I told you Stephanie Kenseth was coming to visit me today? You are not going to believe what she wanted to talk about."

"Let me guess, she wants you to donate to her campaign, or her foundation… or both."

"No, it's not that. She wants me to run for president. Can you believe that?"

"You're not being serious."

"I am serious and so was she. With God as my witness. She sat in my office and asked me to seek the Republican nomination."

After a long pause, Michelle asked "Why would she do that?"

"She thinks the guys who are going to run are bad for the country. She thinks I would be a unifying force on the Republican side."

After another pause. "She *is* running for president herself, right?"

"Yes, of course she is."

"If she wants to be president, would she not want to run against the weakest, not the strongest candidate? Does she think because you have no experience, you would be easy to beat?"

"Who knows what she thinks."

"What did you tell her? You should tell her no. What did you tell her?"

"I told her I would give it some thought, that is all."

Exasperated, Michelle continued, "You should call her now and tell her no. There is something here that does not make sense, Colton. She is cunning… and dangerous. You're the one that told me that."

Colton chuckled. Whether at Michelle's wisdom, or the game in play, he was not sure. "Well I'm not exactly a babe in the woods myself dear."

Tedie paused before continuing, "You are a smart lady, Michelle. That is why I married you."

As planned, Stephanie called Jeffrey from the limousine on the way back to the airport. Jeffrey saw Stephanie's number on his phone and answered with a direct question. "Success?"

"He's going to think about it. But my sense is he may need a little more of a nudge before taking the bait."

"You couldn't convince him? I thought his out-of-this-world ego coupled with your charms would take him exactly where we want him."

"He was blown away by the idea, and by the fact it was me asking. He seemed skeptical. He may fool me and say yes, but I think we're going to need to approach him from a different angle."

Jeffrey smiled confidently and said, "I thought that might be the case, and I've been working on something."

"You're so intuitive. Anything you can share at this point?"

"I'll let you know after we hear from him."

"Done."

For the next seven days, in between meetings and appearances and in the very small amount of contemplative time he had, Colton Tedie considered what it would be like to be President of the United States. He put aside Michelle's counsel to consider the ulterior motive of his encourager, and focused on the mother's milk of politics: money.

He thought about Stephanie Kenseth and the hundreds of millions of dollars he was certain she had generated for herself because of her celebrity and political influence. Though he would never admit it to her, Tedie had a competitor's respect for the tactics Stephanie and her late husband had put to use to create what he assumed was great personal wealth. Campaign finance laws being what they are, or aren't, he understood more than most people that politics is a pay to play racket, disguised as a benevolence society. Bribes disguised as speaking fees, consultants with briefcases full of cash, and access to the public treasury… only a complete idiot, or Puritan, could not make a fortune in this game he thought.

He caught himself chuckling slightly, and shaking his head in disbelief. His thoughts transitioned for a moment to the sheer enormity of the size of the government the President of the United States is responsible for leading. An annual budget of four trillion dollars. Four *trillion* dollars. An annual budget larger than the total value of goods and services produced by most countries in the world. Entire countries he thought. Again, he caught himself shaking his head. As the leader of an organization worth billions, he knew he was one of just a few hundred people capable of fathoming how unfathomable the amount of power four trillion dollars represented. Controlling that amount of money, four trillion dollars; the opportunities for graft and influence peddling were too many for him to even consider.

His thoughts moved to former Vice President Alton Gourley, and how Gourley had successfully leveraged a career in politics into hundreds of millions of dollars for himself by preying on the emotions and fears of the anti-capitalists. He hated the lack of integrity in the guy, but he marveled at his financial success.

These were his thoughts while on his jet flying to Miami. He was going there to meet with several business and government people with intimate knowledge of the business climate and workforce in Cuba. The meeting had been arranged several weeks previous. Many times, both William Kenseth and Stephanie Kenseth had made public statements about the need to ease decades old economic sanctions against Cuba. It was widely speculated they had managed to create real estate assets for themselves on the island while William was governor of Florida. If that were true, an easing of sanctions would be a financial windfall for Stephanie Kenseth. Tedie's meeting today had been arranged in anticipation of her doing just that if she were to become president, which would open the island up to US investment.

Tedie couldn't help but ponder how much a sitting US president could easily, and tremendously, benefit financially from something as nebulous as a change of diplomatic relations with another country. He was certain, absolutely certain that once diplomatic relations with Cuba were restored, there would be an opportunity for direct economic investment on the island. It would be easy to cloak this motivation by saying that he—that whomever was president—was simply doing the right thing for the people of Cuba. Again, Tedie found himself shaking his head. Whether the head shake was because of the simple brilliance of the strategy, or the naiveté of the media and public to be blind to it, he was not entirely sure.

One thing was certain, though. By the time he exited his jet in Miami, he had decided to run for president. He was ready to be president. And he was slightly annoyed with himself for not having made the decision earlier in his life.

The limousine ride to the meeting was short. Tedie was excited. He wanted to call Stephanie and share his decision with her but did not feel he had time. Instead, he sent a short text:

WILL SEE YOU IN NOVEMBER. I'LL CALL SOON TO DISCUSS.

Tedie's limousine quickly reached the hotel where the meeting was to be held. As the limousine pulled into the long driveway, he noticed what looked like 100 people—or more—standing along the sidewalk, most of them carrying signs that simply read, "Say no, Mr. Tedie." He noticed there were almost no young people in the group; almost all of them were his age or older. He thought this a bit odd for a protest.

To no one in particular he said, "What the hell is this about?" as the limousine continued past the crowd and toward the private entrance they had arranged for him to enter through. No one on his team had been alerted to any expected protests. No one in his entourage could offer an answer to his question.

Tedie entered the hotel and was quickly taken to a conference room. Already waiting for him there were government officials from Cuba, Cuban Nationals, and a few Europeans with existing financial interests on the island.

For the next two hours, Tedie and his team were presented with information, pictures, and videos of various places and cities on the island to potentially build new hotels and casinos. Tedie was being offered the opportunity to make substantial investments in properties which would increase tremendously in value when diplomatic relations between the United States and Cuba were returned to a more favorable status.

For two hours, he listened and said very little. This was not normal for Tedie, and his team was somewhat dumbfounded by his silence.

Tedie finally spoke at the end of the presentations. He seemed distracted as he spoke. "I want to thank each of you for making this information available to me today. Certainly, there are opportunities for Cuba to substantially upgrade its hotel and leisure facilities, and attract many, many tourists from the United States and around the world once travel restrictions to Cuba are lifted by my country's government."

Eduardo Perez, representative for the Cuban government, invited Tedie to quickly visit several the locations by air. "Mr. Tedie, we are prepared to fly you and your employees over the island today. We have a plane ready to go at the airport. I am sure you would appreciate even more the value represented by these properties if you saw them first-hand."

"That will not be necessary, Mr. Perez. I'm quite certain I've never been on a plane maintained by a communist country and I'm quite sure I would not feel comfortable about it." His words were direct and emotionless, not meant as an insult, simply reflecting his true thoughts. Now, his team knew he was engaged.

Tedie turned to his staff. "Does anyone know how long we have the room?"

"We have the room reserved for several more hours," came the reply. Tedie was not sure who said it, but it was the answer he was looking for.

"I think we are ready to adjourn here. Again, I thank everyone for making the trip to share your information with us. We have a lot to digest. What I'd like to do is continue in this room with my team only, so that we can discuss what you have presented."

The members of Tedie's team, who had begun shutting down their tablets and zipping up their bags, were now really confused. This was not a tactic they had ever seen from him before.

After handshakes and goodbyes, the room was cleared. Tedie closed the doors and addressed the team leader, Robinson Larue. "Okay, Robbie, here is what I want you to do. I want you to take the limousine out of the complex to where those people were gathered, the ones with the Tedie signs. I'm guessing they are still there. I want you to engage that group, and bring several of their leaders back here, to this room. I want to talk to them."

Several minutes later, Robinson returned with four men and two women from the protest group. Mr. Tedie rose to meet them as they entered the room, and shook each of their hands, asking each of them for their names. He offered them all water and food left over from the meeting. When everyone was settled, Tedie commenced to get an answer to the original question he had asked out loud in the limousine.

With a smile and in a friendly tone, the now jacketless Tedie opened the conversation, "So, I'm minding my own business, visiting a city that I love, on my way to a meeting. And out of nowhere I come upon this large group of people holding up signs with my name on them, asking me to say no. And I'm confused. Say no to what? I've been to Miami a hundred times, I love coming here. It's a wonderful city. And this is the first time I've ever been accosted by a mob of people. A friendly mob mind you, but still a large group of people. It was a little scary and unnerving to quite honest with you." Tedie was still smiling, which allowed a gentle roll of laughter to flow from the group and his team.

"So, tell me now, because you have my full, undivided attention, who are you representing, and what is it that you want me to say 'no' to?"

After looking at the others in the group, the gentleman who appeared to be the oldest rose and began to speak with a heavy Latino accent. "Thank you, Mr. Tedie, for your hospitality. It is an honor to meet you in this way, and have the opportunity to speak to you."

"My name is Jose Garcia. I immigrated to America after Fidel Castro led his armed takeover of my country in 1959." Jose paused briefly, then motioned with his left arm toward the others in his group. "Each of us immigrated after Castro took power and enslaved our countrymen. All our families suffered, as Fidel and his henchmen nationalized our property and businesses and land that our families had worked for generations to own. We are here to ask you to not do business with the Cuban government. Anything they might sell you is stolen! Stolen from the people who rightfully owned it until 1959, when they stole it from the people who had worked generations to build their lives."

Then one by one, after Mr. Garcia finished speaking, each member of the group told their family's story of tragedy after the rise of the Castro led Communists in 1959. Each told of having one or more family members jailed for their political beliefs, or because they would not pay off local police and party officials.

As each person spoke, Tedie experienced a growing level of anger. Anger toward Fidel Castro and the government of Cuba. He was angry that any government would take that which people had worked their whole lives, and their parents had worked their whole lives, to obtain. He could relate to success, and the understanding that material possessions represent something more than just their utility. That they many times are the physical representation of hard work and good decisions and long hours and saving and planning and doing.

Eventually, each of the immigrants talked of their experiences in America. How they had come with nothing more than just the clothes on their backs. How they had found a job, worked hard, earned money for a home, and built a life for themselves and their families. Tedie was struck by the sense of community each of them had and the pride in their heritage. At the same time, they each possessed undeniable pride and love for America, and the opportunities they had realized as a result of being here.

Tedie's anger toward the Communist regime of Cuba transitioned as these people talked. It transitioned into pride for his country. He was proud to be a citizen of a country where a person equipped only with health and a willingness to work hard could succeed and become self-sufficient and create opportunities for their family that they could have never dreamed would be possible.

The Cuban immigrants spoke for nearly two hours. Robinson and the other members of the Tedie team were shocked that Tedie was engaged with them for such a long period of time—and with barely any speaking on his part! They did not know Tedie had decided on a presidential run. They did not realize these people were reshaping Tedie's view of his country and his own relationship to it.

When it was obvious each person had spoken their peace and had nothing left to say, Tedie finally responded. His first attempt at words were choked back by a lump in his throat. He reached for his glass of water and then tried again, successfully this time.

"Thank you for sharing your stories. You are a remarkable group of people and I know you are simply representatives of a larger group of people who all share similar experiences." He paused for a moment to collect his thoughts. His staff had taken note of the fact his signature rapid fire rate of speech was not evident, and that he was truly speaking with these people, not at them.

"I am honestly at a loss of what to say. Hearing your stories makes me proud to be an American. I mean that. So, thank you for reminding me, and actually revealing to me in some ways, what a great country of opportunity this is."

"You know, being from New York, you hear stories of families who immigrated from Italy and Poland and Ireland and Germany and other places. But that was a long time ago for most families, and most of those people were just seeking a better opportunity, and not fleeing a government behaving in criminal ways. I have heard of the stories from Cuba before. But I had never heard *these* stories. I am touched, I really am. My heart is with you."

Tedie now sat a little straighter in his chair, and became more intentional with his eye contact. "You have my word we will do everything we can, everything in our power to not do business with the Cuban government. Cuba represents a huge opportunity for us. We cannot ignore it. But you have my word we will investigate and perform due diligence to ensure that nothing we might buy in Cuba is owned by the Cuban government. The investments we make in Cuba will create jobs for your people and put them on a path toward greater self-sufficiency. Is that fair?"

Jose rose again to speak. "That is fair, Mr. Tedie. Thank you for hearing our concerns. Thank you for being sympathetic to the plight of our people and our country."

Tedie responded, "All of you are great Americans. I am proud to count you as my fellow country men and women. I have thoroughly enjoyed our time together. My staff will tell you it is highly unusual for me to invest more than five minutes in a day to an unscheduled activity. But it was important and I'm very, very glad to have met you. My head of staff for this project is Robinson over here. I would like for you to share your contact information with him. The knowledge you have can be very important to me as we consider our Cuban investments. I would like the ability to reach out to you and speak to you in the future."

Colton Tedie was unusually silent in the limousine ride back to the airport. His thoughts were still consumed by what he had just heard. He felt anger toward the Cuban government, and the plight its criminal actions had inflicted on its people. He empathized with the immigrants who had built their lives in a country blessed with freedom. At that moment, he realized his kinsman ship was with people creating opportunity, not with government restricting it or even taking it away. He began to realize that all his life he had pushed back against the inefficiencies and largesse of bureaucrats at different levels, in order to realize opportunity for himself and others. He was proud of that. He wanted to continue in that role. He did not want to be on the other side of the table, restricting freedom, restricting opportunity. He decided he did not want to be POTUS. And he was proud of his decision.

Colton Tedie waited until he was back in his Manhattan office before calling Stephanie as he said he would. He thought of the text he had sent her, when he thought he would run. He was confident he could spin it.

Stephanie did not hesitate to answer the phone when she saw the caller.

"Hello Colton!"

"Hello Madam Vice President, aka Mrs. Kenseth, aka the next President of the United States."

"Colton, you do know how to flatter a girl. And I am certain that you have made the right decision. You will bring a focus and clarity and a level of sensibility to the Republican Party that is sorely missing. We will be great opponents."

"Whoa, Stephanie, hold on. You are talking as if you know my decision. The purpose of my call to you today is to communicate my decision."

Stephanie expressed her genuine surprise. "Really? I received your text earlier today. That text sounded like you had made a decision, and had made the right decision. Have you changed your mind?"

"No, Stephanie, I have not changed my mind. You obviously misinterpreted the meaning of my text. What did my text say? It said see you in November. That means I expect you to be the next President of the United States. The first woman as President of the United States. That is what my text communicated."

Stephanie quickly adjusted. She was certain Tedie decided to run for the Republican nomination and then changed his mind. To argue the meaning of the text would be fruitless.

"Colton, you are correct. I assumed your text meant you and I would face off in the November election, which obviously meant you would have won the Republican nomination. I am certain if you decide to run for that nomination, you will win. But now I realize your text was not meant to communicate that decision."

"Now we are on the same page," responded Tedie.

"So, you have made a decision? I know many people of the Republican persuasion will be excited to have you as their nominee."

"Indeed they would. And I would be excited and honored to represent them. But I have decided someone else should have that opportunity. I have no plans to run for the nomination or for president. I am flattered, really I am, that you would think to ask me. It would have been a helluva race between us, Stephanie. And, honestly, I think I would have beaten you. But I have full confidence in you to lead this country. Therefore, I will not run."

Stephanie was frustrated. "But, why, Colton? You have a potentially historic opportunity. The Leadership of YOUR party is destroying what makes this country great. Whether unintentionally or intentionally I am not sure. But I am damn sure they are a negative influence on this country. You are sensible, reasonable. You can rally your party behind you and help lead this country to a better place. Will you reconsider?"

"Stephanie, I know everything you say is true. But the truth of the matter is, honestly, I cannot afford to run."

Stephanie quickly interjected, "What, Colton? You will be a fundraising machine. And if what you fundraise on your own is not enough to sustain your campaign, frankly, there are ways we can help you."

"No, Stephanie, you are such a politician. You are getting this backward. It would cost me millions of dollars to take the necessary time away from the Tedie Organization in order to run for president. You make money off government and off your celebrity status and influence peddling. I make money by doing things. By building things. By generating ideas and bringing those ideas to market. I have great people at my organization. But ultimately, I am the decision maker. My involvement here is crucial. I can best serve my country by doing what I do best."
"And I hope, Stephanie, I hope and pray that my decision does not affect our friendship. I greatly value our friendship, which is based on honesty. I've been totally honest with you Stephanie, and I hope you will respect that. Our friendship is important to me, and my conscience is clear with this decision."

"Colton, I thank you for your honesty and I value our friendship as well. That will always remain. I'd be lying to you though if I said I wasn't disappointed. I am disappointed. Disappointed for the country primarily. But also disappointed that I will be facing a lesser opponent."

She continued, "I respect what you are saying though, Colton. I am sure you are the driving force behind your organization. Just for my curiosity and education, how much would it cost for you to be away from Tedie Organization? I mean, for the time you were campaigning and during the primary season, how much would that cost you?"

He thought it odd that Stephanie would ask such a direct and personal question. He was ready for the conversation to be over, so he offered a direct answer rather than an evasive one.

"Stephanie, you are talking about an eighteen to twenty-four-month timeframe. It would cost me a minimum of $10 million to take that amount of time away from my business dealings here. Minimum. That is a lot of money, as you know."

"Yes, indeed it is," Stephanie paused for a moment as she thought. "Colton, I respect your decision. There is still time though for you to change your mind. I hope you will respect me if I don't take no for an answer now, and potentially revisit this with you again in a few weeks. Can we have that understanding?"

"Stephanie, I of all people respect a salesperson who does not accept no for an answer. My father always taught me that no means maybe. In this case, no means no, but I cannot stop you from following up with me in a few weeks if it helps put your mind at ease. I will not be disappointed or angry if we have another conversation on the topic. I doubt you can change my mind, but who knows? I am a reasonable human being."

"That's all I ask. Thank you."

After ending the call, Stephanie immediately hit Jeffrey's number.

Miracle in the Desert

"Hello, Stephanie."

Stephanie spoke very quickly. "He changed his mind. Says he's not running. Says it would cost him too much money to be away from his business. Asshole!"

"Me or him?" asked Jeffrey.

"What? Him, you asshole. You know what I meant. Don't play games with my words when I'm pissed. You know how much I hate that."

Jeffrey grinned. "You said he changed his mind. Colton Tedie almost never changes his mind. What is up with that?"

"He claims he didn't change his mind. Says I misinterpreted his text. What the fuck ever. But he is clear on the fact he is not running. Says it would cost him $10 million in lost income to devote time to a campaign."

"It may cost him more *not* to run."

Stephanie was mad when she called Jeffrey. She felt like Tedie had lied to her. Verbalizing her thoughts had only served to increase her anger. She was therefore only hearing bits and pieces of what Jeffrey was saying.

"What are we going to do Jeffrey? You said before you were working on another plan. What is that? Is that ready?"

"You didn't hear me. I said it may cost him more than $10 million NOT to run."

Stephanie was confused. "What are we talking about?"

"Plan B."

Stephanie paused for several seconds. "Well, are you going to tell me or are you just going to keep talking in riddles?"

Jeffrey grinned again, and bit his tongue. He liked his job, and knew when to be serious about doing it. "I have a Plan B in place. I know how you will get Tedie in the race. He will have no choice. And if we play it right, we might just control him the entire primary season. It's going to be great."

For the first time since she got off the phone with Tedie, Stephanie felt like she could breathe. Her anger abated. It was replaced with a sense of relief, a sense that Jeffrey would once again come through for her, and that she would soon be one significant step closer to the presidency.

She breathed deeply then stated, "You have my attention Jeffrey. Do tell."

"OK. Here's the deal. Tedie is building a new hotel in Vegas. Biggest damn thing you've ever seen. Citibank is providing the financing. The construction is running a little behind schedule. The beauty of that for *us* is, Citibank has covenants in their Loan Agreement that say they can declare the loan in default if specific construction milestones are not achieved by specific dates."

"I'm listening Jeffrey. I'm not following yet, but I'm listening."

"Keep listening. The Loan Agreement says the electrical systems must all be working in the building by June 1. That's just two weeks away. If they are not working by that date, the loan can be declared in default. But here is what's even better. I'm still doing research, but I believe there are several intercreditor agreements between Citibank and Tedie's other banks on other projects. He has something like ten construction projects going on worldwide right now. Most likely, there are cross default provisions in those agreements. If that is the case, when one lender declares a loan default, all lenders can declare default. Declaring loan defaults is bad enough in itself. It's worse for a construction loan, because the lender can force a cessation of construction activity if it chooses. That would cost Tedie millions in extra costs and lost revenue."

"OK, I understand how this is bad for Tedie. How is it good for us?"

"It is good for us because you are going to visit your buddy John Ross at Citibank and persuade him to declare default and call Tedie's loans. That will start a chain reaction of other banks calling Tedie's loans. I can't begin to tell you how costly that will be to Tedie. It will be huge. At that point, you hold all the cards. You force Tedie into the race, while offering him a financial pathway out of his situation. He enters the race, you give him some feel good money from your discretionary campaign coffers, and then get Citibank to remove his loan from default status. The other banks will follow suit."

These was only silence on the other end of the line.

"Stephanie, do you follow me?"

"I think so. You said something about electrical systems and an upcoming date. Sounded like that is the key. How do we make sure those electrical systems are not turned on?

"By calling in some favors. Tomorrow, you will call your friend David Michaels, the Assistant Secretary of Labor for OSHA. You will instruct David to have OSHA inspect the Tedie construction site in Las Vegas immediately. He needs to find a Level 2 infraction. OSHA can always find something that is not exactly perfect, and a Level 2 infraction is fairly common. Also, tomorrow I will call Tom Stenson."

Jeffrey continued to talk, but Stephanie was still digesting all this information. She quickly interrupted, "Who is that? Who is Tom?"
"Tom is the president of Local 357, the International Brotherhood of Electrical Workers Union in Las Vegas. I got his name from our friends at the national AFL-CIO office. I will let him know that the Tedie site will be hit with a Level 2 infraction tomorrow. Per their contract, a Level 2 OSHA infraction allows him to pull his workers off the site for whatever amount of time he deems necessary, up to 30 days, to ensure the site is safe and his workers are not at risk. This ability is already written into their contract. Once his workers are off the site, there is no way the electrical will be working at the hotel by the deadline, which will allow Citi to call a default."
Jeffrey paused, proud of his work. "All wrapped up, with a nice, tidy bow around it."

"Jeffrey, this is brilliant. You never cease to amaze me. How do you know all these things? How do you have these intimate details of Tedie's loans?"

"Madam Vice President, I have a network that reaches far and wide. And, you pay me to know these things."

Early the next morning, after reviewing the file on David Michaels which Jeffrey had emailed her, Stephanie dialed the number for his office at the OSHA headquarters in Washington. "David, this is Stephanie Kenseth. It has been a long time since we've spoken! How are you?"

"I am well, Madam Vice President, thank you for asking. I trust you are as well."

"Yes, never better. And how are Nancy and David Jr?"

David was flattered that Mrs. Kenseth remembered his children's names. "They are great. Nancy has graduated college and is working in DC for the EPA, and David is still in college. He is president of the Young Democrats at Penn."

"Excellent! I am sure you are justifiably proud of them both. David, I'm sure you are busy so I will get right to the point. The reason for my call this morning is twofold. First, I just want to say thank you for your great work at OSHA. I know you have served your country for many years, faithfully ensuring that the nation's workplaces are as safe as possible for our workers. That is a duty to be proud of and I hope you are."

"The second reason for my call, David, is to encourage you and your team to check into the safety and working conditions of Colton Tedie's hotel construction project currently underway in Las Vegas. It would be ideal if an inspection could occur today. Through my sources, I've learned there are multiple safety concerns with this project which are not being addressed adequately. Most likely, I think your team will discover a Stage 2 infraction while conducting this safety inspection. David, am I making myself clear?"

David responded, "Mrs. Kenseth, as always, your concern for the American worker is obvious and commendable. As you know, we conduct multiple unscheduled inspections of construction sites across the country every single day. You can rest assured knowing that the hundreds of workers doing their jobs at the Tedie Las Vegas site will benefit from an inspection today. I also suspect what you meant to say was Level 2 infraction, not Stage 2 infraction. I'm sure we will find one or more during our visit."

"Oh, of course. You are correct. My friend Larry is suffering from stage 2 cancer and I simply got my terms mixed up. Thank you for your dedication to our cause and I look forward to speaking with you again soon." Stephanie Kenseth did not know anyone named Larry who was suffering from stage 2 cancer.

Later that morning, Jeffrey made his own call, to the Local Chapter 357 in Las Vegas. Before doing so, he had called the Washington office of the Senior Senator from Nevada, who provided him Tom Stenson's phone number, as well as other necessary information. When Stenson's phone rang, he did not recognize the number, but he did recognize the Washington DC area code.

"This is Tom Stenson."

"Tom, good morning. This is Jeffrey Saint, Stephanie Kenseth's Executive Campaign Manager. How are things in Las Vegas today?"

"Hot and about to get hotter, Jeffrey. What can I do for you today?"

"Tom, first of all I want to thank you and Local 357 for the generous contributions you've made to Democrat causes throughout the years. Our work in electing the right candidates would not be possible without support from good Americans such as yourself and your members. Thank you for that.

Secondly, I'm sure you are familiar with the new Tedie hotel being built in your city?"

"Yes, very familiar. We have men there now. The project is behind schedule and we are being pushed to meet a deadline. Why do you ask about that project?"

"The reason for my call today is to inform you there is a high probability the Tedie work site will be flagged by OSHA with a Level 2 infraction later today. Now I know the safety of your members is a paramount concern for you. OSHA is inspecting the property today. It is important you are available during this time."

"Thanks for the heads up. Tell me your name again."

"Jeffrey Saint, Stephanie Kenseth's Executive Campaign Manager."

"Jeffrey, not all Level 2 infractions carry the same weight in terms of actual safety concerns. It doesn't take much to reach a Level 2."

"Tom, I understand this. I also understand the union contract with the General Contractor allows you to pull your workforce from the site for up to thirty days after any Level 2 infraction, to ensure the safety of your workers. Is that not correct?"

"Yes, that is correct. But at this point, if we pull our workers for even a day, it is highly unlikely the performance deadlines we are being pushed to meet will be met."

"That is not your problem, Tom. That is the General Contractor's problem and Tedie's problem. I believe your contract also requires the GC to compensate your union for lost work days resulting from OSHA violations. Is that correct?"

"In certain cases, yes that is correct."

"Then you are covered."

There was a pause before Tom continued, "Jeffrey, we occasionally get nut jobs calling here asking us to do crazy things. I'm not going to pull my guys from a job for just anyone. Help me confirm you are who you say you are."

"Certainly, Tom and I understand completely. Before calling you this morning I was on the phone with Charlie Reed, your Senator. He said to pass along his best to you and Maria and the children. He also wanted me to say the Miracle in the Desert would not be possible without people like you."

"Message received and understood, Mr. Saint. You guys keep fighting the good fight in DC and we will do our part out here."

"You're a good man and a great American, Tom. Thank you."

As planned, the OSHA inspection occurred later that day. Several Level 2 infractions were found, all of which were administrative in nature and not physical work condition issues. As required, OSHA informed all the sub-contractors that Level 2 citations had been issued for the site. The following day, only Local 357 pulled off the site. The other sub-contractors remained.

The ensuing conversation between the General Contractor and Tom Stenson of Local 357 was heated. But there was nothing the GC could to. Union contract rules prevailed and the General Contractor was unsuccessful in getting Local 357 back on the job until the day before the deadline for full completion of the electrical work. At that point, the issue was settled anyway. There was no way to meet the deadline. The General Contractor was unaware the deadline was connected to Loan Agreements. It would not have mattered if he had. The situation was beyond his ability to control at this point.

As required, the General Contractor informed its client, Tedie Organization, that a construction deadline was not being met. The General anticipated the electrical for the building would be fully completed and functioning within two weeks. Toby Kaye was Tedie Organization's project manager. He accepted the explanation for the delay and resulting time frame. However, Toby managed the field operations only. He was not in finance. He too was unaware the construction deadline was also tied to Loan Agreement Covenants.

Call the Loans

"You want me to do what?!"

"C'mon John, I didn't stutter. I want you to call Colton Tedie's loans." Stephanie was smiling, but her tone was flat and unaffected.

John Ross, president of Citibank, continued to stare at Stephanie Kenseth across the small conference table in his New York office with a dumbfounded look he was struggling to suppress. He knew Stephanie could be more brash and bold than anyone, but this was new ground. After several seconds of silence, he said the only thing he could think of. "Can I ask why?"

"Sure, you can ask." More silence. No words. Just her signature "you're a dumbass" look.

Squelching the desire to tell her to go screw herself (she could, potentially, be the future president after all), John tried again. "I'd really like to know why?"

"Why is not important John. I just need you to do it. And quickly. Isn't it enough that I am the one asking, John? I mean, I could have sent Jeffrey here to meet with you. Or I could have just sent you a text. But our relationship means more to me than that. I'm actually feeling a little disrespected that I've had to ask twice. And you know, or should know, that I hate feeling disrespected."

John Ross had known Stephanie Kenseth for years. He, his board, and his management team at Citibank had donated hundreds of thousands of dollars to William Kenseth's political campaigns, as well as to Stephanie's charitable causes over the years. That's actually what he thought this meeting was going to be about, and he had come prepared to write a large check either to her presidential campaign, or to the ICSJ Foundation, or both. Her request to call Colton Tedie's loans had certainly caught him off guard.

In his most charming manner, John continued the conversation, "Stephanie, you and I are friends..."

"Yes, we are." Stephanie interrupted quickly.

John continued, "And between you and me I would love to call that pompous bastard's loans. Not just because you want me to, mind you. I'd love to do it just to see the veins in his neck bulge and watch his face catch on fire. But I've got to have a reason to call his loans. I don't have the DOJ at my disposal, you know. A tenth of a second after we call his loans he will have 100 attorneys suing us to death. And you of all people know what that is like."

Stephanie's face offered no quarter at John's failed attempt at humor.

John continued, "I'd like to help you dear friend, but I just don't know how I can."

Unknowingly, John had walked directly into her trap. Stephanie smiled. "John, I *so* appreciate your sincerity. And that's why I'm going to show you how to help me."

John did not like this answer. His heartrate increased slightly and his mouth went dry. Doing his best to mask his physical stress he said, "Well tell me, tell me." And he leaned a little closer in his chair toward Stephanie.

She continued, "Citibank holds the financing on the new Tedie Hotel in Las Vegas. You have covenants in the Loan Agreement which require the electrical systems in that building to be working by June 1, which was yesterday. The Tedie hotel missed that Loan Covenant deadline. Tedie is in default, you just haven't declared it yet."

That Stephanie knew Citibank was the lead financier on the Tedie's new Vegas hotel was not terribly surprising. That was a matter of public record. What was not a matter of public record were the loan covenants, and the hotel's construction progress relative to those covenants. Colton Tedie was the largest borrower at the country's largest bank. It was John Ross's job to be aware of the financial status and wherewithal of his bank's largest credit clients. But Stephanie was sharing detailed information that had not even reached his desk yet. He was at a loss for how she knew it. Before he could protest that Stephanie knew detailed and private information about his biggest client, she continued.

"You also have Call Provisions in all of your loans to Colton Tedie and his many, many connected businesses. One of those Call Provisions states that if Mr. Tedie is declared to be in default in any of his loans, you have the right to place all his associated loans in default. A declaration of default allows you to exercise the Call Provision. See there, problem solved. Isn't that amazing? You can call Tedie's loans after all."

Turning toward her Campaign Manager, Jeffrey, who was standing silently several feet away while looking out of the window of Ross's Manhattan office, Stephanie asked, "I did say that correctly, didn't I?

"Yes, madam Vice President. You stated it perfectly." During their conversation, Jeffrey had made his way closer to John and Stephanie. It was Jeffrey's research which Mrs. Kenseth had relied upon to make her statements.

"Thank you, Jeffrey. That is all." Jeffrey resolutely stepped away from the conversation. John now felt trapped. Trapped by his own words. In his own office. He was angry. No one outside of Citibank and Colton Tedie and his advisors should know the information Stephanie had quoted scripture and verse about. He made no attempt to hide his anger.

"How the hell did you get access to this information?"

Again, a pause. Again, she looked at him as if he were the biggest fool she'd ever met. "Really John? You don't think I can get access to any information I want? Anytime, anywhere?"

John's anger grew. Decorum was melting away. "This is bullshit. You should not be able to access government resources to hack me. We've given you piles of money and this is the respect we get in return? Pure bullshit!"

"Calm down John. I didn't use government resources. And I'll tell you in a minute what you get in return."

John was incredulous. "You're telling me you didn't use the power of the government to hack our privileged and confidential information? I don't believe you. How else could you do it?"

Stephanie leaned further forward in her chair, her hands clasped in front of her in her lap, and she spoke very slowly while maintaining strict eye contact. "John, I did not use government resources to get this information. I used something much more powerful."

She paused. John sat silently, processing what he had just heard. Turning her face away from John and toward Jeffery she said quietly, "Look over there at Jeffrey. Tell me what you see."

Jeffrey was again near the window, head bent over his phone. "I see a guy, probably sending a text or an email. What am I supposed to see?"

Stephanie asked, "What do you know about Jeffrey?"

John paused, not certain where Stephanie wanted him to go. "Well, he's sharply dressed every time I've ever seen him. He's doing well for himself, it seems. He's..."

"Go further. Who do you think he sleeps with?"

John almost choked. Was she for real? "Well, I assume he's gay, if that's what you're fishing for."

Stephanie responded, "Yes he is gay. Do you know why I specifically wanted a homosexual in such a critical role in my organization, John?"

His annoyance caused him to respond with more honesty that he normally would. "I assume for fundraising purposes. But now I'm guessing there is more."

Stephanie continued, "You are right on both accounts. The homosexual community is extremely important to our cause. They contribute tremendous amounts of money to the candidates they believe in. More money per donor than any of our other constituencies. But here's the kicker. Homosexuals are connected by a bond that heterosexuals cannot relate to. They share a common struggle and value system. They relate to and pull for each other in a deeply emotional way. It is an unspoken ideology, much stronger than any other creed or spoken promise of solidarity that I've ever witnessed. We recognize their plight, they support us, so we support them."

"Ok," John responded, "but what the hell does that have to do with my breech of security?" Stephanie paused and raised an eyebrow. John reflected on Stephanie's words. John's mind began answering the question even before Stephanie was able to respond. The look on his face exposed his newfound revelation. Stephanie then proceeded to validate.

"When the homosexual rock star Executive Campaign Director for the Vice President, for the first woman running for president, calls on his network of kindred souls to source information, ideology wins. It was easy, John. I'm certain you have several hundred—maybe even several thousand—homosexuals working for you. It did not take Jeffrey long to find the goods on Tedie. Actually, it took just a few hours and several phone calls. To hell with using government resources to do this research. We have a much more effective network at our disposal."

John felt stupid and powerless at the same time. The CEO of the largest bank in the country was not accustomed to being in this place. Stephanie knew exactly where he was and what she was doing. She let him marinade for a moment as she went back to the private bar to fill her glass.

She did not linger there long enough though to make an enemy. John was a friend and a supporter. That she was using him and his organization to accomplish her desired outcomes was strictly business. She was prepared to reward him for helping her. She sat back down and took a sip from her glass before continuing. "John, what do you think will happen to Citibank's stock when you call Tedie's loans?"

"We both know it will take a dive. Our shareholders will lose millions of dollars. Temporarily at least, and that's assuming the news does not cause a broader decline."

Stephanie responded, "Yes, people will lose money. Unless they have shorted the stock." Shorting a stock is a way to profit when a stock goes down. It is a legal practice, but one that is closely watched by the Securities and Exchange Commission for nefarious activity, such as trading with insider knowledge. Having knowledge that Citibank would call the loans for the bank's largest credit client certainly qualified as having insider knowledge. What Stephanie was suggesting John do was clearly illegal and they both knew it.

"John, you could short Citibank's stock through the Trusts that I'm sure you have, which allow your advisors to trade on your behalf without you being directly involved. I will instruct my friends at the SEC to look the other way. It will be fine, and you will make several hundred thousand dollars. Everyone will win. And in a few days or weeks the stock will rebound as Citibank and Tedie work it out."

John was highly skeptical, but at least now he was being given a good reason to warm to the plan a little. He assumed he better warm to it anyway, because there did not appear to be any other way out. At the same time, the prospect of being convicted of insider trading and going to federal prison did not appeal to him. He turned his glance to the window, then back to Stephanie before responding, "How can you be sure the SEC will look the other way?"

Stephanie now looked directly at him, incredulity written on her face. "John, you disappoint me with your lack of faith." She paused before continuing. "Tell me, do you recall what happened to the stock market in the months leading up to Ingle's election?"

"Of course I remember. No one will ever forget that. The stock market lost nearly half its value, dropping from nearly 16,000 down to 8,000."

"Yeah, I remember that too." Stephanie said with a faraway look in her eyes. "All the economic news being put out was bordering on doomsday. Every day, a constant barrage of negativity. Do you remember what happened almost at the exact time the election was over?"

John responded, "The market starting going up."

"Yes, it did. What if a person had shorted the market when it started going down, and then invested in the upside when Barry was elected? Wonder how that person would have done?"

"That person would have made millions, would have made enough money to live a few hundred years, easily."

"Indeed John. And that is what in fact happened. And some of those who made those millions still work for the SEC. All those news stories that helped to move the market didn't just happen. We made that happen by leveraging our intimate relationships with the news makers. The right people at the SEC know this, and benefitted from it. Trust me, they will look the other way on your little short sale if I tell them to."

John knew Stephanie was powerful. But was she *that* powerful? And taking credit for something that had happened in the past was easy to do. The oldest trick in the book. He was skeptical, but dared not challenge the witch directly.

"Just so I understand, you are saying you engineered an historic stock market decline so that certain people could benefit from both the rise and the fall?"

"No John, of course we didn't engineer the drop. We engineered the media narrative leading up to an election. It was in our candidate's interest to do so. The stock market drop was a predictable casualty of the narrative. It would have been a shame to not profit from a predictable outcome, would it not? We simply let a few of our friends in on the media plan, and they took it from there. Look, John when you start a boulder rolling down hill, you don't know exactly what damage it is going to do. But you know it's going to do damage. In this case, it turned out to be a lot of damage. But we warned our friends, they took counter measures, and some people made a lot of money. That money is my equity, and sometimes I call on that equity. You have nothing to worry about."

As Stephanie was speaking, it dawned on John that he was not among the group of friends who had received advanced warning of this plan as it was hatched several years ago, and therefore he did not participate in the profit taking. He was unsure whether to be upset or happy about this, given the cost of that equity.

"Ok. When? When should Citibank call Tedie's loans?"

"This week," was Stephanie's smiling reply as she stood to leave. "I'll let you choose the day."

Sarcastically John asked, "Oh, wow thanks. Is there anything else I can do for you?"

"Actually, there is John, thank you for asking. After you call Tedie's loans, I want you to demand a $25 million principal curtailment to all of Tedie's financing with Citi, in order to cure the default."

Jeffrey, still standing by the window, pretending to not be listening, was shocked at how high the number was that Stephanie threw out to cure the default. His chin dropped causing him to involuntarily open his mouth. They had not discussed a specific number in their preparatory meetings. He assumed she would offer a much smaller number.

Stephanie turned her face again toward the window "That is the proper term isn't it Jeffrey? Cure the default?"

"Yes Mrs. Kenseth, that is exactly right."

Stephanie now turned her gaze back to the defeated banker and extended her hand. Smiling, she said, "Thank you, John. You've been most helpful. Now don't forget to short Citibank's stock before you call the loans. A quick strike financial crisis in Citi's stock price would be a terrible opportunity to waste."

Tell the Boss Man

Doug Tallon felt physically sick. He was director of all financial relations for Tedie Organization and he had just received the email from his Citibank contact indicating the bank was declaring the Las Vegas Tedie Hotel loan to be in default. Doug was immediately on the phone with Citibank, confirming the email had not been sent in error or as a sick gag. He acknowledged that construction was behind schedule and a milestone deadline had been missed. In this business, missing a deadline for a specific part of the construction to be completed was not all that unusual. What *was* unusual was for the bank to notice immediately. What was even more unusual was the bank declaring default immediately, on a project which was clearly still moving forward.

During his conversation with the representative at Citibank, Doug got the distinct impression that the tenured and high-ranking banker had not been part of the decision-making process, and was acting on orders. This thought made Doug significantly more worried. Still wanting to believe an error had been made somewhere, Tallon picked up the phone and called Toby Kaye, chief construction engineer for Tedie Organization. It took a while to track him down in the field, but they finally connected.

"Hey Toby, this is Doug."

"Hey Doug, what's up?"

"Tell me about the hotel project in Las Vegas. Is everything good there? Is everything on schedule?"

"Well, yes and no. Is everything good? Yes, everything is good. Not great, but good. Is everything on schedule? No, everything is not on schedule. We've had a variety of delays, nothing terribly major but several small things which have aggregated and now we're a bit behind. We are about five weeks behind where we would like to be, but frankly, that's not too bad. The original schedule was overly aggressive and optimistic in my opinion, and I was not consulted when the schedule was created."

Doug was confused. "How is that possible? Wouldn't your opinion be crucial in setting a timeline for your own project? Who set the timeline?" As soon as the words came out of his mouth, he realized the naivety of the question.

Toby laughed out loud. "I cannot believe you just asked me that question, Doug. You know who set it. The boss man set it!"

Doug wasn't about to laugh because frankly, the thought of it made him want to throw up. Rubbing his forehead between his left thumb and index finger he said, "Thaaat just makes this whole scenario even more perfect. Thanks, Toby."

Toby responded quickly, "Wait! What scenario?" but Doug acted as if he did not hear him and hung up. No way was he going to let Toby know that he had failed to inform him the construction deadlines were tied to loan covenants, and missing the electrical deadline was indeed a very big deal.

After leaning back in his chair and staring at the ceiling for several moments, Doug stood and walked over to the cabinet in his office. He drew out the bottle of Garrison Brothers Bourbon that Colton Tedie had given him two years ago, ironically for beating deadlines. He broke the seal, drew one shot from it and threw it back. For two years he had been looking forward to sharing that bottle with good friends, or with coworkers to celebrate a milestone success. "Plans change," he thought to himself. If the rest of this morning progressed how he thought it was going to progress, he was going to need a little bourbon to get him through. He had an inkling of what might happen next, and there was no way he was going to let a great bottle of bourbon go untouched. He returned the bottle to the cabinet and retraced his steps back to his desk where he picked up his phone.

"Veronica, I need to speak to the boss; is he available?"

"Hello, Doug. He has just ended a meeting and has another scheduled in fifteen minutes. I'll see if he will speak with you."

As Doug waited for a voice on the other end of the call, he thought about the potential domino effect of Citibank's declaration of default on this one loan. Citibank was acting irrationally. It made no business sense for them to declare a default at this stage of the project. Therefore, he had to assume Citi would take another irrational action and exercise cross default provisions in all their Tedie Organization financing. Potentially, likely even, Tedie Organization's other lenders, without knowing the details of why Citi had declared default on just one loan, would also follow Citi's lead and declare default on their own loans. Because of the intercreditor agreements, Citi was obligated to tell

Tedie's other lenders about the default. He was fully aware banks tend to follow a herd mentality. No one wants to be the last one out of a burning building. Figuratively speaking, Doug had been in burning buildings before, and he knew this was not one. Which is what made the scenario all the more perplexing.

"What's up?" broke the silence and Doug's nightmare of a thought process.

Doug breathed deeply. "We have a situation."

Tedie could tell Doug was troubled. He paused. "So, handle it."

"I don't understand it, and it is out of my control."

In the ten plus years Doug had served as his Director of Finance, Tedie had never heard Doug say those words. Now Tedie was troubled, and agitated.

"What do you mean you don't understand it? My DF is calling me with what I assume is a financial matter that he doesn't understand? What is it?"

"Citibank has declared a default on the Vegas hotel loan."

Tedie's head involuntarily went backward slightly when he heard the news. He knew the project was behind schedule, but knew of no other setbacks with the project. He had received a status report two days earlier, indicating no concerns beyond normal, typical construction-related issues.

"Why the hell would Citi do that?"

"We missed a milestone deadline. The electrical systems in the building were supposed to be fully functional two days ago. They aren't, but they're on track to be completed within the next few days."

Again, Tedie paused, not believing what he was hearing. "Doug, what is going on? Now I know you are shitting me. There is no way Citibank is declaring a loan default over some Mickey Mouse bullshit item like missing a milestone deadline. Is this your idea of a bad joke? You don't have enough to do, so you call me, interrupt me, for a laugh?"

Doug hesitated. For just a moment he thought about taking the bait. He could apologize and wait this storm out. Tedie was right, there was no way this issue rose to the level of declaring a loan default. That action typically only comes at an impasse, when parties are acrimonious. Doug had received this news via email. Email?! On a performing project. Maybe he could ride the situation out for a bit and see if it got better on its own.

While still wading through this thought process, Doug's eyes landed on his computer screen. His email was open. Since getting off the phone with his Citibank banker, he'd received several new emails. Of concern to him were ones from Citi, Royal Bank of Scotland, and Deutsche Bank. He quickly scanned them.

The email from Citi originated with their internal counsel. Citibank was exercising its cross-default provisions and declaring all Tedie Organization loans in default. And, in accordance with the provisions of intercreditor agreements, Citi would be informing Tedie Organization's other lenders of this default.

The emails from Royal Bank of Scotland and Deutsche Bank, which had arrived just a few moments after Citi's second email, indicated that Tedie Organization's loans should now be considered in default based on communication received this morning from a participating member of the intercreditor agreement. They all promised to follow up with more specific information later in the day.

"Doug, are you there? Did you hear what I said? Is this some kind of sick joke?"

Doug knew his next words would likely be his last while employed by the Tedie Organization. "No, unfortunately it's not a joke and it's probably worse than what I've lead you to believe thus far. I anticipate several of our other banks will also declare default, based on their rights in multiple intercreditor agreements."

Before Tedie could begin yelling, Doug turned on the phone's speaker function, turned the volume all the way up, and slowly placed the handset on the cradle. He had been in similar situations with Tedie a couple times in the past and knew what was about to happen. He wanted his assistant and anyone else nearby to hear the profusion of profanity which was about to follow. At least, he thought, someone could get a kick out of his unfortunate situation.

"Are you fucking kidding me? Get the fuck out of your office Doug! You're fired! Did you hear me? You are fucking fired! I cannot believe the colossal fucking failure that you are, Doug, and the heartache you have just caused me!"

The tirade was just reaching its full crescendo when Doug walked outside of his office with his carry bag over his shoulder, bottle inside.

His assistant Christy tried to remain cheerful. "So, we'll see you in a couple weeks after the boss calms down and wants you to come back?"

"No," responded Doug, "I'm afraid this time is probably different. I don't think he's going to be calling me back. Something's up, I don't know what, but it's serious this time and someone's got to take the fall. Bad luck for me."

Christy had no verbal response. Only a look of bewilderment through her misty eyes.

Tedie's booming voice could still be heard from the speaker phone as Doug walked down the hall toward the elevator.

■■

Three hours later, Colton Tedie was in a conference room with his in-house counsel, Marty Finneman. Marty was intimately familiar with all the Tedie Organization's loan documents. He had also spent the last hour and a half reading Doug's emails from six different banks.

"Marty tell me what we are looking at. Tell me this is some big fucking mistake on some stupid ass banker's part, so that I can go back to running my company."

Marty responded with no emotion on his face, "This is a little more serious, Colton."

Tedie was failing to hide a look of real concern on his face. "How can this be serious, Marty? We are fucking two weeks or something behind some arbitrary deadline for a fabulous hotel that will change Las Vegas forever. And because we miss some stupid ass deadline every bank in the world is calling my loans into default? How is that even possible, Marty?"

"It is a real life small domino to large domino scenario. Technically, Citibank is within their rights to declare a default on the construction loan. Because of the default, they are also within their rights to cease funding on the hotel and your other Citi financed construction projects. The other banks have simply followed Citi's lead and exercised their rights under the intercreditor agreements to protect their interests. Unfortunately, they too can now withhold funding from any construction loans or open lines of credit."

Tedie was getting angrier with every word from Marty's mouth. His face was red, his ears were red, and the veins in his neck were bulging. At various times in his career he'd alternately been at war with, or passionately in bed with, his banks. Banks calling his loans was not new territory. But this was not a fight he had picked. The economy was good, his projects were performing, he had no desire to waste millions of dollars in a protracted legal battle with his banks while they held on to capital he needed. He just could not get over the fact it made no sense.

"Marty, what the hell is going on? This makes no fucking business sense. None whatsoever."

"I couldn't agree with you more, Mr. Tedie. Is it possible something else is at play?"

Tedie looked directly at Marty and exhaled deeply while turning his head left and right. "That's certainly what it feels like. But damn if I know what it is."

"Well Colton, the fact of the matter is, as of this morning, this is a new reality, one that we have to deal with in order to make it go away."

"Find out what Citibank wants and call me. I will try and reach John Ross on the phone in the meantime."

"$25 million," responded Marty.

"What is that?"

"That is what Citibank wants. It came across Doug's email just before I came in here. They want an aggregate principal reduction of $25 million in all of your Citi loans before they will consider unwinding the default."

Colton Tedie shook his head more vigorously. "$25 million, are they serious?"

Marty replied, "I realize that for the average person coming up with $25 million on a moment's notice is a big deal. And I'm your attorney, not your accountant. Is that a big deal for the Tedie Organization?"

Colton Tedie responded while he stared blankly at the New York skyline. "Yeah, Marty, it is a fairly big deal. With a default being declared, all of our credit lines will be frozen. Coming up with $25 million over the course of a couple weeks is not so big a deal. Coming up with it practically overnight, which is necessary to keep projects moving and prevent increased and unnecessary mobilization costs, yes, it's a big deal. We lose hundreds of thousands each day these projects sit idle."

Just then, Tedie's phone buzzed with an incoming text. It was from Stephanie Kenseth.

WILL BE IN NYNY TOMORROW. WOULD LIKE TO SEE YOU, CONTINUE OUR CONVERSATION.

Tedie responded tersely.

TIMING'S NOT GOOD.

Stephanie was unfazed.

I HAVE A MEETING WITH POTUS EARLY AM. SEE YOU AT 1.

Pressure

Stephanie arrived at the White House shortly before 8:00am. She desired to already be in her West Wing office in the event the President wanted to start his meeting with her early, as he often did. President Ingle had only informed her two days previous of his desire to meet at 8:30 that morning. He had not provided an agenda or purpose for the meeting.

Early in her term as Vice President, Stephanie had been more accepting of breeches of decorum from the President. Despite their differences, which they kept hidden publicly, Stephanie was grateful to Ingle for appointing her as Vice President after William's death. He took much criticism for appointing someone who had never been elected to federal office. Her background, gender, favors called in and time in the public spotlight had played in her favor. Increasingly though, she was beginning to sense that Ingle's behavior toward her was a means of keeping her off balance, an attempt to keep her under his control.

At 8:14am, Stephanie's desk phone rang. Caller ID indicated it was the President's Secretary.

"Good morning, Jesse."

"Good morning, Madam Vice President. The President will see you now."

As she rose from her desk she thought, 'See me now? The President had called this damn agenda-less meeting!'

Before leaving her office, she checked her appearance in the full-length mirror she'd had installed in the private lavatory off her office. She was pleased. Her white blouse and grey Armani suit projected the appropriate combination of power and femininity. She tugged slightly on both lapels, indicating the inspection was complete and she was ready to impress.

She made the familiar walk from her office to the Oval Office alone. Each time she made this walk she was aware of the sense of pride and power it engendered within her. All her life she had striven for the highest level of recognition possible. She was only steps away from the President's Office. Her campaign was only steps away from the Office of President of the United States. A great sense of gratification and accomplishment accompanied her into that coveted room.

As she made the right turn into the Oval Office she quickened her pace slightly, which was her means of communicating a can-do attitude; a lesson her father had taught her.

Once in the Oval Office, she continued the right turn toward the President's desk. "Good morning, Mr. President" was out of her dutifully smiling mouth before Ingle's eyes had lifted from his laptop screen. Even though they had now worked together for years and were quite familiar with each other, it was Stephanie's custom to address Barry

Ingle as Mr. President at the commencement of any encounter.

"Good morning, Stephanie." The President rose and extended his hand to meet hers. Stephanie immediately noted the President was attired to do business on the golf course today. "Let's have a seat on the couches."

"Very good," was Stephanie's only reply. She immediately proceeded to the right-hand couch. She knew the President's preferred seating position was near corner, left hand couch. She remained standing until Barry assumed a seated position, then she followed suit.

"So, tell me Stephanie, how is the campaign going? I'm sure you are gearing up to be in full swing."

"It is going exceedingly well. Thank you for asking. My team is well organized and very motivated. As you know, we've been planning for this season for a long time. I believe our execution to date reflects that planning, and I'm pleased with where we are."

"Very good, very good. I know you have been planning for this historic run for some time. And I know you are surrounded by many talented people. That is part of what I want to speak with you about today."

"As we've discussed before, when I appointed you as Vice President upon the unfortunate death of your husband, I did so in order to put you in the best launch point possible to make a run for President. As you know, at the time there were many qualified candidates for VP. Many, frankly, with more credentials than you possessed."

This comment caused Stephanie to reflexively sit a little straighter.

"But I chose you because I believe the time is right for our Party to put forth a female candidate for President. And I believe the country is ready for it as well."

Maintaining decorum, Stephanie responded, "I couldn't agree more, sir."

He continued, "Therefore, to finish what I started, let's talk about how I can help you on the campaign trail. Let's get our people together and determine when we can begin traveling together. As you are well aware, I successfully managed two Presidential campaigns, and I'm prepared to make that a third by helping you."

Here it was. The conversation Stephanie had been anticipating and dreading. Only worse. Even before this meeting she knew she did not want Ingle's assistance on the campaign trail. Except in just a few large cities, Ingle's approval ratings were very low. Except in those few cities, he would be a campaign liability.

Any potential reservations she'd had about not fully engaging the sitting president in her campaign efforts had just been laid to rest. Clearly, he equated her value to her gender, and not her intelligence or life experiences. She had suspected this at times during their relationship, and now he had confirmed it. Clearly, he sought to take credit for her current and future successes, on the fact he had installed her as Vice President.

Ever the politician, she had no desire to create an enemy by saying what she really thought. She chose her words carefully.

"Mr. President, I cannot tell you how much I appreciate your offer. That is very gracious of you. There is no doubt in my mind that your presence on the campaign trail can help. Why, my Campaign Manager and I were just talking yesterday about how wonderful it would be if you would lend a hand. I frankly had hoped this is why you called this meeting. So, thank you." She paused briefly, and proceeded carefully. "My team is still formulating our three-dimensional campaign strategy. I will make my Campaign Manager aware of your desire to be involved and we will work from there. How does that sound?" As she finished speaking she positioned her body in such a way as to communicate the meeting was over and she was ready to leave.

President Ingle paused slightly before responding. His impression was that he had just made a very generous offer, which was received dismissively. He took note, but decided to let it go for now.

He leaned forward and extended his right hand toward Stephanie with his palm facing her. "There is one other item I wanted us to discuss, Stephanie." She now eased back into her cushioned seat.

"Do you recall the conversation we had just prior to my installing you as Vice President?"

"Yes, I do. Quite vividly."

"Then you recall that I indicated in exchange for giving you the position of Veep, there would come a time when I would call in a favor."

"Quid pro quo," Stephanie responded.

"Exactly."

Ingle paused, so Stephanie interjected as a means of taking some control over the flow of the conversation. "At that time, you were unclear on what that favor might be. I'll assume since we are having this conversation now, you've identified the object of your affection."

"Exactly right again, Stephanie. When you are elected as President, I desire to be named Ambassador to the UN. That is a position befitting a former President, and a position from which I can further our interests abroad."

The first thought through Stephanie's mind was to wonder whose interests Ingle was referring to as 'ours.' But this was a secondary issue at the moment. Her bigger concern was the unfamiliar feeling in her gut. Fear. She rarely felt fear. She was politically smart and cunning. She was an expert at keeping herself positioned in such a way as to create a graceful exit, out of an uncomfortable or undesirable situation. That is where she currently was, and at this moment she did not see a good path forward.

She had not yet taken time to speculate what her Cabinet might look like. It was too early for that. But one thing she knew, she did not want Barry Ingle as her UN Ambassador. She did not trust him. She frankly did not understand him. He'd come to power quickly in the Democrat Party, and had done so without paying homage to the traditional power brokers. This was in sharp contrast to how she and William had made their way to the top of the power structure.

There was a force behind his political ascent which made her very uncomfortable. She feared how this force might manifest itself into something even the POTUS could not control, if projected from the platform of United States Ambassador to the UN.

These were her thoughts as she crafted her response. Smiling, she responded, "Really? UN Ambassador? I thought you would aspire to something higher and more permanent, such as a Justice on the Supreme Court. I anticipate one or two openings on the Court during my term. Why UN Ambassador?"

Ingle did little to hide his agitation with her response. Given the directness of the request, and the fact he had placed her in this position, he had expected a direct, positive response. Instead, for the second time in this short conversation, he was feeling disrespected.

His tone was terse and his words were direct. "Stephanie, why does not matter. The fact that it's what I want, and that I am the one calling in the favor you previously agreed to, is all that matters. As fair compensation for putting you in position to ascend to the most powerful elected position in the world, I expect to be your UN Ambassador. Anything else would be an insult."

Stephanie knew her response would set the tone for her relationship with Barry Ingle, the POTUS, for the following months and possibly years. She was indeed grateful to him for choosing her as Veep. But she in no way felt beholden to him or anyone else. She also recognized he had his own politically motivated reasons for choosing her, that choosing her was not an act of sheer benevolence, and that his polling strength had benefitted from the choice.

Contritely, she leaned forward and placed her elbows on her knees, with her hands forward and palms up. She looked directly at him. "Barry, I appreciate how you feel about this. I want us to be clear with each other. I am grateful for the fact you chose me as your Veep. I truly am. I recognize that we have both benefitted from that decision."

She now returned to her upright position, back straight against the cushion. "My recollection of our 'future events' discussion is that I agreed to reward you for helping me. I did not consent to a specific action. That is something I hope we can both agree on. I did agree to a generalized action. I agreed to help you in exchange for your help."

Ingle had now leaned back, his back against the couch. His chin was down, pressing against his chest. He had a look of incredulity on his face.

Stephanie continued, pushing past his obvious body language. "Barry, you and I are soldiers on the same side, in the same fight. We move forward supporting the same cause." She actually doubted this as she said it.

"My commitment to you is you will be highly placed. You will be placed where you can most effectively serve our cause, in my judgment. Whoever I choose as UN Ambassador will be chosen for the same reason. I know that is not the answer you want. I just hope that you understand my rationale."

President Ingle rose, signaling it was time for the meeting to end. Stephanie matched his gesture, and extended her right hand toward his, across the small table separating them. She noticed he grasped her hand more firmly than usual. He pulled her toward him, causing her to be slightly off balance.

"This is something I expect, Stephanie. I know you will make the right decision." He was not smiling.

His words felt ominously like a threat to her. But there was no way she was going to back down or even acknowledge their intent. Smiling, she placed her left hand on his right forearm while their handshake continued. She said, "I appreciate your confidence in me Barry." She now pulled her left hand back to where the tip of her left thumb was touching the fleshy area at the base of Barry's right thumb. She knew this to be a vulnerable part of the body, another trick learned from her father. Still smiling and maintaining direct eye contact, she now applied a quick but intense push with her left thumb. The suddenness and intensity of the pain was enough to cause Barry to reflexively release his grip on her right hand. She turned left toward the door, her back a little straighter than when she had walked in.

Stephanie Kenseth was a student of history. While on her jet traveling from Washington to New York, she reviewed several articles written in late 2012 about that year's presidential election outcome. A common theme was Republican Mike Russell's inability to hammer Barry Ingle on healthcare. In hindsight, Russell, though a skilled and accomplished politician, was the worst candidate the Republicans could have picked to run against Ingle. She contemplatively thought about how she needed her own Mike Russell. She needed Colton Tedie to run.

How It's Going to Be

"Send them in." Tedie rose from his desk to greet his welcome but uninvited and inconvenient guests.

Stephanie walked through the door, followed by Jeffrey. "Colton, it is such a pleasure to see you again!" she exclaimed as she extended her hand to him. They exchanged a firm, slightly-too-formal handshake.

"It is always a joy to see you as well, Stephanie." Unlike the last time they met, Tedie's face did not communicate joy in seeing her. In fact, it communicated the opposite. Sensing this, he mustered up the effort to force a smile for his visitors.

Turning to her left, Stephanie said, "I think you've met my Executive Campaign Manager Jeffrey Saint before, right?" Jeffrey stretched his hand toward Tedie.

"It is a pleasure to see you again, Mr. Tedie."

"And you as well, Jeffrey. Please do come in, have a seat." Stephanie and Tedie sat across from each other at the small rectangular conference table in his office. Jeffrey sat on Stephanie's left.

Stephanie began, "Colton I am so sorry for the short notice. Thank you for making the time for us. I've had our last conversation on the brain and wanted to revisit it with you, and potentially explore a different path. I'm curious if you've had any other thoughts about running for president since our last talk?"

Tedie was slightly agitated that Stephanie was bringing the subject up in the presence of her associate. Bringing it up he had expected. Bringing an accomplice, he had not. He had previously assumed that her suggestion about the idea was exclusively the result of their decades long friendship and business dealings. The fact she was now bringing it up in the presence of another suggested otherwise. He did his best to hide his surprise at her move, which he assumed was strategic.

Before speaking, he leaned back slightly in his chair and raised both palms skyward, an indication that he had very little to say on the topic. His words followed suit. "Stephanie, to be perfectly honest with you, I have a lot on my mind right now. I honestly haven't thought much on the subject. I'm flattered, and I agree that I do have the most potential to unite the Republican Party, as well as lead the country of course." He paused briefly to look down at the table before continuing.

"Stephanie, if we're being transparent here, which I think we both are," he glanced at Jeffrey, "the figure I gave you previously, the $10 million it might cost me in lost earnings to step aside from my organization to run a campaign, well that number is probably lower than reality. You have to understand, that's not small change. I am a wealthy man, but I'd also like to stay that way. So, at this point my position remains the same, I am not planning to run."

Stephanie had maintained her smile throughout Tedie's explanation. "Colton, truly, I can appreciate that. And you know the thing I appreciate even more than that is your honesty. There is not enough of that in our national political discourse. Which is why now more than ever, I believe you are the right person to lead that other party… they're in trouble and you're the guy to grab hold of the reins." Her smile broadened. He seemed resolute, but she was no rookie when it came to breaking down people's defenses. Hesitantly, Tedie smiled back. Her flattery had worked, and the situation with the banks was starting to slip from his mind momentarily.

Stephanie continued, "Colton, how much do you know about my foundation, the International Center for Social Justice?"

Tedie assumed the best way to move the conversation toward a quick conclusion was to just let Stephanie talk.

"Very little. But I know you are doing great work."

"Why thank you, Colton. That is something else we agree upon!" Again, Tedie forced a slight smile.

"When my late husband and I started the ICSJ Foundation, it was our intention to positively influence social, economic, and political factors all across the world. And I am proud to say we have done that, on nearly every continent. We are about to make a significant investment, actually our largest investment to date. And we are going to do that in an area where we never expected to need to invest funds. We are going to do that in our own country. That is how strongly I feel about the current environment in America, and that is how much I love my country."

As Stephanie stopped speaking, she proceeded to open the clasp of the leather portfolio which had been under her left hand. Tedie had not noticed the object as she spoke. During her monologue, Tedie's mind had gone back to the pressing financial matters at hand, and he was searching for a polite way to get Stephanie to speed things up. He certainly didn't need a history lesson on her foundation right now or a lecture on its moral justification.

"Stephanie, you are, honestly, one of my most favorite Americans. Always have been. You are a patriot, and the rest of us should aspire to be more like you. As much as I would love to continue this conversation, and I really must insist, I have pressing matters that I need to get back to. So, if we could get to the point of your visit, that would be great."

As Tedie was speaking, Stephanie had pulled two identically sized pieces of paper out of her portfolio. Tedie had not noticed.

"I understand. But I thought these might help you make a decision on this very important matter of running for the Republican nomination." She pushed the first piece of paper face down toward Tedie and motioned with her face for Tedie to accept it and turn it over.

Jeffrey was having difficulty hiding the look of surprise on his face. This was not how he understood the meeting was to go. Much to his frustration, Stephanie had not agreed to share her discussion plan with him before they entered the meeting, only the follow up plan. He assumed they might offer him some kind of loan, or offer to help him work with the Citi situation—the situation they had caused—but Stephanie had decided to forge a plan on her own. Dealing with surprises was not Jeffrey's strong suit.

With an agitated look on his face, Tedie pulled the piece of paper toward him with his right middle finger. Based on its shape he assumed it was a check, but he was perplexed by the fact that Stephanie would be giving him money.

He turned it over and immediately noticed the amount: $10 million. It was dated the day before. It was hand written on a Bank of the Everglades check, drawn from the account of The ICSJ Foundation. It was signed by Stephanie Kenseth. The memo line read "Worthy Opponent." The payee line, however, was left blank.

Tedie turned his gaze from the check to Stephanie Kenseth's smiling face. His memory quickly went back to the feeling of bewilderment he had experienced the last time she was in his office, when she encouraged him to run for the Republican Party presidential nomination. He was equally bewildered at this moment. He had a sense that he was being toyed with, and this was a feeling he did not like.

He put the check down, shook his head slightly while lowering his chin toward his neck. "What is this Stephanie? Some kind of joke?"

Jeffrey's curiosity was killing him. Despite his best efforts to peer through the paper, he was unable to see the amount on the check. He wondered what amount of money it would take to get Colton Tedie to react like that. Then he remembered Stephanie encouraging John Ross at Citibank to require Tedie to pay down his loans by $25 million in order to cure the default. He wondered if she could possibly be dealing in numbers that large?

Without acknowledging Tedie's question, Stephanie then pushed the second piece of paper, also face down, across the table. Tedie picked this one up more quickly. Again, it was a check. Again, hand written on a Bank of the Everglades account owned by The ICSJ Foundation. The amount of this check though was $25 million. The memo line indicated 'interest free loan.' Again, the check was signed by Stephanie and the payee line was blank.

Momentarily, Tedie was speechless. His mind was racing to figure out the reason she was doing something so odd. At the moment, he could come up with nothing.

He laughed and dropped the second check on the table. This allowed Jeffrey to finally see the amount. For just a second his mouth opened wide in amazement before he caught himself and regained his demeanor.

Smiling, Tedie finally asked, "You want to tell me what is going on? I mean, you have my attention, I will give you that. I frankly do not have time for this today, but you have succeeded in getting my attention. Clearly, you have something you want to say. The floor is yours."

"Tell me Colton, how much strategy and planning goes into making Tedie Organization successful?"

"Thousands and thousands of hours, Stephanie. And millions of dollars. More of both than anyone realizes."

"Well, that same level of strategy and planning is required to successfully influence elections and give your candidate the best chance to win. And that is what we are doing here. All I want to do today is remove all the obstacles that are preventing you from running. I want you to run. It will help our country. And frankly Colton, it will help me."

"Listen…"

"Colton, you make a lot of money licensing your name, correct? I know you do, I see your name on properties that are not even yours, but you are being paid for your name, because your brand is so powerful. I am proposing to buy your brand during the upcoming presidential primary and election season. The money I have presented to you here is a down payment on buying that brand. More will be forthcoming as you manage your campaign in a manner which we mutually agree upon."

"So wait, you want me to run, but you don't want me to win? Am I understanding you correctly?"

"Now you are getting it. When you enter the race and just be you, you will immediately suck all of the air out of the room in terms of press coverage for the other candidates. I want you to appeal to the center core of the Republican base. I want you to appeal to their prejudices. I want you to piss off every other demographic group out there, particularly the Democrat core. Pissing people off is something you are good at. You are really going to love this! In other words, just be yourself. No one else in the Republican field will energize the Democrat base the way you can."

Tedie paused as he tried to get his head around the idea. "And you are going to pay me to do this."

"We are all capitalists in this room, Colton. We just make it and spend it in different ways."

Tedie looked down at the checks again. Even in his world of hundred million dollar deals, $35 million to do something he was already considering doing in the first place was a tempting offer. This would make his bank problems go away, plus give him a little pocket money while he focused on his campaign.

"Stephanie I'm just, I'm just trying to reconcile the fact that you, Stephanie Kenseth, have just put $35 million dollars in my hands. That is, if the checks are good."

"Oh, they are good. And there is more where that came from."

"My mind is recalling an interview you had, with Barbara Trie I believe, in which you told her you were dead broke when William left this earth, God rest his soul. Dead broke, to handing me $35 million is coming a long way, baby."

"Colton, you will note those checks are drawn on The ICSJ Foundation. Literally thousands of people have donated to our foundation in order to help make a positive difference in this world. The money you hold in your hand is the collective and tangible evidence that people believe in the work I am doing, and desire to make a difference."

Tedie was fairly certain that shakedowns and influence peddling had more to do with the origins of this money than people wanting to make a positive difference in the world. But this was not the time to have that debate. He simply nodded.

"Also, I notice the payee lines are blank on each check. What's up with that?"

"They can be made out however you wish. To you, your organization, your campaign, whatever you choose. I did not want to constrain you or do anything to unnecessarily create a tax event for you. Trust me, the money is yours to do with what you want, so long as you agree to run for the Republican nomination."

Tedie still had not come to grips with the genuineness of the offer, so he continued to question her. "OK Stephanie, the $10 million check makes sense to me. That's a number I gave you. But the $25 million, where did you come up with that number? I mean, why $25 million?"

Stephanie repositioned in her chair, which Tedie was quick to notice. He also noticed she was blinking more rapidly than normal. Something was up with that body language, and he was taking note. Whatever she said next would most assuredly be a lie.

"Oh, I don't know Colton, it seemed like a nice round number to me. I mean, we could have made them both out for $10 million. It could have been one check for $30 million. I just thought an extra $25 million beyond what you said it would cost you to run would… help." As Stephanie said the word "help" she shrugged and looked down at her hands. Jeffrey winced, wishing again that she would have bothered to go over the plan with him.

For the first time since his guests had entered his office, Colton Tedie felt at ease. He now understood the game, crooked as it was. He understood why Citibank had taken the actions they had, just the day before. He was certain it was no accident that Citibank was demanding $25 million from him in order to cure a bullshit based loan default, and Stephanie Kenseth was handing him a $25 million bribe to help ensure her victory in the upcoming presidential election. The level to which this woman had her hands in everything went far beyond what he had previously imagined.

That isn't to say it wasn't an impressive feat. He could not believe though, how easy it had been to induce Stephanie to give it away. It was almost as if she never thought he would question the amount on the check. He shuddered at the thought of Stephanie negotiating matters of national security.

During their conversation, he had been looking occasionally at Jeffrey. Tedie assumed the architect of the plan had been Jeffrey. Why else would he be here? If this was the case, he hoped to himself it would be Jeffrey that would be negotiating with the Russians and Iranians in the future and not Stephanie.

"OK Stephanie and Jeffrey, suppose I agree to do this. Suppose I agree to sell you my name and involvement in the Republican race for the presidential nomination in order to pave the way for a Stephanie Kenseth presidency. A moment ago, you mentioned there would be more money coming to me if I run my campaign in a manner we mutually agree upon. That sounds ominous to me to be perfectly honest with you. Tell me exactly what that means."

"Jeffrey, why don't you explain to Mr. Tedie what we discussed on the way over here."

Jeffrey and Colton Tedie now locked eyes. Tedie respected the fact the young man did not seem afraid of the moment at all.

"You will enter the race in late June. We expect as many as fifteen people will run on the Republican side. We will encourage our friends in the press to initially concentrate the bulk of their coverage on you. Whether they continue to do so will depend on you."

"You will do what you do best. You will give the media outrageous sound bites. You'll be bold and brash and loud and unequivocally unafraid. You will campaign to the right of center, seeking to appease gun toting, Bible thumping red blooded Americans, the same ones who raped the Indians yesterday and pollute the air and water today."

"You forgot homophobic and xenophobic," Tedie interjected.

"Indeed, I did. Thank you for pointing that out," Jeffrey said without smiling. He continued, "You do this successfully, and the press will love you and follow you at the expense of every other candidate. We will then help influence the initial polls in your favor. We will instruct the polling agencies to conduct in areas favorably disposed to a white, rich, Washington outsider running for president. We can only influence them for a short period, or the sampling geographies and demographics will be noticed and called out. After we influence them initially, you are on your own."

"OK, I get it. I understand the drill. Now tell me about the money."

Jeffrey's face remained emotionless. "Each week during the primaries that you poll nationally number one or number two, we will remit one million dollars to the domestic or off shore account of your choosing. In addition, we will also orchestrate one million dollars to be donated to your campaign fund."

Tedie's body language communicated that he was intrigued. Jeffrey continued.

"Here is the real money. As we get closer to the primary election, we want you to slowly start to alienate the core members of the Democrat base: women, the LGBT community, immigrant groups, etc. Each time you make outrageous comments about any of these groups and cause national media coverage to converge on your outrageous comments, we will forward five million dollars to the account of your choosing. But only as often as every two weeks.

We need this to sustain. Your comments will energize our base, and drive them to the polls in November."

"And how long do you expect me to stay in the race after this happens?"

Stephanie and Jeffrey looked at each other, then Stephanie answered, "We're going to play that by ear. Ideally you go so far as to win the nomination, even with the hateful comments. At that point, we believe you will have so tainted the Republican brand there is no way you can win in the general election. By the way, the payoff should you win the nomination is ten million."

This caused a raised eyebrow from Tedie, the first physical reaction he had to any of the figures thrown at him so far.

Stephanie continued, "Even if you are unsuccessful at winning the nomination, the tone you will have set during the primaries will cast the Republican Party as being out of touch with a great number of Americans as well as hostile toward their values. The nominee will never recover from that."

Stephanie now leaned forward and clasped both of Colton Tedie's hands in her own. "You will have done your country a great service, Colton. One for which I will forever be grateful, and be quick to reward during my tenure as president."

It did not take Tedie long to decide. He would run. He would get paid a lot of money for his name and his mouth. And he would run to win. "OK. You've convinced me. I'm in. Jeffrey, I need your contact information and I will put you in touch with the appropriate people in my camp."

After Stephanie and Jeffrey left Tedie in his office, there was a call he knew he needed to place quickly. He picked up the phone and called Christy in finance.

"Hello, Mr. Tedie."

"Hello, Christy. I want you to call Doug. I want to you tell him to get his ass back to work tomorrow. Tell him the next time I fire him I will be damn serious about it!"

"Yes Mr. Tedie."

The White House Club

Jeffrey had not volunteered a word since leaving Tedie's office. He had responded in a matter-of-fact tone to questions or comments from Stephanie in the elevator, but had offered nothing extraneous.

Stephanie assumed he was upset, and she thought she knew the reason why. Now as much as ever she needed his emotional engagement. They had just secured a great victory. So as the limousine plodded through New York City traffic, she began the process of reeling him back to the surface.

"Jeffrey, it seems something is bothering you. What is it?"

For the first time since leaving Tedie's office, Jeffrey made eye contact with Stephanie. He held it for a few seconds before speaking.

"I had no idea you would be putting such a large sum of money in his hands today. When we talked about the weekly payments previously, I assumed those funds would self-generate. I assumed those funds would come from fundraising efforts against Tedie and during the campaign. He will be a fundraising gold mine for us if he behaves as we expect he will. But I had no idea you had $35 million at your disposal to drop on him today."

Stephanie was nodding her head as Jeffrey spoke. "Do you disagree with the amount?"

Jeffrey had not expected this question. "No. The amount is immaterial to me. The fact you have that amount of funds available for payment, and I was unaware of it, causes me to think I am not fully in the know."

"And that bothers you," replied Stephanie.

"Yes, it bothers me." He paused. "It causes me to question whether our relationship is based on trust."

Stephanie's assumptions about what was bothering Jeffrey had been correct.

"Jeffrey, of course our relationship is based on trust. There is no one in my life more important to me than you as far as my presidential campaign is concerned. That is a lofty position. There are dozens of qualified people who would kill to be in your role. Believe me on that, because I hear from a few of them daily!"

She continued, "If I did not trust you, you would not be in the position that you are. And this campaign will not succeed if you and I aren't fully trusting of each other. So, believe me when I tell you, you have my full trust." He nodded. "But Jeffrey, I need you to trust me, too. I need you to trust that sometimes, there will be things it is best that you do not know. You're smart enough and you've been in this game long enough to know there is a certain amount of dishonesty that we all must be comfortable with to achieve the greater good. Though it wears on the soul, to be successful, we have to harden our hearts and become numb to it at times."

Jeffrey didn't respond. He knew what she was saying was true. But part of him wanted it not to be. He wanted winners and losers to be determined based on wit and intelligence, not dishonesty and shady dealings.

"I assume that you would agree I am a complex person. I have my presidential campaign, my time as the Vice President, my time as the Vice President's wife, my time as Director of the ICSJ Foundation, my time as a governor's wife, and so on. At each of those points in my life I was, I am, the leader of highly talented and dedicated groups of people. There are elements of each of those experiences which are best if they stay within the realm of those groups. Do you understand?"

Jeffrey did understand, but wasn't willing to concede to her yet. "No, I'm not sure I do."

"Let me put it this way. When we deploy spies, and we have lots of them, they are only given a certain amount of information about what their mission is. In this way, if they are ever caught and subsequently forced to share information, through torture or whatever, they can only share what they know. Their purposeful ignorance is a built-in firewall to protect against greater damage. There are times when I keep you and others purposefully ignorant, to protect you and the greater effort."

Still feinting misunderstanding, Jeffrey continued to probe. "I don't understand how that has anything to do with the $35 million you gave to AWM."

Stephanie chuckled slightly at the reference, and her misplaced perception of Jeffrey's naivety. With an expression of satisfaction born of accomplishment on her face, she took in and let out a deep breath. She looked out of the window of the moving car briefly before responding. Jeffrey made note of what her body language was clearly indicating.

"Jeffrey, let's just leave it with the understanding that my late husband's tenure as Vice President coincided with significant contributions and revenue growth over many years at the ICSJ."

In a purposeful, slightly over dramatized way Jeffrey responded, "I don't understand how those are connected? How did your husband's service as VP financially benefit the Foundation?"

The momentary look of satisfaction on her face now gone, Stephanie returned to the moment. She returned her gaze back toward Jeffrey. "I've told you everything I can, Jeffrey. For your protection, I've told you all you need to know. I need you to trust me. Do YOUR job, and trust me."

"I trust you. We are in this together, to win."

"To win," Stephanie acknowledged.

As the limousine continued, Jeffrey was still reeling from the enormity of the amount of money Stephanie had given Tedie. And she had done so because of *his* recommendation that Tedie should be their chosen opponent! He simultaneously felt a surge of pride that Stephanie would invest $35 million based on his counsel, and a sense of frustration over not knowing how in the hell she had that much money to drop on AWM. He was not surprised that Stephanie had not divulged the source of the $35 million. But he had succeeded in getting a lead out of her. The money's genesis was rooted in her ICSJ Foundation. And he knew just the person to follow up with to find out more. He waited a few moments before pulling out his phone and sending a text. The reply came quickly.

I'D LOVE TO.

■■

After Tedie called Christy to get Doug back to work, he sat back down at his conference table and stared at the two checks. His mind wandered back to the first time he held a million dollars in his hands. He chuckled at how much easier this $35 million had been to obtain.

After his meeting with Stephanie, he was finally starting to understand the amount of string pulling there was in politics. While he was still having trouble believing the Democrat front runner for President of the United States had just put $35 million in his hands to run against her, it was starting to seem a little more unremarkable on the whole. He also needed to temper his excitement until the checks cleared.

After several seconds of reflection, he put the checks down and picked up the phone to call Michelle.

She answered on the first ring. "Hey babe, everything good?"

"Yeah, it's great. Hey, you know when I told you several days ago that Stephanie Kenseth asked me to run for president?"

"Yes, I remember that very well. I remember it didn't make any sense and you were going to tell her no. You did tell her no, didn't you?"

"Actually, I was thinking it might be kind of cool to be president. And you my dear, you would be the hottest first lady ever. Ever."

"Cut it out. You told me you would tell her no. We both know there was something more to her proposal which she was not sharing with you. She is dangerous. Tell me you told her no."

"Yeah, I told her no."

"Good. So, that's the end of the story, right? Except it must not be the end of the story because you are calling me during the day to talk about it and you never call me during the day."

Tedie laughed at the insightfulness of his bride. "Well, the difference now is I know her game."

Michelle hesitated several seconds before taking the bait. A long exhale was audible through the phone before she said, "Which is…?"

"She wants to license my name and my personality. She wants to pay me to run for president. She wants to run against me badly enough in the general election she is willing to pay millions of dollars for me to enter the race in order to motivate her base."

"She's paying you to motivate her base? How does that even make sense?"

"That, my dear, makes perfect sense. That makes the most sense of any of this. The country is sick of Ingle. Many of my Democrat friends who voted for him are appalled at his incompetence, at his hostility toward America the great and his love affair with people and groups who seem hell bent on harming us."

"Stephanie Kenseth, as the Democrat nominee for president, is going to have to campaign through that anger against Ingle. She obviously thinks I am the perfect instrument to get people to forget about this disaster of a Democrat president. She is counting on the fact people will go to the polls to vote against me, at least as much as they go to vote for her."

"So your job is to help her become president by running against her."

"Yeah, that pretty much sums it up."

"And how do you feel about that?"

"Here's how I feel about that. She is going to pay me enormous amounts of money. The first payment of which she made today. I'm going to get paid to say outrageous things, something we both know I am very good at. I'm going to get paid to manipulate the media, again something we both know I am very good at. In the midst of all of that, I believe I can rally people to a pro-American message. I know I can get people to listen to me and I know I can drive the debates. Stephanie Kenseth is willing to pay me to do what I do, and be her opponent. Who knows, before it's all over she may be willing to pay me to get out of the race."

"Wait, so you *are* going to run?"

"Yes, I think so. Are you good with that?"

Michelle smirked and raised her voice slightly, "Does it matter if I am good with that?"

Tedie knew that meant yes. "Hell yes it matters. You know I don't want to do this if you are not on board."

"Bullshit Tedie. You are doing it with or without me, I can hear it in your voice," she said with a smile.

"You know I love you, Michelle."

"Whatever."

"Hey if I win we can join the White House club."

"What is that? Some kind of club in Washington?"

"Sort of. It's kind of like the Mile High Club. You told me once that I was the one to introduce you to the Mile High Club. It's a flattering thought, but I'm not sure I believed you."

"Shut up," Michelle laughed and ended the call. Smiling while shaking her head and looking at the phone she murmured contemplatively, "President Tedie."

How Much?

Jeffrey and Stephanie were back in Washington by midafternoon. He immediately went to his office and began designing strategies to fundraise against candidate Tedie. Tedie was going to be worth millions to Stephanie's campaign in terms of his fundraising value. He wanted to be ready the day after Tedie announced.

Although this work excited him, he was anxious for the day to turn to night. Immediately after learning from Stephanie that the $35 million was generated during her time as Director of the ICSJ, he had sent a text to Amuh Baiden. Amuh was simultaneously employed as William Kenseth's Chief of Staff during his tenure as VP, and Special Assistant to Stephanie Kenseth while she was Executive Director at ICSJ. She had agreed to meet him for drinks at his favorite DC bar, The Heist. Amuh and Jeffrey were longtime friends due to their mutual association with Stephanie. They had never worked together directly, but they had always been in complementary roles, and often swapped stories to blow off steam. It was difficult to share work frustrations with friends that didn't work in politics. They would try to follow along, but having a confidant on the inside —especially one that worked amongst the same group of people—was invaluable.

If anyone other than Stephanie Kenseth knew where that money came from, Jeffrey knew it would be Amuh.

Although Amuh was previously married to a congressman, she had a reputation in the gay community. She was referred to as a "fag hag." It was a harsh term, but one that Jeffrey thought was pretty accurate. He knew Amuh had tried to seduce, sometimes successfully, several of his gay friends and colleagues in Washington. Sometimes when they were hanging out together, he sensed that she was coming onto him. A lingering touch on the arm or a flirtatious look, nothing offensive. Nothing he wasn't able to ignore. He wondered how often she fucked men to get what she wanted. Politics is a sick and sordid business, thought Jeffrey as he pushed open the door to the tavern.

Jeffrey had invited Amuh for drinks for the stated purpose of catching up, but he had more in mind. He wanted information from Amuh. That was the real purpose of their meeting tonight. Specifically, he wanted information about money. Everyone who knew Jeffrey knew that he was fascinated with money. He craved it. He loved to spend it. He enjoyed the finer things in life money helped him to buy. He had piles of money in his uptown apartment in the form of designer clothes, shoes, furniture and art.

Seeing $35 million slide across the table in front of him, money that he did not know Stephanie Kenseth possessed, had really gotten to him. The shock of it was now fading into awe. He wanted to know how she generated that kind of money, and how she could so nonchalantly slide it across a table. He wanted to know how much was still left in the kitty.

Stephanie handed it over so easily he assumed there was much more behind it. His desire to know about the origins of that fortune grew into a small obsession as the day had worn on.

Jeffrey wondered if the reason Amuh had responded so quickly and affirmatively to his text to meet was because she secretly wanted to seduce and claim him as another male homosexual conquest. He suspected it was. He considered that possibility when he texted her to meet up, but he just couldn't ask the kinds of questions he wanted to ask over the phone or email. He wasn't afraid of sex. On the contrary. His little black book was nothing to be ashamed about. There's nothing men find more attractive than powerful men, and he was using that fact to his advantage. He wasn't even afraid of having sex with a woman, although it had been many, many years since he had done so. Amuh was beautiful and sophisticated, and it certainly seemed like she was experienced, but he had no desire to sleep with her.

Still, his desire to learn more about the origins of the ICSJ money were very intense. To get the information he wanted, he had to be prepared to give her what she wanted in return. He knew her well enough to know that she would make a game out of it.

As usual, Jeffrey had arrived early to ensure he would have enough time to control the situation, to pick his preferred seating arrangement, and to play the part of the host. He knew this place well enough to know there were three specific tables there with unique protections and sight lines, and he wanted to make sure he got one of those tables.

When he arrived, he recognized the hostess, though he couldn't remember her name. He had clearly made more of an impression on her, however.

She greeted him excitedly by name, and let him know that his party had already arrived.

This is strange, he thought. He was annoyed. He followed the hostess, hoping she had made a mistake. His hope diminished as they rounded the corner and he caught sight of Amuh, who was seated with her back to the wall at one of the more conspicuous tables. Jeffrey smiled through his frustration as Amuh rose to greet him with a light embrace. He did not like how this was going already.

After a quick but friendly embrace, they exchanged a light kiss on each cheek. Jeffrey tried to quickly but inconspicuously slide into the seat where Amuh had been perched with her back to the wall. However, instead of securing his preferred seat, all he managed to pull off was an awkward half dance followed by nervous laughter. She retook her seat, eyeing him suspiciously. Jeffrey slunk into the chair opposite hers, with his back to the expanse of other tables. He was uncomfortable. She didn't care. They were in the midst of a power play, and they both knew it.

"Jeffrey, I was *so* excited to get your text. It has been far too long since I have enjoyed your company. How have you been?"

"Very well, thank you Amuh. Life is busy, as you can imagine. We are coming into season and there is so much behind the scenes work to do. But you know all this. How are you? What are you up to?"

"Happy, but a little bored. My time at ICSJ with Stephanie was awesome. I miss it. ICSJ just was not the same after William died and Stephanie accepted appointment as VP from the President."

Jeffrey asked, "Remind me what you are doing now?"

"I am the director of special projects for three different senators. Stephanie and the DNC helped line it up. It keeps me busy. My plan, of course, is to work for Steph again once she is back in the White House. So... I'm counting on you, Jeffrey... make it happen!" As she said this, she reached across the table and firmly grasped his left wrist with her right hand. "Be your usual brilliant self and help her win this election!"

The waiter now arrived to take drink orders.

Amuh started, "I'll have a Bearcat please, and my friend will have a..." Amuh could not recall Jeffrey's drink of choice.

Jeffrey looked up at the waiter. He looked familiar. "I'll have a Robert the Bruce."

"Excellent. I'll have those right out for you." They *had* met before. The circumstances of that meeting rushed back to him and he felt a slight flush wash over his face.

"So, who do you think Stephanie will be running against? There's what, fifty Republicans running for the nomination?" She laughed.

Jeffrey smiled the way a person does when they know a secret. "Who do you think?"

Amuh sat back in her leather chair slightly. "Well I assume Sutton. He has the most money and name recognition."

"No, I don't think so," Jeffrey said, somewhat smugly.

Perplexed, Amuh responded, "Wilson? Has he declared? He hasn't declared, right? None of the others really have the fundraising abilities, do they?"

"No, I don't think it's going to be Wilson. He played his hand and lost. He's smarter than to try that again."

The conversation was briefly interrupted by the delivery of their drinks.

"Bearcat for the lady. Robert the Bruce for the gentleman." As the waiter placed Jeffrey's drink in front of him, Jeffrey made eye contact with him. The waiter shot his gaze over quickly toward Amuh and then back to Jeffrey, while widening his eyes as if to communicate danger.

"Thank you," Jeffrey replied verbally to both the warning and the delivery of the beverage. Amuh's reputation must be well known in this place, he thought.

Jeffrey turned his gaze from the waiter, who was now sauntering away from their table, back over to Amuh. She was stirring her drink, and he had to admit... he'd forgotten how stunning she is. He noticed, for the first time, the plunging neckline of her blouse and the gold necklace she was wearing. Her shoulder length jet black hair and low-cut white blouse framed her face perfectly. "Hey. You want to know a secret?"

Amuh leaned forward in her seat and widened her eyes. "Yes! Tell me."

"I know who the Republican nominee is going to be."

"No way."

"Way," said Jeffrey as he widened his eyes playfully and consumed more of his drink.

"Jeffrey, you are so good. I mean, the Republican convention is what, a year away, and you already know who it is? How do you know this?"

"I know this because I am the one who is going to make it happen. The plan is in place, and in motion. I am going to determine who the Republican nominee is."

Amuh's tone now changed from playful to skeptical. "Jeffrey Saint is going to determine the Republican nominee? I had no idea you were so powerful."

He backed up, but only slightly. "Let's just say that with the vast human and capital resources at my disposal, I am going to significantly influence who the opposition candidate will be."

"Okay, not to undermine how impressive it is that the Executive Campaign Manager for the Democrat nominee has that power, but why do you care this far in advance who you're eventually going to be running against… assuming Steph gets the nomination?"

Jeffrey now leaned forward in his seat to emphasize his point. "Let's be honest, Amuh. The Democrat Party—and therefore the nominee—are starting this election cycle from a bad place. A really bad place. Barry Ingle has done significant damage to the Democrat brand. His real poll numbers are terrible. He has succeeded in causing way too many people to wonder where his allegiances lie, including many in our party. Add to this the fact that people do not trust Stephanie, and not only that, she is not a likeable candidate. I'm just being honest. The Damascus situation, the missile technology issue that just won't die, her public comments about various religions, those things have hurt Stephanie's credibility with large groups of people and have the potential to hurt even more during the election."

Jeffrey paused to take a sip of his drink.

"But despite the momentary issues presented by Ingle and Stephanie, our base will eagerly coalesce against an opposing candidate, even when they have a hard time rallying around our candidate. That is the power of ideology. That is the value of party affiliation as a replacement for religious affiliation, something our party has been working on for years. Our side, our leadership, has this figured out. The opposition has not. They practice church on Sundays in quaint structures. We practice church in the hallowed halls of government. And the people who believe as we do love us for it. Therefore, finding and inserting the opposition candidate who we can demonize as a heretic, who rallies our base, is always critical. It is especially critical this year, with all these negative factors present for us."

Amuh was fascinated by Jeffrey's insight. She knew he had a reputation for brilliance, but they had never spoken of politics at a core level. He spoke about politics with a blunt and clear honesty she rarely experienced, especially in this town. His words connected with her, and to be honest, she was starting to feel aroused by his confident sense of command over the entire scenario. When she was preparing for this meeting, she momentarily fantasized about it ending in a rendezvous. Now she desperately wanted to sleep with him. And not just so she could add him to her list of homosexual conquests. She found herself genuinely and intensely attracted to this sexy, very confident man.

Absorbed in this reverie, Amuh realized he had finished speaking and she was still staring at him. She blinked and quickly tried to regain her composure. "So… are you going to tell me who it is? Who is this Republican heretic who will also be the unwitting savior of our party and our way of life?" There was a playfulness in her words, as the booze and the sensuality coursing through her veins started to take hold on her.

"I suppose maybe I could tell you."

"Maybe? Don't play with me! Tell me!"

Jeffrey responded, "I will. But first tell me what I want to know. I think you have some information I'm looking for, too."

Amuh felt a satisfying sense of control return to her side of the table. "OK. Tell me what *you* want to know."

"I want to know how Stephanie created so much cash for the ICSJ Foundation during William's time as Vice President."

The flirtatious smile on Amuh's face disappeared quickly and was replaced with the same poignant look as the one found on Jeffrey's face.

"I don't know what you are talking about. What makes you think the ICSJ Foundation benefitted from William's tenure as Veep?"

"Oh, I don't know. Maybe it was the two eight figure checks I saw written out of the Foundation recently. Or maybe it was the fact she told me the two are connected."

"She told you that?"

"Oh yes. In a weak moment, while basking in self-glorification, she told me that."

Amuh was quite familiar with the fact that Stephanie was terrible at keeping secrets and was known to overshare, especially when she was feeling on top of the world and untouchable.

"How big were the checks?"

Jeffrey leaned forward wide eyed, and with put both fists on the table said, "Thirty-five million."

Jeffrey then quickly noted that Amuh had no facial or other reaction to the amount of the checks. This spoke volumes to him and deepened his intensity to know more.

Amuh then asked, "Who did she…"

"Colton Tedie."

This she did react to. "No way!"

"Oh yeah way. I was there."

Amuh finally broke eye contact and turned her gaze up and to the right as she thought. Jeffrey could see the impression of the tip of her tongue pressing against her lower lip as it slowly went back and forth. She was clearly processing some information, and taking a fair amount of time deciding what to share.

He sensed that if he kept pushing her, he could break down any last defenses she was holding onto. So, he pressed. "Now you tell me. Where did that money come from?"

Amuh's eyes now returned to Jeffrey's. The calculations in her brain continued. He could tell she did not know quite what to say, or how much to reveal.

She looked down at the table briefly and let out a long exhale before returning her eye contact to him. A wry smile had returned to her face, as if re-living a fond memory. "Jeffrey, you have no idea."

Jeffrey recognized the stall tactic and quickly moved to disarm it. "I'm aware I have no idea love, which is why I am asking you. Now, I told you what you wanted. It's your turn."

"She gave those checks to Tedie because he's the guy you are promoting as the Republican nominee?!" Her surprise was genuine. She had not made the connection. He didn't respond.

After turning this over in her mind for a moment, she snapped back to reality and twisted her stir stick between her long, elegant fingers. She reminded herself of her original purpose in wanting to meet tonight. "What you are asking for is a top shelf secret. Its value is much greater than knowing who the Republican nominee might be. I could find that out just by waiting and watching the news."

"Amuh Baiden, I cannot believe you are reneging on your word."

"Whoa, hold on right there, Jeffrey. I never accepted your deal. You put it on the table and then began talking. I never agreed."

Not that it mattered at this point, but Jeffrey knew she was correct. His calculated gamble to guilt her into talking had come up short. Now he knew he was essentially down to his last card. But he was not yet ready to surrender.

"I cannot believe you are keeping information from me. We've known each other for years, and we share this great, mutual respect, and you are treating me like a piece of garbage on the street."

Amuh liked the direction of the conversation. "The only garbage here is the fact you are full of it. You know damn well I didn't agree to any terms." She paused briefly. He could tell she was formulating a plan, and he had a feeling he knew what it was going to involve.

Amuh took a sip of her drink then turned her eyes toward Jeffrey's choice of libation. "Robert the Bruce. Remind me of who that was?"

Jeffrey was confused by this change of course. Still realizing he was likely down to his last card, he decided to go with it. He looked down at his nearly empty glass, then back at Amuh. "He was king of

Scotland a long time ago. He united the Scottish clans against the British who were an unwanted and ruthless occupying force."

Amuh was smiling and nodding her head in affirmation. "Yes, I remember now. Didn't he also switch allegiances before he became king, and fought with the British? Didn't he betray, oh, what was his name, William Wallace?"

Jeffrey could not believe what had just happened. What he had just allowed to happen. He gritted his teeth briefly before speaking. "Yes, he did fight with the British before fighting for Scottish independence. There is some controversy over whether he actually betrayed William Wallace."

Amuh now looked directly at Jeffrey. "So it seems that sometimes it is a wise move to switch allegiances to get what you want."

Jeffrey again looked down at his drink and tilted his head slightly to the left, before returning his look to Amuh, "So it would seem."

"So, Robert the Bruce… will you agree to my terms?"

Jeffrey knew that if he was to get what he wanted, he would have to agree with whatever she said next. "Name them."

She leaned in, and again placed her right hand on Jeffrey's left forearm. "I admire and respect you, Jeffrey. You are talented, funny, and smart. It's been a little lonely and devastatingly boring in my apartment lately. You have always excited me, Jeffrey. I want to experience you and our relationship in a new and… fun way. Come home with me, I think you'll enjoy yourself, despite your 'natural' tendencies."

Now it was Amuh who went for the presumptive close. She picked up her purse, straightened her back and twisted her body in her chair, preparing to stand. When Jeffrey's movements did not follow suit, she gave one final attempt to persuade him.

"Come with me Jeffrey. Do this for me and for yourself and I will tell you everything you want to know about the Foundation and the cash." Jeffrey hesitated only slightly before rising from his seat.

■■

Amuh was dreaming, floating on the last leg of that wretched trip between deep, satisfying sleep and consciousness. She smelled coffee and bacon in her dream. She rolled her head to the other pillow and smelled the scent of a man. This caused her to open her eyes slowly. Her dream was over, but the smell of bacon and coffee, and the scent of Jeffrey, remained.

Fully awake now, she rolled and propped herself up on her side just in time to see Jeffrey enter the room carrying a tray containing two cups of coffee and two plates covered with crisp bacon and scrambled eggs. Jeffrey was only wearing yesterday's boxers and Amuh made a conscious effort to capture what he looked like in that moment. There was just something about gay men. They had their shit together. They always looked so damn good, even first thing in the morning after getting very little sleep.

"Oh my god, Jeffrey, aren't you just the domestic goddess? You are awesome."

"Yes, I am love. Awesome, that is. And if you did not know that before last night, you certainly know it now." Jeffrey set the tray down on the nightstand. "Do you prefer to eat in the buff, or would you like me to find you some clothing?"

"Just throw me your t-shirt." Jeffrey picked up his crumpled white undershirt that he had been wearing last night and tossed it at Amuh. She pulled it over her head, then tried to smooth her hair, but the effort was futile. Jeffrey handed Amuh a plate as she sat up. He sat down on the bed next to her, cross legged, his plate between his legs.

Jeffrey, never the subtle type, got right down to business. "Alright, girl. Time to talk. I walked the walk last night. Now you must talk the talk."

"Can I at least finish my breakfast first?" Amuh said through a mouthful of eggs. "Geez."

"My dear, this morning, I have clear, firsthand knowledge of how talented your mouth is. I am certain that you are very capable of talking and eating at the same time. So, give it up!"

Amuh responded coyly as she took a bite of bacon, "It was pretty good, wasn't it? Speaking of good, these eggs are excellent. Thank you for breakfast."

"I have to say, it was fabulous. You might, might, *might* even convince me to trip the light fantastic with you again sometime. But for now, I need you to talk!"

"Well, that certainly is something to look forward to." Amuh now sat up a little straighter, and placed her plate to the side. She squared her body towards Jeffrey's before she began talking.

"What do you know about the ICSJ Foundation?"

"Stephanie and I have never directly discussed it. I know it's there and that's about it. I have no real knowledge of it."

"OK, I will tell you about the highlights only. If we discussed all the sordid details, we'd be here several days." She took a sip of coffee and began. "When you are the spouse of the Vice President of the United States, and your spouse has well-known aspirations to be President, and when you are as politically and internationally connected as someone with Stephanie Kenseth's background, clearly you have access and influence. Many people in the world are willing to pay for access for your current, and future, influence. The Foundation was a perfect and totally legal cover for Stephanie to get paid for influence peddling on the part of the Vice President. Even after William's death, Stephanie continued to sell access and the promise of future influence. She has been very up-front with people around the globe that she expects to be President, and that she will reward in the future those who reward her now. There are going to be many upset people around the world who have paid a lot of money, some of whom with access to guns and ships and missiles, if Stephanie is not elected president and cannot deliver on her promises."

"Like what kind of promises?" Jeffrey asked.

"I can't answer that completely because I was not involved in the discussions. But I'll give you an example of one situation that involved current and future influence. Have you ever heard of the company Uranium One?"

"No, should I have?"

"Not really. Unless you are into Russian Uranium."

With that piece of information, Jeffrey's eyebrows raised substantially.

"While Stephanie was Vice President, a Russian company which later changed its name to Uranium One bought a Canadian company which controls the mining rights to about 20% of the United States' uranium supply. Because of the national security implications of a transaction like that, the Office of Vice President is required to sign off on the deal. Not only did Stephanie give her approval for the deal, she helped fast track it through the system. Literally a dozen people, from Russian government through Canadian industry, gave money to the ICSJ Foundation, which she alone controlled, during the process."

"How much?"

"About $40 million."

"Holy shit!"

A confident smile emerged on Amuh's face. "Pretty good number, huh? I'm kind of surprised you didn't know about that. The Times reported on it, which really pissed Stephanie off."

"The New York Times reported on it and she still got away with it? How'd she pull *that* off?"

"You tell me. She's Stephanie Kenseth. She and William had a way, and she has continued that after his death. But that's not even the motherload."

"She scored a bigger number than $40 million?!"

"Add a zero. Actually, probably more."

Jeffrey was wide-eyed and silent.

The smile returned to Amuh's face. She continued, "OK, if you don't know about the Times report on the uranium, I'm guessing you don't know about the Inspector General's report on the $6 billion missing from the White House budget."

Jeffrey could hardly speak. "Stephanie Kenseth took $6 billion from the White House budget appropriation?"

Amuh laughed at the ridiculous look of bewilderment on his face.

"No, goofball. She didn't take all of it. She got some of it, though. I can't believe you don't know about this!"

Amuh was talking about these incidents like they were common knowledge. Even still, Jeffrey was a little embarrassed he didn't know about them and was starting to get a little defensive.

"Look love, while you and Stephanie and others are trotting around the globe, making the world a better place, or just lining your pocketbooks, I'm stuck here building the relationships and networks that make it possible for our people to win elections. Forgive me for being engrossed in the much more honest work I do." Jeffrey punctuated his point with a rightward tilt of the head and flash of the eyes. "Now tell me about the $6 billion!"

Amuh returned Jeffrey's smile. "Easy tiger. No one is diminishing the great work you do. Sorry if I gave you that impression."

She continued, "The White House has a budget of around $20 billion annually. All of that is spent ultimately at the direction of the President and Vice President. A lot of that budget is spent on contracts for all types of aid in foreign countries, as well as domestically. When you consider that William or Stephanie was the Vice President for nearly eight years, the fact the Inspector General could not account for $6 billion over that time is really not a huge deal. I mean, it's about 4% of the total budget over that time."

"So, what happened to it?"

"Most of it, I have no idea. Some of it was laundered into the Foundation."

"What do you mean laundered?" Jeffrey asked honestly.

Amuh now looked at Jeffrey as if he were a child. "Jeffrey, you are so precious. Some of the money was provided to people and businesses and foreign governmental agencies and made to look like contracts. But there were no contracts. These people were political friends of Stephanie and William, and they were in essence paid money from the White House budget, with the understanding that they would then give some of that money, usually half, back to the ICSJ Foundation. It was a way of laundering US tax dollars into the possession of the Kenseths, via the Foundation.

Jeffrey was nodding his head and looking at Amuh through slightly squinted eyes, an involuntary habit when his brain was processing unbelievable information. "A classic kickback scheme."

Amuh affirmed, "Classic kickback. Jeffrey, do you recall the Everglades scandal Stephanie endured when William was Governor of Florida?" Jeffrey slowly shook his head to indicate he did not.

Amuh continued, "After William was first elected Governor, Stephanie made Save the Everglades her pet project. Millions of dollars were raised from across the country. The money was to be spent in specific counties to protect and improve water quality. A county official in Dade County, I think, accused Stephanie of requiring quid pro quo donations to her husband's re-election campaign, in order to receive funds from Save the Everglades. Kind of the same scenario as now, just 20 years in the past."

Jeffrey responded, "Now that you mention the details, I do recall this. But she was never convicted of any wrongdoing, correct?"

Amuh rolled her eyes. "Convicted, no. Having access to millions of dollars given to Save the Everglades will buy you a lot of friends. So, convicted, no. Guilty? You tell me."

Jeffrey's mouth was shut, but his face was speaking volumes.

"Oh, and the guy in Dade County who made the accusation… his car and his shoes, and *only* his car and his shoes, were found on the bank of Lake Okeechobee, which only happens to have the highest concentration of alligators of any lake in Florida. Imagine that, a guy from Florida with intimate knowledge of the area decides to walk barefoot in an alligator-infested lake and was never heard from again. I'm sure *that* happens all the time."

"Damn," was all Jeffrey could say.

Amuh continued, "So the Inspector General's report uncovered the fact there was a lot of money spent from the White House budget for which no contracts or invoices could be found."

Jeffrey asked, "And that amount totaled $6 billion?"

"That was the total identified in the IG's report."

"How much of that did Stephanie get do you think?

"It's almost impossible to tell. But ten percent would be a good guess."

"That's all?"

"Six hundred million is not impressive enough for you, Jeffrey? C'mon you greedy bastard! That is a *huge* number!"

"I know that's a huge number. And yes, I *am* a greedy bastard! I just meant I can't believe Stephanie was only able to get ten percent of the total."

"Some of that lost and unaccounted for funding identified by the IG is real. The White House's accounting systems and financial accountability in general are a mess. It was only because of that fact that we were able to hide her activity. Again, you're only talking about 4% of the White House's budget over a multi-year period, and Stephanie's portion of that was ten percent. So, four tenths of one percent has Stephanie's fingerprints on it."

Jeffrey was dumbfounded. "Unbelievable. So there is upwards of… what would you think, seven hundred million dollars at the Foundation?"

Amuh responded, "More than that."

"How the hell is it more than that? What else did she have going on?"

Amuh hesitated. She wished she had let it go, and let Jeffrey believe his own conclusion. Jeffrey could sense she was calculating how to end the conversation where it stood, and he knew she had more to share.

"Tell me, Amuh. You can't just leave me hanging like this."

"Jeffrey, it might be best that you don't know. I mean, this is some pretty serious stuff. Let's just drop it."

Jeffrey paused before speaking, as if contemplating how to evade the yield sign Amuh had just erected. "No freaking way, love. You want to tell me, I can tell. And frankly you *should* tell me. I want to know and you should tell me!"

Jeffrey was sitting cross legged in the bed directly in front of Amuh, who was also cross legged. He put his hands on her knees, leaned forward, and kissed her on the chin. While he kissed her, he moved his hands from her knees up her thighs and gave her hips a squeeze. This served to slightly disarm her. Playfully now she asked him, "What makes you think I want to tell you?"

Jeffrey paused, reached to his right and picked up the last piece of bacon from his plate. He slowly brought it to his mouth, bit off a third of it and continued with no emotion on his face. "Because telling me lessens the likelihood the police will find just your shoes and just your car on the banks of the Okeechobee." He widened his eyes and smiled wickedly.

"Shit! Shit you are right!" Her eyes were darting quickly back and forth across the room. She was unsure of whether to be scared to death, or laugh at the flippancy with which Jeffrey had just revealed the tenuous position she was in and previously unaware of.

With her left hand, she now grabbed the rest of the bacon out of Jeffrey's hand and wielded it at him like a policeman's baton. She pointed it at his face as she said, "You can't tell anyone what I'm about to tell you! Do you understand me?"

"I understand," Jeffrey said is his most contrite tone of voice.

"I'm serious. This is serious shit. No messing around. This stays between us girls. I have to have your word." Her tone *was* very serious.

Jeffrey leaned forward, took a bite of the bacon Amuh was holding, took his right hand and made the sign of the cross and said with bacon still in his mouth, "Just between us girls, I swear."

Exasperated, Amuh now threw the remaining morsel of bacon at his face and said, "You are such a loser. I cannot believe I am going to tell you this." She rolled her eyes and cursed herself for her utter lack of willpower. Jeffrey did his best to force a serious look.

Amuh closed her eyes and took a deep breath and exhaled before she began. "You know how Stephanie told you the ICSJ made a lot of money while she was running it and while William was VP?"

"Yes."

"You remember the attack in Damascus on the US Consulate when the ambassador and several others were killed?"

"Yes. That was horrible."

"Yes, it was horrible, and those two things are related. Some of the money at the Foundation, and Damascus."

No longer did Jeffrey have to force the look of seriousness look on his face. "Okay…" was all he could muster in response.

Amuh began to explain. "When William was Vice President, he asked for and received permission from the President to make Middle Eastern relations his pet project. He was allowed to direct some of the discretionary White House budget to that region. A lot of it went to Syria, and most of that through Damascus. At the same time, Stephanie set up a field office for ICSJ, also in Damascus. Together they established a pay to play environment, somewhat similar to the Everglades project. In this case,

William would direct White House funds only to groups who agreed to give some of it to the ICSJ Foundation as a donation."

Jeffrey sat in only mild disbelief for a few seconds then responded, "Classic kickback again."

Amuh hesitated slightly before acknowledging. "It gets worse."

Jeffrey only needed to raise his eyebrows to prod Amuh further.

Amuh continued, "The Foundation's role in Damascus was to distribute food, clothes, and medicine. The people there are in such terrible shape because of the civil war. But the Foundation was not just distributing humanitarian aid. It was distributing guns and weapons which it sold to the highest bidder, regardless of political or religious affiliation. The Foundation was actually helping perpetuate the civil war which the Foundation was supposedly there to help ease the pain of."

Jeffrey was dumbfounded. "That is truly awful."

"Yes, it is. But again, it gets worse, and that's how the consulate was involved in the attack. You can imagine, with a civil war raging and control of the streets of Damascus changing hands sometimes daily, there weren't many secure places for the Foundation to hold its cache of weapons while they were being marketed."

Jeffrey's eyes grew wide as he said, "The consulate…"

"You got it. Somebody, maybe Assad's forces or the Alawites or Sunnis or who knows who else, got wind of where a bunch of weapons were. No one knows whether the attack was to obtain the weapons, or stop their ongoing distribution. Either way, the

Ambassador and his staff were killed in the hours long attack."

"That explains why no Marines or Seals or anybody else was sent to help them. It would have blown the façade and exposed the consulate as an armory."

"Ha! Not just an armory, Jeffrey. A for-profit weapons distribution center being funded by laundered U.S. Government funds, being managed by a humanitarian aid organization, all under the umbrella of U.S. diplomatic protection, with all trails leading to William and Stephanie Kenseth."

Jeffrey sat in stunned silence for several seconds. He knew Stephanie was a highly-complicated animal. But he had no idea she was capable of something as complex as this. Suddenly his mind was jolted back to the question that had started the conversation. "So how much money do you think the Foundation really has? A billion?"

"As big a number as that is, that's probably a good guess."

Jeffrey's mind was racing. He was having trouble imagining a number as large as a billion. No wonder Stephanie so easily slid $35 million across the table to Colton Teddie.

"Who controls the account?"

"Only Stephanie. No one else that I am aware of has access. I mean, I know there is an account. I was notified when money came in, via an email. The email contained information on the sender and the sender's bank, which I archived for Stephanie. But I've never seen statements or other documentation of the actual account the money goes into. I just know it exists. It could be held offshore for all I know. But Stephanie is the only one with direct access to it."

Jeffrey jokingly said, "So William didn't have access to it?"

Amuh almost had her coffee come through her nostrils. "Right. If that happened, at least we'd know what a billion dollars in hookers looks like." Jeffrey roared, then thought some more. "So, the $35 million she gave Tedie was really just pocket change."

"Yeah, as crazy as it sounds, $35 million is a fairly small number when you consider what is available in that account."

Amuh continued, "It is a small, but impressive investment to help ensure four to eight years in control of a $4 trillion-dollar U.S. budget from the office of the President. Given her past success at laundering, the possibilities of what she could scarf from the total budget are pretty mind numbing." Jeffrey repeated, "Mind numbing."

Run for President

As planned, Colton Tedie formally announced his candidacy for the Republican nomination for President on June 16, 2015. The announcement was of course held at The Tedie Hotel in New York City. Tedie made his grand entrance by descending on an escalator, giving the appearance he was entering the race straight from heaven. The DNC acknowledged Tedie's entrance into the race by declaring that he brought a seriousness to the field that had been lacking.

It did not take long for Tedie to begin implementing the plan Jeffrey had laid out for him. The heart of the plan was Tedie grabbing headlines by making inflammatory statements, aimed particularly toward women, immigrants, and the LGBT community. However, the timing had to be right. He had to win everyone over. He couldn't seem like a joke or simply an attention hound. Therefore, in his initial speech as candidate Tedie, he kept things pretty tame, and only briefly once mentioned drugs and crime being brought over to the United States from Mexico.

Jeffrey watched the well-attended press conference via Periscope. The feed was being provided by longtime friend Marvelous Marvin Brown, who was covering the event for the Landon campaign. Jeffrey was pleased with Tedie's delivery and his light touch on the immigrant issue. Republicans would defend him on this, but it certainly set the tone for future sound bites that they had planned to make about Mexican immigrants, and many other hot button issues.

A week after Tedie announced his candidacy, there was a scheduled conference call for some members of the PTL Committee. It was an opportunity for them to compare notes and discuss their impressions of how the plan was unfolding, seven days after the official launch.

Jeffrey was leading the call. "OK folks there's no agenda here other than to discuss what we are hearing, seeing, and witnessing in Tedie's campaign. Who wants to kick us off?"

Jeremy Lamb began, "Looks like it's working perfectly so far."

Amy Lackey was next, "I agree totally; so far we are achieving exactly what we wanted."

All the ensuing comments were positive. After several minutes, Jeffrey summarized his observations and research. "None of the other Republican candidates are trending anywhere near the level of Tedie. Our man is attacking where we want him to, and in stark contrast to career politicians, also not backing down from his comments when he is attacked. The media is responding exactly how we assumed they would. I also sense our base is beginning to coalesce against Tedie. It's early, but so far, we are perfectly on track."

No one objected. This was almost too easy, thought Jeffrey. "We will have a follow up call at the end of July. I'll send you the time and date. Thanks, everyone!"

The call that took place at the end of July was pretty much the same, just with more data and results to discuss. Before they ended the call, Tommy LaRusa asked Jeffrey to share his private polling numbers.

"Tommy, they beat anything from any candidate I've ever seen before. In the two weeks following his announcement, Tedie went from less than 8% to over 11%. A month later, he is commanding a 25% share of a very crowded field. This kind of movement is unprecedented."

"Why do you think that is?" Tommy asked.

"Clearly, he is striking a chord with a large number of people. What is most unique about Tedie as compared to traditional candidates is that he is not backing down when attacked by the press. That is obviously playing well to his base. The more negative his press coverage, the more his supporters are drawn to him. I've never seen anything like it. I am certain any other candidate we might have chosen to promote would have wilted by now under this kind of negative coverage."

Tommy asked an additional, important question. "Jeffrey, how has Tedie's entrance into the race affected our fundraising?"

"Great question, Tommy. The effect on fundraising tracks with his ascension in the polls. Outstanding. Business is as good as expected!"

Per their original agreement, Tedie's polling success meant additional payments were sent his way from the ICSJ Foundation. His deposits to date were now over $50 million. In addition to these payments made directly to him, the Foundation was helping finance his campaign.

On the first Monday in August, Jeffrey was in high spirits. He'd just finished a seven-mile early morning run around Arlington and the District. He loved the feeling he got while running through the nation's capital. It was now late morning and he was preparing for his Monday check-in with Stephanie. He knew she would be interested to hear the latest on Tedie's polling, and even more importantly, what his strategy was to douse the flames of her most recent controversy.

Many months ago, a story had been leaked to the press from an unknown international source, which suggested Stephanie Kenseth may have personally benefitted from the sale of weather satellite technology to the Tunisians. The sale was highly controversial, owing to the fact the same technology which enables a satellite launch can, with slight modifications, also enable offensive ballistic missile capabilities. The Tunisians did not possess ballistic missile technology at the time, and several countries within the range of a mid-level ballistic missile voiced grave concern over the sale. The loudest opposition came from the Israelis.

The story, which had been all but dead, had been revived this week with new information identifying three high ranking Department of Defense officials who had signed off on the sale, along with Vice President Stephanie Kenseth. This was highly classified information, which could logically only originate from within the Pentagon, or Vice President Stephanie Kenseth's email server. It was again suspected the Israelis were the source of the leak. Most damning, however, was the assertion that funds paid to the ICSJ Foundation from an unnamed Tunisian government official, supposedly for philanthropic purposes, were actually a bribe for the missile technology. How the Israelis obtained the information was unknown. The exposing of named individuals was significant because it created reasonable suspicion that if Stephanie had indeed benefitted financially from the sale, she may not have been the only one to do so.

As always, Jeffrey called Stephanie one minute later than their scheduled start time. It was all about control.

"Hello, Jeffrey."

"Hello Mrs. Kenseth. How are we today?"

"I am rushed today. Busy morning. Tell me quickly what you have in store for this week. I'm especially interested in hearing your plan for dealing with this weather satellite issue and getting it off page one."

"The story will be old news by the end of the week."

Stephanie quickly interjected, "Well I look forward to that. You sound very confident. Care to share how you plan on accomplishing what no one else has been able to yet?"

"It will go away because we are going to unleash our friend Mr. Tedie this week. You're obviously aware the first live Republican debate is being held this week. We are about to launch Phase II of his Alienation Plan. Morgan Smalls is one of the debate hosts. My sources at Fox assure me she will attack Tedie on his historical comments on women. Tedie will receive a directive from me before the debate to go after Smalls, as part of our plan to have him alienate the female vote. The confrontation between those two prima donnas will immediately bury the satellite story."

Stephanie thought for a moment before she spoke. "You indicated you are going to give Colton Tedie a directive to do this. The Colton Tedie I know does not take directives. He gives them. Tell me how *that* is going to work."

"With respect to the Colton Tedie you know, Madam Vice President, the Colton Tedie I know likes money. He likes it a lot. The directives I give him make him money, thanks to your Foundation. He will do it, because he knows it will drive the polls and create another paycheck from you."

Stephanie chuckled slightly. She knew everything Jeffrey had just said was true. "Outstanding. I like it. Fortuitous for us the debate is this week. Great job leveraging Smalls for our purposes. She won't even know she is helping our cause."

The day before the debate, Jeffrey sent a text to Tedie. "Pick a fight with Morgan Smalls tomorrow night. This is part of the plan. Based on her anticipated comments it should be easy."

However, Tedie did not end up picking a fight with Smalls. He didn't get the chance. Morgan Smalls took the fight to him with her first question. She reminded him of the demeaning and mean-spirited comments he had made against women in the past, just like Jeffrey knew she would. Her comments were fact-based, poignant, and appropriate given the likelihood of Stephanie Kenseth being the Democrat nominee.

At first, Tedie appeared to be taken off-guard by her immediate and direct line of questioning. He initially responded with humor, which the crowd responded to with sustained applause. The applause was so long, in fact, that Smalls had to refrain from continuing her questioning for several seconds. Jeffrey and the other Democrat strategists took special note of the audience's reaction. They were clearly less affected by Smalls' comments than they were by Tedie's own defense of his statements, and his easy humor in the face of this serious evidence against him. He did not apologize. He did not back down. Tedie's response to Smalls' questioning was exactly what Jeffrey expected. The fervor of the crowd's reaction, though, was not something he had anticipated. There were plenty of supporters in this crowd, but there were also plenty of Democrats.

Through the rest of the debate, Tedie continued to receive pointed questions from all the moderators, but especially from Smalls. It was fairly clear to anyone watching that he was being ganged up on, but at no time did he back down.

In the days following the debate, Tedie took the fight with Morgan Smalls to unprecedented levels. He attacked her on Twitter. He attacked her on competing networks. He made it personal. Jeffrey was enormously pleased with this. Tedie's actions went well beyond good taste, and well beyond what he had directed Tedie to do. Jeffrey momentarily worried that the fervor of this fight might be counter-productive for his purposes, and damage Tedie's chances against his Republican rivals.

When the polls came out after the debate, he was shocked to find out that the opposite had happened. Despite this very public feud with one of the leading female journalists in the country, Tedie's poll numbers were soaring. The day before the debate, Tedie had been polling at 25%, more than double his closest competitor. Within two weeks, after numerous attacks on Smalls from Tedie, his polling was up to 30%, with an 18% lead over his closest opponent. He was now virtually the only Republican in a crowded field receiving substantial media attention. This was exactly the execution the PTL envisioned many months ago.

Money from the ICSJ Foundation rolled in as he drove the media narrative with his attacks, all while continuing to lead in the polls. By the end of August, he had personally received over $60 million from the Foundation, including nearly $10 million in laundered campaign contributions.

Throughout the Fall and into Winter, Tedie maintained a commanding lead in the polls over his rival Republicans. Tedie was capitalizing on every major news story, and it seemed there was one at least weekly which supported his assertion that America the great had become America the weak due to the policies of the Democrat party and Barry Ingle's administration. Privately, Jeffrey marveled at how opportunistic the man was behind the microphone. Even with all the private celebrations and congratulatory emails and texts he had been receiving from those who knew the game that was being played, Jeffrey began to worry if perhaps he had miscalculated the mood of the country. The depth and breadth of the chord Tedie was striking exceeded what even he had imagined was out there.

Unplug the Monster

Despite the increasing Springtime temperatures, Jeffrey's times on his early morning seven mile runs in the District were continuing to improve. Typically, around this time of year his run times would slow due to increased heat and humidity. But this summer was different. It was June, and he was becoming more worried about the AWM monster he had created. He suspected his accelerated run times reflected the anxiety he was feeling, and the burgeoning need to take corrective action. He liked the faster times. He didn't like the reason why.

By all indicators, barring an unprecedented revolt by the Republican super delegates at the Republican convention in July, Tedie was going to be the Republican nominee. This is what he had predicted over a year ago, when he led the PTL team to focus on Tedie. What he had not counted on was the degree of Tedie's popularity. His incendiary speeches and attacks on large voting blocks had done very little to divide the Republicans against him. He had, however, coalesced a loud subset of Democrats against him. But not enough. In Jeffrey's privately funded polls, Tedie was polling well ahead of Stephanie for the presidency itself. So far, he had not shared this fact with anyone.

Excluding Jeffrey, everyone on Stephanie's team, and especially Stephanie herself, was giddy at the likelihood of running against Tedie. The national media polls had Stephanie slightly ahead in the matchup. Jeffrey knew better. He did not trust national polls conducted by major media. He understood their bias. What he trusted was his pragmatism and his political sense. He recognized that Tedie was touching a raw chord with a large swath of the electorate, including many Democrats. He feared he had underestimated President Ingle's and Vice President Stephanie's negatives. He also seemed to have underestimated Colton Tedie's ability to rally people around a message.

This morning, Jeffrey reached a decision he had been avoiding for several days. There was no other option, and time was quickly running out. He determined that he must destroy the candidate he had helped to create. Since he had been running past the World War II Memorial when he made this decision, he planned to call the action Operation Overlord, which was the code name for the allied invasion of Normandy in June 1944. He thought there was symmetry in the fact it was currently June, and that he was also going to be toppling a burgeoning power. "The end of the beginning," he recalled Churchill appointing it at the time.

With both conventions looming and the general election only a few months away, Stephanie and Jeffrey were spending more time together. He knew Stephanie was in Washington today, though she had not told him why. He suspected it might have something to do with damage control she was trying desperately to manage over the satellite technology sale to the Tunisians. There was growing evidence the Tunisians had quickly turned around and provided the technology to the Iranians. Operation Overlord was something he wanted to discuss with her in person, not over the phone. Her presence in Washington today made that possible.

They met in his Arlington office in the early afternoon. "Stephanie, it is fortuitous that that you are in Washington today. I have a few very specific things I'd like for us to discuss. But before we commence, is there anything I can help you with regarding your unscheduled stay in DC?" Jeffrey's inquiry had less to do with actually helping Stephanie than it did with trying to discover the nature of her visit.

"Thank you, Jeffrey, but no. I am working on personal matters which require me to be here."

They moved toward the small conference table situated in Jeffrey's office near the window. Stephanie continued after they both sat down. "I picked up a sense of urgency in your email about needing to meet. Tell me what is on your mind. From my perspective, we are right where we want to be, right where we thought we'd be. I get the sense you may be at a different place."

Jeffrey moved forward in his seat uncomfortably. "Stephanie, as usual, your keen sense is spot on. I am concerned about the monster we have created in Tedie."

With genuine surprise Stephanie responded, "Really? Because I am thrilled with him. He's been everything we wanted, and so much more. He has absolutely motivated our base, and painted the Republican Party with the broad, negative brush that you put in his hand. What concerns you about him?"

"He's motivated the elites and the very young of our base only. Unfortunately, he is attracting the non-urban, non-affluent part of our base. Farmers, factory workers, teachers, people in the heartland. His message is resonating with them. He seems to have the Reagan effect."

Stephanie straightened in her chair. "You're not concerned he could win the general, are you?" She paused, and stared at Jeffrey's blank look for several seconds. "So that's why you asked me here, isn't it?"

At this point, Jeffrey looked Stephanie squarely in the eye. He did not do this often. Most people were too intimidated by her to attempt such a power move. His prolonged eye contact communicated as much as any words could. He then pulled up his laptop screen and placed it on the coffee table in front of them.

"Stephanie, these are the polling results we pay for. I've sent you these via email but I don't know whether you've seen them. In each of the last six polls I've done, once weekly over the last six weeks, Tedie wins head to head against you. And his margin of victory is outside the statistical margin of error. This is serious. I can potentially see a scenario in which you actually win the popular vote, but lose the Electoral College. You poll great in the metro areas, not so great elsewhere."

Stephanie donned her reading glasses and looked intently at the information. She had seen the emails from Jeffrey, but had not taken the time to review the polling information. She had been trusting the national media's polling data, which showed her winning in a head to head matchup against all the Republican frontrunners. The one thing she trusted the most about Jeffrey was his judgement, however, and she knew they would not be having this conversation if he were not legitimately concerned.

Stephanie turned her gaze from the screen back to Jeffrey and waited for him to continue speaking. Jeffrey seized the opportunity. "He is continuing to pack out stadiums, drawing more than 10,000 people consistently in towns that have about 10,002 people in them. Even worse for us, he's doing this in states Ingle won in 2012. He's insulted everyone we've asked him to insult, many times over. But instead of this rhetoric hurting him, it seems to be propelling him."

Stephanie sat back in her chair and stared out the window. She let out a long exhale. "You believe this is sustainable, and that he is a threat to us in November. Yes?"

"I absolutely do. He has tapped into a vein that we underestimated."

"Indeed… he has." She paused thoughtfully and looked directly at Jeffrey. "So, what is your recommendation? What do we do now?"

"We can still undo what we have created. We have two torpedoes that we can potentially put into him. One, we can let the world know how his candidacy began. We can let it leak that he was in financial trouble, sought us out for money, and he agreed to run for pay. That should significantly damage his credibility."

Stephanie pursed her lips and looked down her nose at Jeffrey. He was expecting this.
"Two, perhaps the bigger opportunity for us, is to leak the news that some of the money we have put into his campaign coffers has come from China. It is cloaked, but we can de-cloak it. Whether it's illegal or not is up to interpretation of the laws, because the laws are intentionally vague. But the news that he's

taken foreign campaign contribution should damage him significantly."

Stephanie now stood and walked over to the window overlooking Arlington. It was an unusually clear day for June, and the view was stunning. She spoke into the window. "So, we let it leak that we paid him to run. How does this not potentially damage us?"

Jeffrey spoke to Stephanie's back. "That is a great question. One, our media friends will treat us favorably. They don't want a Tedie presidency any more than we do. They will focus on Tedie's sin, not ours. Second, the answer to the question is yes, the Foundation paid him. The Foundation was being true to its mission. The Foundation identified the best, worst candidate for the country. We, like everyone else, were later shocked and appalled by his actions, and decided to withdraw support."

"If we take these actions and undue Tedie as you are suggesting, what are we then up against? King?"

"Yes, most likely King. But whether it is King or somebody else, I don't think it matters. Tedie has commanded almost all the media attention during the campaign, and is the favorite among most of the Republican voters. He has succeeded based on his personality and the strength of his message, which is unique to him alone among their candidates. There is no 'light version' of Tedie on their side. If Tedie is successfully damaged to the point that the super delegates at the convention choose King or anyone else, it will create a firestorm for the Republicans internally that will overshadow their candidate for weeks. Tedie voters will stay at home in droves on election day if Tedie is not the nominee. And then, voila! It's November, and you are elected President."

"Are you sure, Jeffrey? We have invested so much in Tedie. And your plan, what you predicted would happen, has happened. Shouldn't we just stick with the original plan?"

"I think this is actually a better plan, Stephanie. We have successfully installed their front runner, and we have done so while having inside information that is damaging, potentially fatal, to his campaign. He is absolutely vulnerable in ways we can exploit. He has galvanized support around himself, not his party. This is actually the perfect point at which to burn him to create the best chance for you to win."

Stephanie thought as she continued looking over Arlington, then spoke. "Brilliant. The media would certainly go nuts over this." She now resolutely turned back toward Jeffrey. "What is your plan for timing?"

"It will be leaked in the days leading up to the Republican convention. The story has the potential to overshadow the whole event. Tedie's delegate count is within the margin controlled by the super delegates. Most of the super delegates are anti-Tedie to begin with. They hate the fact he has created his campaign, and his candidacy, on his own and outside of their traditional network. They will jump at the opportunity to install another candidate, a candidate they can control."

Stephanie summarized, "So we inflict a mortal wound on Tedie before the convention, creating turmoil. The convention picks another candidate, their base is now alienated, and our base is ecstatic that AWM has been toppled. Our challenge at that point is to keep our base as engaged through November, as they are now."

Jeremy finished, "Which is what you pay me to do."

"Which is why I pay you, Jeffrey. So, how will you do that? Keep our base engaged. How will you do that once Tedie is gone?"

Jeffrey laughed audibly. "I cannot believe what I just heard you say. There is no such thing as Tedie gone. When we successfully topple him from the perch he is currently sitting on, the perch we helped create for him, he will lash out like no other. He will come after us like a woman scourned. And the louder he screams, the less relevant he will become."

"The only avenue he has for coming after us is the media. And we own the media. Our kinsmen in the press will help us paint him as a raving lunatic, one not fit to govern. You will seize upon that as a reflection of the entire Republican party. Even as he is relegated to political obscurity, he will help you get elected President."

Stephanie was nodding and smiling confidently. Jeffrey was a master puppeteer, and she always enjoyed listening to him predict the future. "I like it, let's do it. And speaking of payments, since this is our new plan and we don't need AWM anymore, we will stop paying Tedie immediately. He'll reach out to you when the money stops. Tell him we changed our minds. He won't like it, but he'll get it."

As soon as Stephanie left his office, Jeffrey was on the phone to Jeremy Lamb of the New York Times. Lamb recognized Jeffrey's number.

"Jeffrey, how are you?"

"I'm good, but not nearly as good as you are about to be."

"Well I like the sound of that. Tell me more."

"Jeremy, we need to get together this week. I'm going to hand you a story that will win you another Pulitzer. I'm in DC all week. Meet me here."

"Jeffrey, you are such a tease!"

Jeffrey quickly responded, "That I am, but have I ever let you down? I don't think I have."

"Not once. See you in DC tomorrow. And thanks."

On Sunday July 17, it was no surprise the New York Times committed significant ink to the Republican National Convention, which was set to commence on Monday in Cleveland. What was a surprise, a complete bombshell, was the highly detailed, page one story by Jeremy Lamb detailing how Colton Tedie had been paid tens of millions by the ICSJ Foundation to seek the Republican nomination.

The story contained pictures of the two original cleared checks, totaling $35 million, which had gone from the Kenseth Foundation to Colton Tedie himself. Routing and account numbers were redacted to protect the Foundation of course, but everything else on the checks was crystal clear.

There were copies of emails (minus the names), which appeared to originate from inside of Citibank, clearly indicating that Tedie's loans had been called. There was detailed information on the $25 million loan pay down requirement in order to induce the bank to forebear any other legal action. The article left no doubt the $25 million check from

The Foundation bailed Tedie out of a $25 million hole he was in at Citibank.

Potentially most damaging of all, was a detailed accounting of how laundered money from China and Russia had found its way into Tedie's campaign accounts. If this were proven true, it would be a violation of campaign finance laws and draw into question Tedie's true allegiances. Various entities, circumstantially believed to be Chinese and Russian, had bought $1 million blocks of pre-paid credit cards in $250 increments, and those funds had been deposited into Tedie's election campaign accounts. In contrast to the funds from the ICSJ Foundation which contained a great number of specifics, the information on the potentially foreign money simply referenced unnamed sources.

Included in the article was a statement from the Kenseth campaign. It simply read, "In early 2015 Colton Tedie reached out to Stephanie Kenseth for assistance in funding a contemplated presidential run. Based on the decades long friendship between Mr. Colton and Vice President Kenseth, and a belief that Mr. Tedie would promote values in his campaign which were reflective of their shared New York ties, the ICSJ Foundation agreed to help fund Colton Tedie's campaign. Funding of a political campaign is consistent with the mission of the ICSJ, and demonstrates its true neutrality in matters of politics. The funding ceased after it became clear Mr. Tedie allowed the seduction of power to alienate himself and the Republican party from a large number of honest and hardworking Americans. Further, Vice President Kenseth condemns the acceptance of foreign funds to finance his presidential campaign, and now strongly questions if Tedie can be trusted with promoting American values."

The story was immediately the hottest news item on the planet. What should have been a news cycle of positive press for the Republicans and their upcoming convention was turned into a free-for-all in which the narrative was being driven against them, not for them. It was a perfect storm, all engineered by Jeffrey and the Democrats.

Colton Tedie and wife Michelle were home in New York when the story broke. They each received text messages from friends alerting them of the news story. Each of them silently scanned the article privately.

After reading the story, Michelle sought Colton out in his study. She was angry. The last thing she wanted was a tainted image, a tainted name. Their son would have to endure even more taunts and bullying from his politically aware school friends. She walked more resolutely than normal into the study and entered without knocking.

"I'm assuming you've seen the story by now?"

Tedie tried to hide his agitation at her bold interruption. "Yes, my dear I have."

"I told you not to get into this relationship with her! I told you she was evil and could not to be trusted. You didn't listen, and now we have this bullshit to deal with as a family."

"Michelle my dear, you are right and wrong. Yes, you did warn me, and you were right. I knew it at the time. We both knew it at the time. But where you are wrong is in thinking that I did not listen to you. Just because I didn't *do* what you wanted me to do does not mean I didn't listen. I listened, I just went a different direction than you wanted me to go."

Michelle was quickly going from agitated to full-blown irate. His smug calmness and his egotistical response infuriated her. "Whatever, Colton. What are we going to do about it? What are *you* going to do about it? These are serious charges you are being accused of."

"What WE are going to do about it my dear, is get our asses ready to go to Cleveland, God help us, and accept the Republican nomination for President of the United States."

Michelle rolled her eyes and did her best to bite her tongue. With all the restraint she could muster, she pressed him further, "Seriously Colton, what are you going to do about this?"

Now smiling, he responded, "Michelle I am a little disappointed you ask that question. What am I going to do? I'm going to do the two things I always do. I'm going to fight. Then I'm going to win. You know this. Trust me, everything is going to be great."

Early Sunday afternoon, the Tedie campaign issued a brief statement. It read, "Colton Tedie will respond to today's politically motivated attack at the appropriate time in the appropriate manner." The ambiguity in that communication only served to feed additional speculation.

The only outreach on the issue Colton Tedie made outside of his inner circle on Sunday was to Jeffrey Saint. He thought about sending a text, but he did not want his text potentially being forwarded. He called instead.

Jeffrey saw the number and hesitated. He was not sure he wanted to take Colton Tedie's call today. He assumed Tedie would blitz him for leaking the information which made today's NYT's article possible. Still, it was not every day that you get cursed out by one of the biggest names in business. He would consider it a badge of honor.

"Hello Mr. Te…" was all Jeffrey was able to say before he was cut off.

The message from Colton was quick and to-the-point.

"Well played, Jeffrey. Well played. But the game is only just beginning." Tedie ended the call before he could respond.

That, thought Jeffrey, was even better than being cursed out. Game on.

A Crazy Woman

During the first two days of the Republican Convention, Colton Tedie kept a low profile. He was not even in Cleveland. Nor was he campaigning. His spokespeople were all over the convention though, continuing his message of America is Ready for Tedie. When they were asked about the NYT story, they indicated Mr. Tedie would respond fully in his speech scheduled for Wednesday night.

Entering the convention, Colton Tedie had amassed just under 1,450 delegates, about 200 more than he needed to secure the nomination. But there were over 400 super delegates at the convention. The super delegates were not bound by the voting results from their states. The Tedie story had brought these super delegates into play and given them more power than usual. The fate of the convention and the selection of the nominee was in their hands.

The person expected to benefit the most from the super delegates potentially breaking with their state's electoral results was Ricky King. King was the favored candidate by the old guard Republican establishment. The Republican power brokers, those behind the scenes individuals who yield significant power, hated and feared Tedie. Tedie had made the traditional party power structure impotent with his direct appeal to the voters and primarily self-funded campaign. He had not played their game, not respected their decades old power structure, and had won in spite of their influence. If Tedie won the nomination, their role as the guardians of the party power structure would be exposed as unnecessary. They needed King to seize on this moment and claim the super delegates now in play. Everyone assumed they were in play. No one on Monday or Tuesday thought Tedie could recover from the recent revelations.

As part of the original scheduling for the convention, Colton Tedie was due to speak in prime time, 9:30pm on Wednesday night. As a result of the damning article, the Republican party leadership began campaigning to have King speak in this slot, and Tedie speak sometime in the midafternoon. The difference in audience viewership was stark between these two times. Advertising rates reflected these differences in audience size. The party leadership was ready to make this move… until the television networks stepped in.

Colton Tedie had proven to be a financial windfall for the networks during the debates and during the entire campaign season. Ratings for the debates, and subsequently advertising rates, had soared due to Tedie's involvement. The networks wanted Tedie during prime time. They made sure the party leadership knew to expect solar flares to disrupt satellite transmissions during King's speech should Tedie not be allowed to speak as originally planned at 9:30. The Party leadership got the message and backed down, keeping Tedie in his original time slot. He received dozens of requests for interviews leading up to his Wednesday evening speech, but Colton Tedie participated in only one. In typical Tedie fashion, he engineered this interview to have maximum impact.

He agreed to be interviewed by Fox News only, and demanded the interview be conducted by Morgan Smalls. This demand caused two news stories to become one. The first story was the fact Colton Tedie was conducting his first interview after the incriminating article. The second story was that fact that he didn't just agree, he demanded, to be interviewed by Smalls, the same person he had carried on a very public feud with since the first Republican debate almost a year ago.

In addition to requiring that Morgan Smalls conduct the interview, he mandated that the interview be done standing up, and that it occur during King's speech. Fox News protested vociferously at this expectation, but Tedie ultimately won the argument when he threatened to allow another network to conduct the interview instead.

Midafternoon on Wednesday, Fox News began advertising that it would have an exclusive interview with Tedie immediately after King's speech, which was scheduled for 5:30pm. This provided them with a cover for when the interview began "early" beyond their control.

At 5:44, in the midst of King's speech, Fox News broke away to a shot of Morgan Smalls standing in front of a backstage curtain. Tedie was with her, also standing. Because they were standing, Tedie was in almost complete control of the interview. Smalls and Fox knew they were being used, and at King's expense. But Tedie was a ratings magnet, and at this moment in time, he was in command.

Smalls had no idea how long Tedie would agree to be interviewed for. She assumed the interview could end at any moment with him simply walking out of the shot. He had pulled this move before. To give the best chance of getting the answers she wanted, she front-loaded her most important questions.

"Mr. Tedie, for several days the political world has been waiting to hear your reaction to the recent New York Times story, that Stephanie Kenseth paid you to run for the Republican nomination, and that your campaign has illegally accepted funding from foreign countries. What is your response to these allegations?"

"Well first of all, I think you are selling me short. You said the political world has been waiting to hear my reaction. Based on what I have seen and read and experienced this week, including stories on your own network, the *entire* world, not just the political world, wants to know what is going on. And I am going to make it all clear tonight in my speech."

He continued, "But for the benefit of our brief time together right now and for your audience, which I am sure is huge right now, I can sum this whole thing up in one statement. Stephanie Kenseth is a liar. She is a serial liar. She has made a career out of lying."

"So, you are denying the allegations?"

"Morgan, I will fully address the allegations in my speech tonight. I will be very honest, and very clear. There will be no ambiguity in my comments. I will not hide behind a New York Times reporter or a press release the way Stephanie has done."

Tedie then made a move to step away from Smalls but she pressed on, "Mr. Tedie what do you expect will happen next, after your speech tonight?"

Tedie stopped and turned back toward Smalls. "I expect to be named the Republican nominee for President tomorrow. And in November, I expect to win the Presidency. And then I expect to help return America to greatness again, along with the help of the millions of people who support me and believe this country was once the greatest on Earth. That is what I expect to happen after my speech." He then walked off camera.

Fox garnered a seventy-five percent share of the television market during Tedie's brief interview, an astounding number. Only ten percent of their audience remained to watch the conclusion of the King speech. Social media feeds blew up. In contrast, King's speech did not even register as a trending topic. The Republican leadership, despite their clear bias for King, could only watch as Tedie continued his mastery over their game.

Later that evening, Colton Tedie took the podium at the Republican National Convention. Most of the gathered delegates in front of him were on their feet. The applause was extended, fitting for a presumptive nominee. Tedie was smiling. He had the look of a man who was about to turn over the ace of diamonds to reveal the last card in a royal flush. He made no effort to stop the applause, which lasted a full three minutes.

Finally, he began his speech. "My fellow Americans, thank you. Thank you very much. As much as I would like to think that all this applause and love that I feel in the room is for me, I know it is not. I know this because I have spent the last many months traveling this great country, and speaking to many, many great Americans. So, I am fully aware that your applause and your cheers emanate primarily from a realization that the nightmare of this eight-year amateur hour that we've all had to endure is soon coming to a close!" Everyone in the room, not just the Tedie supporters, now stood and applauded wildly.

"Together, we will bring America back to that special place of freedom and opportunity for all!" More applause. At this point, Tedie backed a half step away from the podium. He peered across the room and tilted his head upwards slightly. His gaze was mostly skyward, and his lips were curled in slightly. He had the look of a person who was about to tell a scandalous story. He stepped back to the podium and waited for the last of the applause to die out. He put both hands on either side of the podium and recommenced his speech.

A smile came across his face. "You know ladies and gentlemen, a funny thing happened to me on the way to the convention this week." Mild laughter could be heard, as well as some jeers. Tedie was still smiling. "I actually had to change my speech. I mean, I had this great speech written out. Those of you who know me well know I make a living being prepared. One of the tenants of my enormous success is being prepared. So, naturally, I had tonight's speech prepared well in advance. And then this... thing happened, this story came out, and it seems to have captured everyone's attention." More gentle laughter in the room as Tedie paused for effect. "So, I thought maybe I should address that here. Just between us, in this elegant, intimate setting."

Tedie paused before continuing. The pause highlighted the silence which had settled upon the previously rancorous crowd, as they all waited with baited breath for his next sentence. "I love this country. It is the greatest country on Earth because we are blessed with so many freedoms. This country, our country, has historically had the highest level of political, religious, and economic freedoms of any country in the world. This country has provided so many opportunities to so many people, because we have freedoms. Or we did, I should say." Tedie paused, and applause filled the void.

"Many of you know, probably all of you know, I have considered running for president in the past. And I've considered doing so because I love this country, and because I believe the country and my fellow citizens would prosper under my leadership."

"I was not, however, planning to run for president in 2016. Yes, our beloved country is in quite a mess. Yes, many trusted colleagues that I respect immensely suggested that I should run. Even still, I was not planning to run. I am happy with my life, my business ventures are successful, and I thought the best way for me to help the country was to just continue doing what I was doing, creating jobs and paying taxes. I, like everyone else, was praying that the right candidate would come along, a candidate that reflected the values of the great people gathered in this room and watching on television."

"So, there I was, minding my own business, and this crazy woman shows up at my door." Tedie paused, and a slow rolling laughter filled the room as the reference to Stephanie Kenseth began to take hold.

"I was literally minding my own business and this crazy woman shows up at my door. She wants to come in. I'm a nice guy, so I let her in. Wouldn't you know, this crazy woman has something very interesting with her. She has a bag full of money. A huge bag full of money. And the only reason I know she has money in the bag is because she opens the bag and shows it to me! She says to me, 'Here, take a look at all this money!'" Laughter quickly echoed throughout the room.

"You guys are laughing and I'm not even to the funny part. Now I said she was crazy. The reason I know she was crazy is because of what she said to me. This crazy woman with the bag full of money says she wants me to run for president. So, I asked her, president of what?" The laughter in the arena was now growing.

"She said 'President of the United States.' I said, 'these United States?' I mean, I wanted to be certain the crazy woman's United States were the same United States that I am familiar with. And she said 'Yes, these very United States.' Then before I could answer, she said, 'I will pay you to run.'"

He paused to let that sink in.

"I said, 'Wait a minute. You are going to *pay* me to run for president?' I thought, what a great country this is after all! So, I asked her, 'Tell me, why are you going to pay me to run for President of the United States?'"

In an instant, Tedie's smile disappeared from his face. It was replaced with his signature scowl. He paused for people to understand the tone of his story had switched. Laughter slowly gave way to captivated silence.

He began speaking very deliberately, as if speaking to each specific person seated in that arena. "She said, 'I'm going to pay you to run for president, because you are the guy I think I can beat. I want you to run for president because my people will hate you. They will hate you more than they dislike me. Their hatred of you will overshadow their ability to recognize the glaring nature of my failures and the bankruptcy of my failed ideas. You will cause my people to come out in droves and vote *against* you. Only simpletons and hicks will vote for you. I want you to run for president, and lose, to me. And I am so confident in my ability to manipulate the American people and win this election, I am willing to pay you a lot of money because I think you are the right loser.'"

Tedie paused now for several seconds. His facial expression did not change. The gaze of his eyes scanned the arena, seeking to make direct eye contact with everyone he could through the blinding stage lights.

"My fellow Americans, if you do not know anything about me, know this. I. Do. Not. Lie. I do not lie. I exaggerate, sometimes. I am from New York, it's what we do. But I do not lie. Believe me when I tell you that Stephanie Kenseth sought me out many months ago to run for the Republican Party nomination for President of the United States. She sought me out. She offered me several million dollars to seek the Republican nomination. Now you tell me this…" Tedie backed up slightly from the podium and threw his arms wide with his palms up toward the sky, raised his voice and continued, "what would you have done? What would you have done?"
At this, Tedie backed up further from the podium and crossed his arms and began nodding his head. The crowd rose to its feet in unison and applauded lustfully. Several shouts of "Take the money! Take the money!" rose from the floor.

After several seconds, he retook the podium. "You're damn right, I took the money!" Again, he backed away from the podium to allow the applause to cascade. His scowl was now replaced with a broad smile.

"If you read the newspaper article you saw the number, $35 million. That is true. That is the amount Stephanie Kenseth put in my hands to run for president. And she was very clear, she expected me to lose. Her arrogance, ladies and gentlemen, is greater than you can imagine. She thought, and still believes as far as I know, that people with our American values are the minority in this country, that we are the problem. Well, it's Stephanie that now has the problem. Like so many enemies of this country before her, she is learning she has picked a fight with the wrong opponent!" Sustained and boisterous applause again erupted and the convention was on its feet.

Tedie interrupted the applause. "The only strings attached to that money, ladies and gentlemen, the only strings attached to that money were that I be myself. Trust and believe that I have been true to myself and my red, white, and blue beliefs during this campaign. You, the American people have responded to that by voting for me in greater fervor and volume than any other candidate in this race. I am honored and humbled by that, and I am clearly the candidate the people who comprise the Republican Party wants to have as its presidential nominee." Again, the crowd rose to its feet and offered extended applause.

"If you've read the article from that failing newspaper, Stephanie essentially made three accusations. One, that I sought her out; that I sought her assistance and funding to run for president. That is a lie. Two, that I accepted money from her to run for president. That is true. I will admit to being a smart enough businessman to accept $35 million dollars from someone who asks me to do something I am more than capable of doing. Third, she accused me of accepting illegal, foreign campaign contributions. Stephanie Kenseth, by the way, is an expert on accepting illegal, foreign campaign contributions. She is uniquely qualified to make this accusation." More rancorous applause.

"As part of her efforts to have me run for the Republican nomination, Stephanie agreed to send money to my campaign accounts. Those funds were laundered I now believe through Chinese and Russian sources. I don't know the original source of the funds, I assume they come from Stephanie's own campaign war chest. But those funds did in fact come to us from thinly veiled foreign sources. It was a trap. It was clearly a trap and it took my team less than one hour to uncover it. Again, this woman's arrogance is beyond fathom. She believed we were dumb enough to fall for a trap that she herself invented, fell into, and that her own husband was caught in previously during her crooked career."

"Over the course of many months, her campaign sent my campaign several million dollars which were handled at some point through foreign operatives. In each and every case, these dollars were summarily rejected by my campaign within forty-eight hours of receipt. Before this week's article was ever published, we volunteered this information and all our campaign records to the Federal Elections Commission. We passed their audit with perfect marks. We have run the cleanest campaign in the history of this country, and we will run the most effective administration in the history of this country!"

At this revelation, and from the comfort of his living room, Jeffrey raised his eyebrows and said, "Well played, Mr. Tedie" to no one except his iPad and his dog.

Tedie was now ready for the close. "My fellow Republicans and my fellow Americans, I stand before you tonight because of two phenomena. The first is that I love my country, and believe I am uniquely qualified to return America to her rightful place of prosperity again. The second, and more important phenomena, is that a majority of people in the primaries, and I believe a majority of people in the country, are fed up with the utter and complete lack of leadership coming from the White House, coming from the Democrat Party, coming from Washington, and are tired of having the American values they hold so dear ripped to shreds by people whose only purpose in life is to perpetuate their political careers on the backs of taxpayer dollars and at the expense of their God-given, Constitutionally protected freedoms! Together we will return America to glory again!" The ensuing applause was so intense that Tedie appeared to be pushed back from the podium by its force. He thrust his right fist into the air twice, and exited the stage to the outstretched arms of Michelle, who had tears streaming down both cheeks.

The following night, to no one's surprise, Colton Tedie was declared the Republican nominee for President of the United States. Every single delegate won in his favor in the primaries was awarded to him in the nomination process. Like everyone else in the arena, and millions of viewers across the country, the super delegates were swayed by his dynamic and transparent speech.

Truman

Exactly one week later, the Democrats held their convention in Philadelphia. There was no drama in the election of Stephanie Kenseth as their candidate. There was however, course-altering drama in the days that followed.

With great fanfare, Stephanie Kenseth accepted the nomination of her party as its presidential nominee on July 28. In doing so, she became the first woman to accept the nomination for President of the United States from a major political party. What had commenced many months previous as a foregone conclusion was now a reality. What Stephanie Kenseth had dreamed of for decades was now a reality. Team Stephanie could now shed the illusion there was any concern over winning the nomination, and focus on Colton Tedie and the Republicans as their opponent.

On the Monday after the convention, Stephanie's phone rang at 9:05am. As usual, Jeffrey was late in delivering his 9am call. She could not understand how anyone with Jeffrey's superlative management skills could be so consistently late in calling her for their scheduled conferences. She dispensed with the cordial and went straight to business. She knew Jeffrey had polling information to share with her. "Tell me what you see" substituted for any good morning pleasantries.

Jeffrey jumped right in. "I see Tedie ahead by anywhere from three to seven points. In each of our polls he is leading outside of the statistical margin of error. His convention speech both lifted his numbers and hurt ours. Our convention did very little to give you meaningful lift."

"That's not what I'm seeing on the news reports. The numbers aren't that bad."

Mildly exasperated, Jeffrey responded, "That is because the news agencies you're focusing on are our friends. They poll where, and until, they get results which are helpful to us. They are fans, and they want to see you succeed. I, on the other hand, am the voice of reality that you need to listen to. I am the mayor of Realville. The real polling we conduct is done without bias. And today, with just a little more than thirteen weeks before the election, Tedie would beat you in the election. Right now it is looking bad for us, and we need to change the momentum, and fast."

Jeffrey paused, expecting to hear a response from Stephanie. Hearing none, he continued, "Over the weekend I worked on several strategies to deal with the issue of Tedie's response to the Times article. I've got several ideas for both attacking his credibility as well as..."

Uncharacteristically, Stephanie interrupted him. "Jeffrey, please email me your ideas. I'd like to have the opportunity to review them before we talk again. Please send them today and I will follow up with you by tomorrow. Thanks." Stephanie abruptly ended the phone call.

Jeffrey was more than a little dumbfounded. It was highly unusual for Stephanie to not want to hear his ideas and follow his lead on such matters immediately.

Several hours later, Jeffrey's phone rang. It was Stephanie on the other end. He assumed she was calling to discuss the polling information and new strategies he had emailed her after their morning call.

He started, "So what do you think?"

"About what?"

"Oh. I thought you were calling to discuss the strategies I emailed you this morning."

"We can discuss that later. I'm sure the strategies you proposed are fine. I'm calling to tell you I need you here tomorrow. I received a call a few minutes ago from Amuh Baiden. She has sourced a donor for the campaign and the Foundation who wants an audience with me tomorrow in New York, at my home. He can only meet tomorrow, and I am on the road for several days after tomorrow. He insists on meeting with you as my Campaign Manager as well."

"Any idea why?"

"I assume he's like everyone else who believes he has great ideas and wants to share them with us. According to Amuh, he is bringing a seven-figure check with him. For that amount of bling, he gets a date with the two of us. I need you here at 2pm. Amuh will be here as well."

"What's his name?" Jeffrey asked with skepticism in his voice.

"Amuh said he goes by Truman. I'm sure we'll get his full name when he gets here."

"Let me make sure I understand. You want me in New York tomorrow to meet with a guy we've never met, whose last name we don't know, and who wants to give you seven figures from and unidentified source. Am I understanding that correctly?"

Stephanie, feeling a bit temperamental, rose up. "Here's the deal, Jeffrey. I don't want you in New York tomorrow, I *expect* you in New York tomorrow. And I expect you here on fucking time and with a pleasant demeanor. We are in a bad place right now due in no small part to your recommendation that we pick Tedie as the loser. Maybe this Mr. Truman or whoever the hell he is has some great ideas. We seem to be lacking in great ideas at the moment. But right now, anybody with a million dollars and my name on a check gets an audience with whoever the hell they choose on my team, and whenever the hell they choose! Are we clear?"

"I look forward as always to seeing you in New York tomorrow."

Jeffrey was not sure what he was expecting, but Truman certainly did not meet his expectations. He was young, in his early thirties by Jeffrey's estimation. Generally speaking, people with a million dollars to donate to a political candidate are a little older than Truman.
And he certainly was not dressed like a typical man carrying a seven-figure check. No jacket, no socks, and it appeared no shave today. Jeffrey reminded himself that money speaks louder than appearances, and clearly, this guy speaks well.

The four sat around a coffee table in the sunroom of Stephanie's home. After introductions, and after Truman had awkwardly placed an envelope in Stephanie's hand, he began discussing the real reason for his visit.

"Back in the year 2000, Congress approved funding for states to update their voting machines. You may recall 2000 was the year of the hanging chad, and the results of the presidential election were delayed as a result. Congress immediately tried to guarantee that scenario would never happen again."

"But, as with most things the federal government undertakes, the fix to the problem created another potential problem. That is where I come in. My firm specializes in leveraging opportunities from problems. The funding Congress provided for these updates allowed states to purchase electronic voting machines. Those voting machines went disproportionally to the most populated counties in the United States, which makes sense when you think about it. You want your newest, best equipment in the locations where the largest number of people are going to be voting."

He paused and took a sip of his water.

"Fast forward to 2008. You may recall a Princeton study done on electronic voting machines. Do you recall that?" Truman looked first at Stephanie, then at Jeffrey and Amuh. All three had looks which clearly indicated they did not know what Truman was referring to. Barely hiding his disappointment, Truman continued, "I was the team leader for that study. We learned how easy, how very easy, it is to hack voting machines to create the results you want."

An awkward silence followed. Amuh and Jeffrey alternated looking at each other, then back at Truman. Stephanie's eyes stayed fixed on Truman. Jeffrey broke the silence.

"Truman, let's back up a step. Tell us, why are you here?"

Truman appeared truly surprised at the interruption to his story. "I'm here because you're going to lose the election, and I can help you change that."

Amuh chimed in, "You can help us change that how?"

Again, Truman looked confused. Don't these people ever just let someone talk? "I can help you change that by influencing the voting machines in the most populated counties in the country."

Amuh continued, "You're suggesting we commit voter fraud, with your help? Am I hearing you correctly?"

Truman now had the bewildered look of a man who was starting to doubt everyone was in on the same secret he was in on. "Don't tell me you guys don't know voter fraud goes on. It's as old as prostitution."

Jeffrey responded, "Truman, I think we're all sure that both sides have overzealous supporters who may break election laws in some fashion. But in no way do those activities ever reach the level of the candidate's knowledge. You've heard the term plausible deniability? It's a thing for a reason."

A look of regret flashed across Truman's face. He looked dumbfounded. "Well, um, can I just work with you two?" he asked, pointing alternately at Amuh and Jeffrey.

Jeffrey rolled his eyes and put his hands up in a "whoa, buddy" position. "Let's start over, why don't we? How about you start by telling us who are you, where you got the money you gave Mrs. Kenseth today, and what you do for a living?"

"Sure. I have a PhD in mathematics and computer science from Princeton. Partly due to the

2008 study I worked on while at Princeton, companies hire me to help them protect their networks and thwart hackers. It's very high-level stuff. I can't tell you who my clients are due to confidentiality reasons. But you'd recognize the names of most of them."

"The money in the envelope is written to the Kenseth Foundation. I can change it around however you might like. It's all legit money I've earned through my company. When hackers have a company by the short hairs and they need help getting their operation back functioning, they pay a lot of money for my services."

Amuh now spoke, "So you're just a Stephanie supporter wanting to help the cause however you can?"

Truman smiled thankfully, "Yes, and sort of. Yes, I support Stephanie. And I hate Tedie. I cannot believe people believe anything he says. I'm also a capitalist, and a pragmatist. And it's not hard to determine that you people are in trouble. Based on what I see, you are going to lose the election. I have access to insider private polling and it is clear, you are going to lose without some sort of extraordinary event. I can provide that event."

Jeffrey took note of Truman's reference to private polling. "Let's just say for kicks and giggles we believe everything you say, that an election can be stolen through the voting machines. How would something like that even work?"

"Think of it this way, anything electronic can be tampered with. So, making a voting machine record Kenseth, when someone chooses Tedie is not hard. What *is* hard is covering your tracks and not getting caught. Every voting machine that was purchased with those year 2000 funds was made by one of two manufacturers. The designs are easily known. Almost every voting machine in the country will be tested between now and November. My company will supply most of the subcontractors which will conduct the testing. Meaning, my people will be inside the voting machines in the most important counties in the next ninety days."

Truman now paused to see if anyone had a question. He looked directly at Stephanie, then Jeffrey, then Amuh. Receiving no resistance, he continued.

"It is not difficult to install software in those machines that switches votes. And it is not difficult to design that software to only engage during a twelve-hour period. If the machine is tested before or after November 8, the vote switch is not engaged."

Jeffrey and Amuh looked at each other. Amuh then spoke, "You make this sound so easy. It can't be that easy."

"It actually is pretty easy, but only if you have all the elements in place to make it happen. Because of my work in 2008, I have the best network of anyone in the United States with local Boards of Election. My company is also one of only three which are approved by the U.S. Government to do this kind of work."

Jeffrey was ready to bring the conversation to a close. "Truman, this talk is the stuff of fantasies and movies. Because we've had this conversation, if voter fraud on the level you are describing does happen and we got caught, we'd all be in federal prison for years. But just so we can bring this fantasy tale to an end, and to satisfy our curiosity, if a candidate were to employ you to program the voting machines as you have described, assuming you are not doing this solely for God and country, what would you expect in return."

"One hundred million dollars."

"Oh, is that all?" responded Jeffrey sarcastically. "And I'm sure you would expect for this to be paid up front."

"Paid up front, no. Delivered up front, yes."

"What's the difference?" Amuh asked, with an annoyed tone in her voice.

"The difference is a pay for performance account which would be established in a Cayman Islands bank. In this arrangement, the client delivers an agreed upon sum to the bank and opens an account under the names of both parties. Up until an agreed upon date, only the depositing party can withdraw the funds. After an agreed upon date, the second party can withdraw the funds. If the funds disappear before the agreed upon date, the desired action does not occur. If the funds disappear after the agreed upon date and before the second party, in this case me, can withdraw the funds, then news media all over the world learns of how Stephanie Kenseth tried to commit massive voter fraud."

"But that would incriminate you as well," responded Jeffrey.

"Jeffrey believe me, if I am good enough to pull this off, I'm good enough to be completely invisible in the process. There are dozens of subcontractors who will perform the voting machine tests and install the program that I provide them. There is no common denominator there. The only link to me is the programming, and it's easy enough to make it look like the software came straight from India or Russia or Iran and was never touched by me.

If I hand you the election and my money somehow disappears, trust me, the world will soon enough know the results were fraudulent."

He paused, then smiled. "But I really don't know why we are talking in these terms. I'm sure we are all very honorable people here. And as you have already said Jeffrey, this is the stuff of fantasy, and your campaign is not interested." He rose to leave. "My card is in the envelope I gave you, Mrs. Kenseth. I wish you much success in your campaign. It's been an honor to meet you, and you as well Amuh and Jeffrey. I can see myself out."

As soon as Truman left the room, Jeffrey was down Amuh's throat. "How in the *hell* does a guy like that get past you and in front of Stephanie? Don't you understand how dangerous a guy like that potentially is for us!?"

Amuh fired right back. "Lighten up! My friend at Princeton called me. She said there was a seven-figure donor to the university that wanted to meet Stephanie and give us a lot of money. I talked to him. He could only meet today in the next thirty. Where we are right now, knowing those details was all the vetting that was necessary for me. He is naïve as hell. Brilliant I'm sure, but very naïve." She took a breath and continued, "I cannot believe though that he came in here with a plan to alter hundreds of voting machines. I just hope he doesn't call Tedie next."

Jeffrey was not ready to go there just yet. "What time did he call you yesterday?"

"About 11am. Why?"

"Just curious." Jeffrey had sent his most recent polling information to Stephanie around 10am, which indicated Stephanie was behind Tedie and was gaining negative momentum. He assumed there was a connection between the timing of the email he sent to Stephanie, and Truman's reference to his own private polling. Jeffrey knew all the players in the polling industry, and he had never heard of a software company or voting machine company commissioning their own polling. He wondered if Stephanie's email had been compromised and Truman was viewing Stephanie's emails. He wondered if others were as well.

He rose to leave but directed a question to Stephanie first. "Your server is safe, yes?" Stephanie was opening the envelope Truman had delivered to view the check inside. She did not make eye contact with Jeffrey when she dead panned, "Of course it is." She paused then continued, "We put a condom on it."

Jeffrey was not in a mood for cheap humor. "Very funny. I mean is it secure?"

"You've asked me this in the past, and the answer is always the same. Yes, it is very secure."

The meaning of certain terms change over time. Secure is one of those terms. Sixty-five year old Stephanie Kenseth believed the computer server in her New York home was secure because it was behind a locked door. In that sense, it was secure. And that was the only sense in which it was secure.

Squeeze Play

"So what'd you do?"

"David, I did exactly what you're supposed to do in that situation. I threw the ball at his face."

David paused before responding, "What the hell?"

"Yeah. It's a helluva reality check for the batter. But it's what you're trained to do. In a suicide squeeze play all the batter is trying to do is bunt the ball in play. Anywhere in play. If he can bunt the ball in play, the runner already on the move from third will score. There's no way to stop it once the batter bunts the ball. So, your only defense is to prevent the batter from making contact. It's tough to make contact with the baseball if you're lying on your backside looking up at the sky, thankful for the fact you still have all your teeth."

"So, you didn't hit him?"

"No I didn't hit him. Didn't have to hit him. With a 90 mile per hour fastball coming at your face, instinct takes over. He ducked out of the way, the catcher caught the ball and easily tagged out the runner coming home."

"Wow, amazing. Now that you recount it, I remember that play. That was the last out of the game, wasn't it?"

"Last out, bottom of the ninth, game seven of the National League Championship Series. I was pressed into service as a reliever in the eighth inning, something I had never done before in my career, or ever did again in my career."

David paused. He was temporarily caught up in the moment. He was a huge baseball fan, and he always enjoyed hearing Tedie's stories. While he was struggling to remember how the conversation that was supposed to be about the campaign had strayed to baseball, Tedie reminded him.

"So, as I was saying David, that is what I was determined to do with my speech at the convention. Stephanie Kenseth and her team thought they had created an advantage by leaking information to the press. So, I decided to throw a fastball at their face, see if that might change the dynamic. Based on the polling results you've emailed me, I'd say my strategy worked."

David was now quickly back in the original conversation. "Change the dynamic? I'd say that's putting it mildly. You put them on their ass, looking up at the sky, same as you did that batter."

"Looking up at us David, looking up at us. Hey, I know you emailed me David, but remind me of the polling numbers since the convention."

David knew that 'remind me' meant Tedie had not read the email. He had become accustomed to Tedie's fly by the seat of the pants style, and was not surprised in the least that Tedie had not read the report which was to be the basis for their scheduled telephone meeting this morning. David also recognized that Tedie very much enjoyed hearing, rather than reading, positive results that he had personally engineered.

"Certainly. Heading into the convention, you were essentially tied with Vice President Kenseth in all major polls. You were leading in some states, primarily those which are less populated. And you were losing in other states, primarily those more urban and densely populated. Immediately after the convention, you established a three to five percent lead. The composition of the lead change was across the board. What is most impressive though, is you have maintained this lead several weeks after both conventions. The lift, so far, has proven to be more than just a convention bounce. It's impressive, it really is."

Tedie was smiling. "Do you recall our first conversation, David? Do you recall what I told you about my organization?"

"Yes sir, I do."

"I told you that we win. Team Tedie wins. Whether it's building and managing commercial properties or producing entertainment product or running for President of these great United States, we win. And with your help and the help of other great people, we're going to win in November."

It was now David who was smiling. He too believed that Tedie was going to win in November. There had been plenty of times since becoming Tedie's campaign manager that he had wondered if he could corral Tedie and actually do his job and lead the campaign. Somewhere along the way he began to realize there is no corralling Tedie. His thought process was interrupted by Tedie's voice through his ear piece.

"And David do you know what is the kicker about all this? Here I am, a political novice, not a babe in the woods by any stretch of the imagination, but still a political novice. And with just a few weeks remaining before the next 'most important presidential election of all time' a political novice is leading in the polls against an entrenched and powerful political figure. And do you know why?"

David sensed this question was not rhetorical. He decided to reply in a light-hearted manner. "You mean other than the fact you have an awesome campaign manager?"

Tedie chuckled. "David, you certainly are an awesome campaign manager. Stephanie Kenseth has a pretty good one too. But you truly are great, and I'm very glad you made that outreach to me many months ago." David took note of Tedie's reference to Jeffrey Saint. He wondered if Tedie's comment was a generalization, or if he really knew Jeffrey.

Tedie continued with his analysis. "But that's not the reason my poll numbers took a critical turn after the convention. The reason I am leading in the polls is simply this: I told the truth. I told the American people the truth! Everything I said in Cleveland was the God's honest truth. Everything I have said on the campaign trail, at these rallies where we have twenty or thirty thousand people, is the truth."

He continued, "Most Americans, particularly those who have to work for their money, are not dumb. They know bullshit when they hear it, see it, smell it. They know when they are being fed it. And for years, many years David, Washington DC has been serving them crap. And they're tired of it. They are tired of the lack of honesty from politicians, and from the press."

"Stephanie Kenseth, God love her, is a sham. And the American people, at least the ones who are voting for me, recognize this. Stephanie was a friend of mine before the campaign and I hope she is still one after the election is over. But Stephanie is a sham. The American people see it, they are pissed that the press won't call it for what it is, and they are flocking to me because I am unafraid to say what millions of Americans are already thinking. It's not rocket science David. It's really not."

"Mr. Tedie you unquestionably have tapped into a vein that most in Washington did not know existed. And it appears your discovery of this is going to pay off big in November."

David's choice of words caused Tedie to have a verbal reflex reaction. "That's potentially not the only payoff that's going to occur between now and November." The words were out of Tedie's mouth before he even realized he was saying them out loud. Catching his mistake, he now spoke quickly.

"David, keep up the good work. Your planning and execution are laudable. I'm able to do what I do, because you are so good at what you do. We'll talk later."

David had become accustomed to abrupt endings with Tedie by now. But this phone call was cut short even by Tedie standards. He wondered about Tedie's payoff comment. What did he mean by that? Given that the arena was politics, the possibilities for that comment's meaning were widespread.

He was still lost in this thought when his phone indicated an incoming text. It was from Jeffrey Saint. He and Jeffrey communicated occasionally, to jab each other and maintain professional relations.

NICE JOB AT THE CONVENTION. GREAT LIFT.

THANKS. WISH I COULD TAKE CREDIT. THAT WAS ALL TEDIE. HIS INSTINCTS ARE MAYBE THE BEST I HAVE EVER SEEN. I'M JUST HANGING ON FOR THE RIDE.

Then David quickly followed with another text.

HAVE YOU EVER MET HIM?

Jeffrey considered not responding. But he did not want to be rude to his friend.

YES.

"Hmm" was David's barely audible response upon seeing the text. He was fairly certain the brevity of the response spoke volumes.

Coronation and High Crimes

As of October 2016, Stephanie Kenseth had been under investigation by the FBI for many months. The FBI was actively considering whether actions surrounding her ICSJ involvement in Damascus, as well as the circumstances of the sale of missile technology to the Tunisians which she approved as Vice President, rose to the level of criminal activity. At Barry Ingle's directive, the FBI was providing him with weekly updates on the investigation and its findings. The public was aware of the FBI probe. The public was unaware the White House was intimately familiar with its details.

Jeffrey first noticed the Breaking News story on CNN at 8:30am on Monday, October 3. The scroll read "FBI close to initiating a criminal investigation into the Tunisian missile technology sale and Vice President Stephanie Kenseth." This was the boldest statement to date from the FBI. Except the quote was not attributed to the FBI. It was attributed to unnamed sources.

Jeffrey was immediately on the phone to trusted friend Trina Banks at CNN.

"Hello Jeffrey. I've been expecting your call."

"Yes, I bet you have! I saw the headline. Is there more information coming?"

"I am led to believe yes, but I've not been told what to expect."

"Where is it coming from? It must be a credible source if you are running with it."

"Well, you didn't hear this from me, but it's out of the White House."

"Oh, shit."

"Yeah, I thought you'd like that one."

"Thanks, Trina." Jeffrey was well aware Stephanie Kenseth had made many enemies during her political career. He was also aware that Barry Ingle and Stephanie had never been on the best of terms, despite his selection of Stephanie as the VP after William's death. Even considering this, he was at a loss as to why the FBI probe leaks would be coming from the White House.

Over the next seventy-two hours there was a steady stream of new leaks from "unnamed sources."

"FBI pursuing new evidence linking bribes as the motive for Tunisian missile technology sale."

"FBI getting closer to linking deadly raid on United States Damascus compound to VP Kenseth ICSJ Foundation and illegal weapons."

"FBI investigating Tedie claim that foreign campaign donations, later sent to him and turned over to FEC, were funneled through operatives associated with Kenseth campaign."

By the close of the news cycle on Friday, Stephanie's polling numbers were five to ten points behind Tedie. Privately, she was furious and looking for someone to blame and hold accountable for the news reports. Publicly she stayed on offense and appeared impervious to the accusations. It was just another scandal, in a career filled with scandals, that she would withstand. She knew her supporters would not abandon her.

The following week provided no relief. Monday's headlines were potentially the most damaging to date: "FBI investigating potential arms dealing in Damascus with ties to ICSJ funding." The headline was actually a watered-down version of what some in the FBI believed was really true; that the only ICSJ employee suspected of running a for-profit arms operation was Stephanie Kenseth. In the opinion of many in the FBI, the four Americans who died during the attacks did so because military help during the attack was refused, for fear the arms and illegal dealings would be discovered.

Late in the day on Monday, the White House issued a statement indicating that due to the seriousness of the allegations against Vice President Kenseth, President Ingle was convening a meeting between himself, the Director of the FBI, and Stephanie Kenseth. The private meeting would be held on Wednesday.

Jeffrey was the first on Team Kenseth to see the headline about the Wednesday meeting. He thought it quite odd that he knew nothing of this meeting before it was announced to the general public. It was not on Stephanie's calendar, and in fact, it conflicted with campaign stops in North Carolina that were already scheduled. He immediately called Stephanie.

"Hello, Jeffrey."

"Did you know you've been summoned to the White House on Wednesday, the same time we're supposed to be in North Carolina?"

"What are you talking about?"

"I just saw it on CNN. The President has scheduled a meeting with you and the Director of the FBI."

"Son of a bitch."

"I'll clear your campaign schedule and find out the exact time they want you there. I'll also put out a statement regarding the cancelled events."

Jeffrey's press release on behalf of his boss went out immediately. It read, in part, "Although I regret not being able to meet with our amazing friends in North Carolina this Wednesday, I am looking forward to meeting with FBI Director Smith. It is unfortunate the allegations against me are being handled in this manner, and I find it unsettling that unsubstantiated accusations against me are being released to the press in the midst of a presidential campaign. The people and assets of the FBI should not be used as political weapons."

That evening, while pacing alone slowly on the portico of her New York mansion, Stephanie took stock of her current situation. Except in a few large cities, her poll numbers were in a steady decline. Her media team, for all its talent, was proving inadequate to overpower the scandal narratives dominating the current media discourse. 'Tedie's Army' was picking up momentum everywhere he spoke, and her team's attempt to topple the monster which they had created had failed.

She decided in that rare quiet moment what she must do. She resolutely covered the distance between the portico and her first-floor study. She found Truman's card on the desk where she had left it. Based on the current variables, she believed it was time to fund the insurance policy. She hurriedly tapped the number sequence into her phone.

"Hello, this is Truman."

"Truman, this is Stephanie Kenseth."

"Hello Mrs. Kenseth. It is a pleasure to hear from you. How may I help you?"

"Truman I think it's time to engage your firm for the benefit of my campaign. I'd like you to perform the services you discussed in our initial meeting. Is that still on the table?"

"Yes it is, Mrs. Kenseth, but we must move very quickly. I will need half of your payment immediately, and I will need the other half two weeks from today, on the… 24th. Both payments will be held until the 24th. It is fortuitous that you called today because after the 12th we probably would not have had enough time to inoculate the necessary number of machines."

With a chuckle, Stephanie responded, "Inoculate. What a clever use of the term. How shall I send you the money?"

"Wire for the first $50 million is best since we must move quickly. I will send you an encrypted text with the wiring instruction."

"I will text my banker today to send you the money. His name is Lee Roy Butcher; he is the president of First National Bank of the Everglades. "

"Very good. You will not be disappointed. Thank you for calling and trusting us. We are all pulling for you."

Stephanie Kenseth arrived at the White House with her attorney on the 12th one hour before the scheduled start time for her meeting with the President and FBI Director. They went to her West Wing office for final preparations. While there, the office phone rang. Caller ID indicated it was Sid Wilson, head of White House security.

Stephanie answered the phone. "How can I help you, Sid?"

"Mrs. Kenseth, I have been instructed to inform you your attorney is not invited to your meeting with the President and the FBI Director."

Stephanie paused before speaking. "Well then I guess they can meet without me."

"The President thought that might be your response. He said for me to inform you the choice is yours. However, the meeting is taking place with or without you. If you desire to have an influence on the outcome of the meeting, he recommends you attend."

Stephanie hung up without acknowledging Sid. "Bastard" slipped easily out of her mouth as she hung up the phone.

When Mrs. Kenseth left her office, she was greeted by White House Security immediately. She thought this was odd and highly unusual. They led her toward the Oval Office, but to her surprise, they turned into the Roosevelt Room, which was directly across from the Oval Office. They motioned for her to follow.

When she entered the windowless room, President Ingle and Director Smith rose from the table to greet her. They had previously been seated at the right side of the rectangular conference table. Each wore a dark suit, white shirt, and tie. Director Smith kept his jacket on.

After handshakes and greetings, which were completely void of emotion and sincerity, Mrs. Kenseth continued toward the conference table. On it, she noticed three identical, unmarked red folders. Two of the folders were opposite each other on the right hand side of the table where President Ingle and Director Smith had been seated. The third folder was at the opposite end of the conference table, several feet from the other two.

The President asked Mrs. Kenseth to sit on the right side of the table where he had been seated opposite Director Smith. President Ingle took the seat at the left side of the table toward the far end, a good distance away. The whole thing struck Stephanie as very odd.

Director Smith sat first, followed by President Ingle then Mrs. Kenseth. Stephanie sat forward in her chair, her back straight. She rested her forearms on the table and clasped her hands together. Her chin was tucked in slightly as she began speaking.

"Director Smith, I'm assuming this meeting was your idea and with respect, I just have to say I find it questionable and unfortunate that I would not be given any more notice for the meeting, and have to learn of its existence through the media. Furthermore..."

"Vice President Kenseth!" Came the firm voice from the end of the table. What followed was delivered in a more subdued, but no less direct tone. "In due time, you will have the opportunity to say whatever it is you wish to say. You were given the same amount of notice for this meeting as Director Smith. Now, in the essence of time, my recommendation is to allow Director Smith to share what he came to share with us."

Mrs. Kenseth neither acknowledged nor challenged what she had just been told. She simply turned her eyes back toward Director Smith and forced a small smile.

Director Smith then opened the folder in front of him and encouraged with a slight nod that Mrs. Kenseth to do the same with her folder. She complied. In a matter of fact tone, the Director proceeded to highlight several pieces of information in the folder. Copies of emails originating from her indicating the amount and method of payment to the ICSJ Foundation for consideration of missile technology sales to Tunisian. Copies of cryptic emails to the personal email accounts of the three DOD officials who, along with her, approved the sale. The emails insinuated they would be well compensated. There were copies of her emails from her ICSJ server to and from known arms manufacturers in Europe and Africa, discussing payments and shipments to the US consulate in Damascus. They had copies of texts and other correspondence from the night of the Damascus attack, in which she urged then Defense Secretary Lanny Patella to not send military assets to engage in the Damascus fight. Records of deposits made by anonymous sources into whisper accounts (an account opened and closed in a short time period, to avoid detection) owned by ICSJ which were traced back to arms sales financed by ICSJ.

As he went through the items in the folder, Director Smith's tenor was that of an Executive Summary, similar to the way one prosecutor shares information with a fellow prosecutor before a trial. He employed no emotion with his words, just factual data with the occasional tactical explanation of how the information was gathered. He also implied that there was more supporting material than what he was sharing.

After Director Smith had finished his remarks, President Ingle addressed a question toward him.

"Director Smith, in your professional opinion, based on your thirty plus years of service to the United States at the Federal Bureau of Investigation, if the FBI choose to formally initiate criminal charges against Mrs. Kenseth on behalf of the United States, what is the likelihood the charges would include treason?"

Stephanie Kenseth's gaze had been fixed upon Director Smith while President Ingle had been speaking. Though her teeth had been clinched, she maintained a forced smile. When the word treason came out of President Ingle's mouth, she involuntarily jerked her head toward him, and stared him down, cold. The illusion of a smile was gone.

"Mr. President, based on what I know about the transfer of missile technology to Tunisia, I believe there is sufficient evidence to pursue the charge of treason. That technology was illegally sourced with her help, and is now in the hands of known enemies of the United States and her allies."

"Thank you, Director. At this point I'd like to speak one-on-one with Mrs. Kenseth."

Director Smith hesitated. Given the nature of the information he had just shared, he thought it unwise for the President and Mrs. Kenseth to have discourse without a witness present. Ingle sensed his hesitation, and he calmly nodded toward the door. "You may leave, Director Smith. I can handle this."

"Certainly, Mr. President." Director Smith now turned to face Stephanie before standing to leave. "Good day, Madam Vice President." Stephanie gave no verbal response as he turned and left the room.

The room was silent save for the sound of the door closing behind Director Smith. Stephanie maintained her perfectly straight posture while keeping her eyes fixed on the wall in front of her. President Ingle sat somewhat slouched in his chair.

His legs were straightened in front of him. His right arm was folded across his abdomen. His left elbow rested on the back of his right hand, his left thumb and index finger touching his lips. His index finger moved back and forth slowly across his lower lip. His brown eyes were fixed on Mrs. Kenseth. Except for his dismissal of Director Smith and his rebuke of Stephanie's failed attempt to coop the meeting, he had not said a word since the meeting began. He had not even opened his folder. They both knew he held her fate in his hands.

As the President sat there in his contemplative pose, he was reminded of how proud he had been in 2008 when he beat William Kenseth in the primaries to win the Democrat nomination for president. At this moment, he realized that he valued that political victory even more than he valued winning his first and second presidential elections.

In 2008, William Kenseth had been considered invincible. Behind the scenes, he and his wife were notorious for their dirty, win-at-any-cost political tactics. During the primaries, he and his family had endured intimidation, threats, and lies about his background and his work in Detroit. He knew most of those threats and rumors had come out of the Kenseth campaign. The fact that he was a black man and the Kenseths were from the South made the intimidations and his victory over them even more poignant.

He was proud of the campaign he had run in 2008. Smart, new age, relevant, and above board. He had made William Kenseth look old, and more importantly, irrelevant. The only reason he had chosen Stephanie William as his VP was to keep peace within the party. He was proud of the scandal-free way in which he had lived his political career.

In the past few months he had found himself becoming increasingly contemplative about his life in politics. Politics had been good to him. Very good. But one thing kept weighing on his mind. It seemed petty, but he couldn't get past the fact that he had not benefitted financially from his time as President in the same way he had seen so many other politicians do. He had not participated in any of the "sort of" legal schemes available to people in power. During these recent career reflections, he had found himself wondering if he had made the best choice in this regard. He had seen so many people leverage their position in politics to create significant wealth. Yet he had not done so.

These were his thoughts as he considered his next move with Mrs. Kenseth. There were two very clear options in front of him. The question was, which was he going to take?

Stephanie sat in silence wondering when Ingle would speak. Her thoughts were betraying her. Her entire married life she had sought to emerge from William's shadow. And since his death, she had done so with great success. She was the first female Vice President. She had many firsts, and many accomplishments. But at this moment, she yearned for William to be in the room. He was so skilled at disarming an opponent and diffusing seemingly hopeless situations. She recognized those were not her skills and right now, she needed them. She was great at ignoring criticism, intimidation, even threats. All she could do in this moment is tap into those skills. But she could see no angle for a bluff.

She maintained her gaze on the artwork in front of her. She chose to not physically acknowledge the fact that Barry Ingle was holding all the cards.

Finally, after what felt like ten minutes of silence, the dealer spoke. He had settled on a path, and he was going to take her down it with him. "Kenseth, have you seen the movie *American Gangster*?"

The nature of the question caught her off guard. She hesitated, turned her face toward him and spoke, "I don't believe I have."

"Came out in 2007. It's based on a true story about a guy named Frank Lucas. Lucas was a black man who became one of the country's most prolific drug dealers at a time when most black men never rose above street-level dealing."

Now Stephanie was very confused. "That's interesting." She paused. She was anxious, so she pressed, "Is there a parallel here that I'm missing?"

"Not yet. You'll understand my point in a minute I think. Anyway, in this movie there is a crooked cop named Trupo. Trupo hates Lucas. He's on Lucas's payroll, but he hates him. One day, Trupo and his cop buddies raid Lucas's house. He wants the getaway loot. He knows that every gangster, every half decent crook, has a stash of money always available to either get away or save his ass with when the total shit has hit the fan."

Ingle paused, but maintained his eye contact with Stephanie. Stephanie was alternating her look between the table and the wall and occasionally Ingle. Finally, she asked, "Well did he find it?"

"Yes, yes he did. He found it hidden under the dog's house. Big ass German Shepherd. Trupo had to shoot the dog to get to the money."

Ingle waited a few seconds, then picked up his phone and made a call. "Send Charles in."

Thirty long seconds later, Charles Hurt entered the room. Stephanie had never seen this man before, but he had the look of an accountant, albeit a wealthy one. His suit was expensive, perfectly tailored, and his eyeglasses, cufflinks, and tie were all designer. He was more finely dressed than most people she encountered in Washington. She smiled at him as he entered as if nothing at all unpleasant was transpiring, and she rose to shake his hand.

Ingle made the introductions. "Charles, this is Vice President Kenseth. Stephanie, this is Charles Hurt. He works for the Inspector General's office. He and his team did the good work that uncovered the $6 billion that went missing from the White House budget under your watch."

Stephanie felt her stomach twist. She fought the urge to respond to his insinuation, but surmised it was best to allow the situation to evolve naturally, before giving any acknowledgment to Ingle's offhanded accusation.

Ingle continued speaking, "Charles, if you could please tell Mrs. Kenseth what you have been working on for me over the past twenty-eight months or so."

"Yes sir, Mr. President. As you know, Mrs. Kenseth, in April 2015 the Inspector General identified $6 billion of funds that went unaccounted for from the White House budget over a multi-year period. I served as the lead investigator for that IG report."

"Upon release of the report, President Ingle assigned me to find it, to find where the money went… at least as much of it that could be found."

Enthusiastically, Stephanie said, "That's very interesting, Charles. I'm curious to hear what you found."

"Well, I actually found most of it. Or, I didn't exactly find it, instead I found where it went. A lot of it went to contracts that were simply not documented properly. So, essentially, it got spent where it was supposed to be spent."

Stephanie started to reply, but was cut off.

"Some of it, though, appears to have been spent on fraudulent activity."

She remained calm, "Are you completely sure of your findings, Charles? That is a very serious assertion you're making."

"I am sure it was not spent on official White House business. I can trace how almost $2 billion of it left the White House bank account for which contracts were not fulfilled. And I can trace how most of it was dispersed from that point. The disbursements from the no contract payments almost always went in two directions. Part of it, usually half, went to different banks in many different locations. All across the United States, and some to Puerto Rico, and even some to Cuba, which was very interesting."

He stopped and looked at Ingle for a moment. Ingle nodded at him to continue.

"In almost all cases, the other half of each of those transactions went to a single bank, in Florida, First National Bank of the Everglades."

"How fascinating. Can you tell whose account the money went to?"

"No. Without a warrant, I cannot obtain that information. The Inspector General's office is not empowered to obtain warrants. We only know the bank. Not who received it, not even the bank account number."

"Well Charles, let me congratulate you on the great work you've done. The integrity of our republican systems is buttressed by people like you."

"Thank you, Mrs. Kenseth."

"Charles, I echo what Mrs. Kenseth has said. Thank you for your service to me as President, and to the American people. I appreciate what you've done here. I'm going to need a few minutes to speak with Mrs. Kenseth alone at this point."

The silence which had followed Director Smith's exit from the room returned after Charles left. What changed was the focus of Mrs. Kenseth's eyes. Instead of alternating between the table and the wall and the floor, her eyes were fixed primarily on the leather-bound folio which lay on the table in front of her. It was her personal folio, a gift from her staff when she had been President at ICSJ. She carried it everywhere she went. She rarely opened it in the presence of others. She was considering whether she needed to open it at this moment.

Just as he had before, President Ingle broke the extended silence. "Kenseth, you of all people, I am sure, can understand the dilemma I am in… as well as the predicament you are in. On the one hand, you've got the FBI ready to charge you with treason. Treason! That'd be a hell of a legacy for the first female Vice President to leave behind, don't you think?"

Without waiting for a response, Ingle continued. "Understand, they know there was money leaving the White House and finding its way to you. They just can't prove it. They don't need that information, mind you. What they've got on Tunisia alone is enough to charge you and likely convict you."

Stephanie turned her face toward Ingle and opened her mouth to speak. He raised his right hand to indicate he was not finished. In this moment, she thought it best to acquiesce.

"On the other hand, you've got the IG's office who, thanks to my insistence that Charles get to the bottom of this, knows almost exactly where the money from the White House went. Almost, but not quite. You know what I bet? I bet if Charles and the FBI had a conversation, somebody just might put two and two together and get a warrant, and determine exactly who in Florida, or from Florida as the case might be, illegally benefitted from that money. What do you think?"

Stephanie was thinking she had been in this place before. Still staring at her folio and fingering its clasp, she thought back to the times she had to buy her and Bill's way out of trouble. She hadn't been honest with Ingle. She had seen *American Gangster* and she was quite familiar with getaway money. She and William had used it in the past. This was different. She had never been in this much trouble. At the moment, she was trying not to consider the depth of her plight, only her escape.

She knew Ingle was enjoying his moment of control right now, and that disgusted her. She was reminded of the hate she had felt for him and her subsequent depression once she realized that he, not William, would win the 2008 party nomination for president. Vice President was not what William deserved. It was an insult. However, she quickly figured out how to turn the situation into a financial windfall for them. When the money started rolling in, she forgot her hatred for Ingle. She forgot that he existed, for the most part. But now, she remembered how much hate she had for this man who was sitting across from her.

Rage did not look good on her, but it was not a new emotion. Every time she learned of a new woman in William's life, she felt the same burning, helpless wrath inside her. With no choice but to squelch it and move forward with her head held high, she was a master of control. Nothing scared her more than letting her anger loose. She feared what doing so would do to her judgement, and her wits.

She did her best to remain calm and calculated. Without prompting, she cleared her throat audibly then asked, "How much?"

"Kenseth, I'm so glad you asked. It shows me you are thinking. But unfortunately, that is the wrong question. It's absolutely the wrong question. The right question, and what you need to ask yourself is, how much is your freedom worth? How much is your family's reputation and legacy worth to you?"

She now turned her body in her chair to more squarely face her Trupo. "Name the price, Barry. Let's just get this over with."

Ingle smiled. "I don't want it all, just my fair share. You and William stole all that money while in the VP role because I put you both there. Consider it a finder's fee, only in reverse."

"Reverse, forward, neutral, park, drive, what the fuck ever. Name the number so we are not here all fucking day."

All the playfulness left President Ingle's face. "Two hundred fifty million dollars."

"What?!" Stephanie laughed as she slammed her open palm right on the table. "Are you out of your fucking mind? You have been given very, VERY bad information if you think I actually have access to that amount of money!"

"Kenseth, you should be thankful I'm not a greedy man. You should also be thankful I don't get insulted easily. Because if I did, your initial response to my benevolent offer would have been met with a Secret Service agent showing you the door, followed by newspaper headlines you wouldn't even be able to fathom tomorrow morning."

He straightened in his seat. "The price today is two hundred fifty million. And here are my terms: should you refuse my offer or need more time to consider it, the price doubles to five hundred million. Should you be wise and accept my offer, you will pay me one hundred million dollars today, and fifty million each Friday over the next three Fridays, beginning next week. I'm being generous and cutting you slack this Friday."

Stephanie Kenseth *was* actually relieved at the terms. However, she was still not through trying to talk him down.

"How in the hell do you expect me to get you one hundred million dollars today?"

"Here's how. You're going to open that folio that is in front of you, the one that's with you almost every time I see you in high level meetings, and you are going to pull a check out of it. On that check, you're going to write one hundred million dollars. It's just as easy as that. I think I know you well enough to know that you keep your getaway money right at your fingertips, and not under the house of a big ass German Shepherd."

Ingle continued, "And starting next Friday, and for the following two Fridays, you will Fed Ex a fifty million dollar check to me here. Once you do so, your two hundred fifty million dollar get out of jail free card will be validated."

Stephanie Kenseth felt trapped and relieved all at the same time. She saw no way around paying off Ingle in his shakedown, and that made her furious. But she was relieved the cost was not higher, and that she indeed had access to the funds, despite her protestations.

She reluctantly opened the clasp to her folio and pulled check number three from a zippered inside pocket. "How shall I make the check out?" was her only question.

"Make it out to BIOLT. That's the acronym for my newly formed trust. Your check will be the initial deposit, so thank you for that."

Stephanie was trying hard to ignore Ingle's flippancy.

Ingle continued to speak as Stephanie wrote. "Kenseth, there is one other thing you need to do which is very important. I don't want there to be any issues with these checks clearing your bank. Therefore, you need to contact your bank, and make sure they do not delay processing such large checks for any reason. But here is the kicker: I would recommend you call your banker. Don't email him. I suspect the FBI or somebody else may be watching your emails. If you email your banker, you may give them enough clues to find the money I know they are looking for. If you make it easy to find, they will."

By this point, Stephanie had finished writing. She had one more question to ask before handing the largest check she had ever seen over to her most bitter opponent. "What assurance do I have this money causes the FBI probe to end and all their files and information to find their way to me?"

"You don't have those assurances. That's not part of the deal. But here is what I am going to do. Tomorrow, I will publicly announce that I am ordering the FBI to stand down their investigation. I will tell the American public I am doing so because I believe the investigation to be rooted in politics and not in the pursuit of truth."

"Director Smith will be incredulous. I suspect he may resign in protest. His resignation and my order will cause the FBI to lose sight of the investigation for several weeks. If you play your cards right, a few weeks from now you will be President. And with history as my guide, I'm certain you know how to obtain FBI files and deep six them."

With that, Stephanie Kenseth slid her check in President Ingle's direction. He stood and walked the several feet separating them. Without examining the check, he picked it up and placed it in his chest pocket.

"You've made the best choice, and I knew you would. Let me be clear though, call your banker. There can be no glitches in these checks clearing."

Before her driver had reached the Potomac, Stephanie Kenseth was on the phone to Florida.

"Hello Mrs. Kenseth! How are you today?" bellowed the pleasant voice of Lee Roy Butcher, President of First National Bank of the Everglades.

"I am wonderful, Lee Roy. How are you? And how is Nancy?"

"We are just as fine as we can be, thank you for asking. How may I help you today?"

"Lee Roy, I just wanted to make you aware there are going to be some rather large withdrawals coming out of the Foundation account soon. Beginning tomorrow, actually. I wanted to let you know to expect them and to ensure they happen without incident or delays in processing."

"That is very wise of you to let us know. We pay strict attention to your account and would likely have questioned any type of sustained debit activity, as we did earlier this year with two other large checks if I recall. But I have pulled up your account and have made a notation on it so my staff is aware they should process the upcoming withdrawals without question."

"Thank you. By the way, what is the approximate balance in the Foundation account? I'm having issues with my computer and may not be able to check the balance online for a few days."

"I have that information right here, Mrs. Kenseth. The balance is just slightly over eight hundred fifty million. Do you want the exact amount?"

"An exact amount is not necessary. Thank you, and please give my best to Nancy and the children."

Consider What Happens Next

Since their initial introduction many months
ago, Jeffrey Saint and Colton Tedie had developed a
mutual respect for one another. Though they were
opponents in the political arena, they recognized and
valued the unique and refined attributes which made
them outstanding in their field. This mutual respect
had developed through short text communications, as
well as witnessing the tactical moves engineered
during their respective campaigns. They had not yet,
however, had a one-on-one conversation. Colton
Tedie was going to change that, and he was choosing
today, the day before the big meeting between the
President, the FBI Director, and Stephanie Kenseth,
to reach out.

Jeffrey was circling the Jefferson Memorial on
his morning jog when his phone rang. It was not
unusual for him to get calls while he ran. Almost all
of them he ignored. His early morning jog was church
time for him. He needed it, guarded it, and rarely
allowed any intrusions into it.

Without slowing down, he checked the caller
ID. It was Colton Tedie. It was still very early,
6:18am. Why would he be calling him at this hour?
Jeffrey broke stride and decided this is a call he
would take.

"Good morning, Mr. Tedie."

"Good morning, Jeffrey. And please feel free to call me Colton. I had a suspicion you are someone who gets at it early. How are things in our nation's capital?"

"Things in DC are excellent, as usual, Mr. Tedie. I was just finishing my morning run and I'm standing with the Jefferson Memorial behind me and the White House about a quarter of a mile in front of me. This is a great city."

"Yes, it sure is. I know exactly where you are standing. It is truly awesome the way Mr. Jefferson has a watchful eye on the White House. I am lucky enough to be heading to DC tomorrow and I would like to spend some time with you. Do you think that would be possible, for us to spend some time together?"

Jeffrey was intrigued, and thought it extremely odd that Colton Tedie would want to have a meeting with him. "Yes, we can make that happen. What is it that we will be meeting to discuss? And do I need to bring anyone with me?" The anyone he was referring to was Mrs. Kenseth, which he assumed Mr. Tedie would infer.

"No, I'd like for it to be just the two of us, and even further than that, let's make sure no one else is aware of this. What I'd like to discuss are the hits Stephanie is taking from the FBI reports, and what should reasonably be expected to happen next in that regard. 11:00am at the Jefferson Hotel? I'm sure you know where that is."

"Yes sir, I do. And 11:00am can work."

"Good. Ask someone at the front desk which conference room C. Jones is in. That is where I will be. I look forward to seeing you then."

Before Jeffrey had the opportunity to say good bye, Mr. Tedie ended the call.

Since he had broken stride anyway, Jeffrey took just a moment to enjoy the tree lined view of the White House that is available only from the Jefferson Memorial. He then turned 180 degrees and looked at the larger-than-life statue of Thomas Jefferson. He wondered what the venerable author of the Declaration of Independence would think of the present-day nature of politics. He was lost in this train of thought until the sound of a truck horn from East Basin Drive jolted him back to reality. He let out a long exhale, then re-initiated his stride and headed back toward Arlington. He was perplexed why Colton Tedie would want to meet with him, alone, and under an assumed name. When he got back to his office and before he showered, he checked every news source possible, and none of them had Colton Tedie being in DC tomorrow. Now his curiosity was even more piqued.

Jeffrey arrived at the Jefferson Hotel in Downtown DC at 10:55 the following morning. Upon approaching the front desk and asking for C. Jones, a very tall and trim black woman rose from the seats located in the lobby near the front desk. She was beautiful and professionally dressed. She called Jeffrey by name and introduced herself as Bequeeta. She spoke with an accent which Jeffrey thought he recognized as Jamaican in origin. She asked him to follow her. Jeffrey estimated she was close to six feet tall, and based on her build, she could be a body guard. She led him to a first-floor conference room, knocked three times on the door, and then opened the door. Inside the room was a small conference table where Colton Tedie was seated. He immediately looked up from his tablet.

"Thank you, Bequeeta" were Tedie's only words to her. She smiled, stepped back into the hallway, and drew the door closed after ushering Jeffrey inside.

Tedie rose to shake Jeffrey's hand. "Jeffrey, thank you for agreeing to meet with me on short notice. I know you are very busy managing Stephanie's campaign, so I assume you had to make accommodations and rearrangements to make this meeting work. I want you to know I really appreciate it."

"The pleasure is mine, Mr. Tedie. What brings you to my town?"

"This meeting actually. I am in DC for the sole purpose of meeting with you today." Tedie motioned toward the small circular table. "Let's have a seat."

Jeffrey spoke as he sat. "Well this is quite unusual. You certainly have my attention."

Tedie waited for Jeffrey to be seated before taking a seat himself. He was smartly dressed in a blue suit, white shirt, and red tie. He began, "Jeffrey, do you know what makes this country great?" Jeffrey assumed the question was not his to answer, and he remained silent. Tedie immediately continued, "Freedom and opportunity are what make this country great. We have the greatest level of economic, political, and religious freedoms of any people on the planet. We have the freedom to act on opportunity as we see fit to better our lives."

"This minute, in this presidential race, there are a number of unique factors which are quickly converging. They portend great opportunity for the people who are able to see them and execute on them. Opportunity is a funny thing, Jeffrey. It does not wait around. It's there, then it's gone. Sometimes it's gone because someone else captures it. Sometimes it's gone because by its very nature it is fleeting, and no one capitalizes on it. Sometimes—and this is the really tricky part—there is great risk in not capitalizing on the opportunity."

Jeffrey was certain he had no idea where Tedie was going with this. But he assumed it would be made clear, and therefore did not interrupt.

Tedie now paused, pushed back from the round table slightly, and looked inquisitively at Jeffrey before asking a question. "Do you like going to the theatre?"

Jeffrey shrugged his shoulders slightly. "As much as the next person I suppose. The opportunities to enjoy and appreciate the theatre certainly are not as prolific here as they are in New York. There are many days where I feel like my job is more fictional than real. So I suppose I scratch my itch for drama simply by coming to work in this town."

Tedie chuckled. "That is very clever and astute, Jeffrey. It's funny you put it that way, and yes you are certainly correct about New York. My father introduced me to the theatre when I was a child and I have loved it since. It was painful, living in Los Angeles when I played ball. The so-called entertainment capital of the world has no idea what cultured entertainment really is."

Tedie now pulled back closer to the table, and his face took on a more serious expression. "Right now, you and I, Stephanie, and a few others are players on a stage. The stage is eternal. It was there with other players acting on it before we showed up, and it will be there when we are irrelevant. But today, we own it."

He continued, "On this stage, right now, there is tremendous opportunity for you and me. There is also great peril. But the peril is yours to suffer, not mine." Tedie pointed his right index finger at Jeffrey to emphasize his point. "However, if we act upon this opportunity, and execute successfully, I think the potential exists for great riches. If we fail to act upon this opportunity, if either of us chooses to ignore our moment in time and not take action, I fear what happens next for you may be an unpleasant thing."

Jeffrey recoiled slightly. "Mr. Tedie, that sounds like a threat."

"No Jeffrey, it's not a threat. Quite the opposite. It is a warning. I'm not in a position to threaten you and I have no reason to threaten you. I am however in a position—I think—to help you capitalize on an opportunity that is before you, one that you may not even realize is there."

Jeffrey had a suspicion he was being led down a path. But he trusted his wits and judgement. He sat silent for several seconds, his eye contact locked with Tedie's. "I'm listening..." was his invitation for Tedie to continue.

Tedie now repositioned slightly in his chair, as if signaling a new phase of the conversation was about to commence.

"Jeffrey, I am a very observant person. I notice things. I am particularly observant of other people. When you and Stephanie first came to my office to buy my entry into this presidential race, I noticed several things about the situation, and about you."

Jeffrey smiled slightly and responded, "Do tell."

"I noticed you were very surprised when Stephanie slid those two checks across the table toward me. I noticed you were very interested in seeing the amounts on the checks. I intentionally hid the amounts from your view for several minutes just to examine how hard you would work to see them. I noticed that the checks were numbered one, and two. And, I noticed Stephanie Kenseth herself wrote the checks."

"Now, I am certain that you are aware, capitalizing on an opportunity requires more than just observation. A person has to be able to interpret what they observe, and then develop and execute a plan based on their interpretation." Tedie paused for a moment to test Jeffrey's present level of engagement.

"And what did your observations of that meeting cause you to interpret?"

Tedie was pleased. Jeffrey was following along. "I'm glad you asked that question. First, I interpreted that Jeffrey Saint enjoys the finer things in life. He likes what money can buy. The exquisite clothes you are wearing today further confirm this. Secondly, I interpreted that Stephanie was acting on her own. Her actions were not something that you and she had discussed beforehand. The fact her actions surprised you leads me to believe you are a good manager, one who takes pride in controlling the scenario and delivering great work. But my third and most important conclusion, was that Stephanie Kenseth has access to, and is herself in control of, a huge pile of dirty money."

Jeffrey was impressed, but he did not want, nor did he allow, Tedie to see that.

"Why do you think Stephanie Kenseth's money is dirty? She's had a very successful political career, as well as a lucrative career as a public speaker and executive."

Tedie laughed out loud. "It's precisely because she's had a successful political career that I believe her money is dirty!" Jeffrey laughed also while acknowledging the larger point. "No, seriously, Jeffrey. I know Stephanie Kenseth's money is dirty because I know Stephanie Kenseth. If you don't mind me asking, how old are you?"

"Thirty-seven."

"Thirty-seven means you were born in 1979, correct? Don't take this the wrong way, and I am not patronizing you, but Stephanie Kenseth has been dirty and trying to get filthy rich since before you were born. She lusts the two things 99% of all politicians lust: money and power. And she figured out a long time ago that either one of those is easier to get when you have the other. In her case, the appetite for both is insatiable to the point of being dangerous. Especially to the people closest to her, which includes you." Tedie emphasized this by pointing at Jeffrey with his right index finger.

"Those checks she wrote were drawn on the ICSJ Foundation. The New York Times of all papers exposed a story on the fact monies were being paid to the ICSJ Foundation by people and governments she dealt with while Vice President. I mean, come on. The level of corruption has to be enormous for the Times to write that story about their standard bearer. Add to that, the $6 billion that went missing from the White House budget while Stephanie was VP, and William before her?"

Jeffrey involuntarily raised an eyebrow when Tedie brought up the IG's report.

Tedie continued, "Yeah I know about that. Just because that story didn't last long in the media doesn't mean it didn't get noticed by a lot of us." He looked smug. "So, you asked me how I know Stephanie Kenseth's money is dirty? I know Stephanie Kenseth. She's had access to great power while VP, which put her in a position to gain access to huge amounts of money. When desire and opportunity come together..." he raised his eyebrows as if to say "you know the rest."

Jeffrey paused contemplatively before responding. He held Tedie's eye contact as he did so. "OK Mr. Tedie, let's say for argument's sake that you are right, and there is a pile of dirty money somewhere. I don't understand how what happens next might be an unpleasant thing for me."

Now it was Tedie who allowed an involuntary emotion to show. He chuckled slightly, and the right-hand corner of his mouth turned up in a slight grin.

"Jeffrey, where is your boss, right now?"

"She's at the White House. She was summoned there to discuss the potential FBI investigation. I'm sure you already know this. Why do you ask?"

"That, my friend, is a great question. Why would I ask you to answer a question we both already know the answer to? I'll tell you. Because the real answer is not something that is even on your radar yet. I told you, I'm observant. I can tell you have not yet considered what happens next. Jeffrey Saint needs to wise up and consider what the future holds. What *his* future holds. What do you think happens next, after her meeting today?"

Jeffrey paused for a moment and looked down at the table as he thought. "Well I suppose since we are in Washington, a deal may get cut."

"A pretty good chance of that, I'd say. Who's at the table?"

"Ingle, the FBI, and Stephanie."

Tedie paused. "For a deal to work, everybody has to get something they want, right? What's in the deal for Ingle?"

Jeffrey continued to look down at the table as he tried to get his mind to stop racing long enough to settle on a feasible answer. "Potentially a place in her administration? Potentially a Supreme Court nomination?"

"C'mon, Jeffrey. You really think Ingle wants those things? After you've spent eight years as POTUS, do you really want any of those things?"

Jeffrey was stumped.

"What does Stephanie have to offer that would be valuable in making a deal? Think fear and greed, Jeffrey. The two emotions that drive almost everything each of us does. Fear and greed. What does Stephanie have to offer?"

Jeffrey looked up. "Money."

"Exactly," Tedie said as he again pointed his right index finger in Jeffrey's direction. "She has that huge pile of dirty money. And Ingle doesn't. I'll hand it to him, he's run a very clean administration. I don't agree with many of his policies. In fact, I probably disagree with 99% of them. But he does not appear to have used the public treasury to make himself rich. So, good for him. But now he's thinking about life after POTUS."

Jeffrey continued the thought, "And he's looking to cash in."

"Can't blame him. If he's half the politician I think he is, he knows about that pile of cash, or has enough suspicions about it that he's willing to place a bet." Tedie rose from his seat and began slowly pacing around the conference table, his left index finger tapping his chin as he spoke. "So, now that we've established what Ingle gets out of a potential deal… what does Stephanie get?"

"She gets cleared."

"Well, not exactly. But you are on the right track." He stopped pacing and leaned over the back of the chair opposite Jeffrey to look him directly in the eye. "I'm not thinking she gets cleared. You see, it has to be established that something nefarious has occurred in order for someone to get cleared. That has not yet been established. That is actually what the FBI is seeking to uncover in their investigation. No, what I think she gets is Ingle offering to deep six the investigation. He'll kill it so that it does not interfere with the election, which is what Stephanie wants."

Tedie waited a few seconds, allowing Jeffrey to continue processing this information before he continued. He straightened up and began pacing again.

"So, we've established what Ingle gets. We've established what Stephanie gets. How many groups are at the table, right now, as we speak?"

"Three."

"Three. Okay, what does the FBI get?"

Jeffrey shrugged. "Screwed?"

"Screwed! The good law enforcement officers of the FBI get screwed because a political outcome hoses their sincere efforts to catch a career criminal. And then what does the FBI get?"

Jeffrey thought for only a second. "They get pissed."

"Screwed, then pissed! Then what?"

Jeffrey's eyes followed Tedie as he slowly walked back and forth in front of the large wall of windows. His brain was not keeping pace with Tedie's analysis, and this fed his anxiety level. He could not find the words.

"Jeffrey, let me short circuit this exercise. Ingle can order the FBI to kill the investigation, but that doesn't mean they are going to. He's a lame duck president. No one listens to a lame duck president. The FBI is a great organization with a tremendous amount of pride. They'll double their efforts if told to back off. They'll do it quietly and behind the scenes, but mark my words, they will not back down if they think high crimes have been committed."

Tedie sat down again. He leaned back in the overstuffed leather chair, and crossed his right leg over his left knee. It was a casual power move. Tedie was clearly in his element holding all the cards.

"Your boss has done some really stupid, really dangerous things. If half of what has been reported in the media is accurate, Stephanie is in really deep shit. William and Stephanie built their careers by slipping the noose. But now you're dealing with the FBI. The FBI, Jeffrey! And now, it is just Stephanie on her own, not the two of them. People liked William. People do not like Stephanie." Tedie paused to let that sink in. However, it wasn't new information to Jeffrey. He knew many people hated Stephanie. It was his job to know how many and which kinds of people hated her. It was his job to create wins despite that fact.

"As I examine this whole FBI scenario with your boss, as new revelations come out about potential crimes, incompetence, lapses in judgement, and potential cover ups, I am convinced of two things. One, somebody is going to jail... or worse. And two, that person isn't going to be Stephanie Kenseth."

As much as Jeffrey did not want to hear what Tedie had just said about Stephanie's plight, he knew it was true. For months, he had been completely immersed in her presidential campaign. This had allowed him to easily ignore the Congressional probes and FBI engagement with Damascus and Tunisia. Tedie's words were a stark reminder that Stephanie was indeed in serious trouble, and this time it was with an enemy she might not be able to defeat. He had never considered that the fallout from it could affect him in any way other than having to find a new job. Was Tedie suggesting that it was he who would go to jail?

"Mr. Tedie, if I'm understanding you correctly, and I think I do, you're mistaken. I'm not in any danger. I've not done anything wrong."

"I'm not saying you have done anything wrong. But here's the thing – it really doesn't matter whether you've done anything wrong or not. If Stephanie and her team of lawyers—along with a press that is sympathetic to their Joan of Arc figure—can paint the picture that you or anyone else close to her is dirty, that person or persons is going to jail, or worse."

Jeffrey was getting slightly irritated. "You keep saying 'or worse.' What do you mean 'or worse?'"

"Jeffrey, how well versed is your knowledge of Kenseth history? Have you heard of a guy named Michael Griffey?"

"Of course I know who Michael Griffey was. He was the Kenseth's personal attorney and he committed suicide."

"Did he? I mean, how do you know that? Because a newspaper sympathetic to the Kenseth's ideology told us so? Why would the man pen the note, 'No one will ever understand the innocence of the Kenseths' as his suicide note? And even if he did commit suicide, why was his body moved before the police got there to investigate? No one disputes that his body was moved, but why? So many why's surrounding the death of a man so closely associated with the Kenseths for so long. How about Cindy Thomas? You've heard of her? Where is she right now?"

"Prison, I think. Is she in prison?"

"Yes, she's in federal prison for obstruction of justice, for protecting the Kenseths from being prosecuted for bank fraud and accepting bribes while in Florida. And her husband? Do you know where her husband is?"

Jeffrey responded without conviction, "Dead, in a hit and run car wreck."

Tedie snapped his right thumb and forefinger crisply to emphasize his point. "Dead, just like that. While William Kenseth was Governor and Stephanie Kenseth was the unofficial official governette, under investigation for taking bribes. You know, I heard they never found the hit and run perp. That's amazing, don't you think?"

Jeffrey did not respond.

"Here's my point, and I think you know my point already but I'm going to say it anyway. Michael Griffey, Cindy Thomas, Jimmy Thomas, a dozen others we've never heard of or have already forgotten about, they are dead, or they've had their lives ruined, because of the Kenseth's corrupt machine in Florida. And when the truth comes out, and believe me I think it will any time now, we will learn that what the Kenseths did in Florida was child's play compared to what happened at the ICSJ Foundation while William and then Stephanie were in the Vice President role."

Jeffrey was growing increasingly agitated with the direction of the conversation. "But I haven't done anything wrong!"

"Jeffrey, that doesn't matter one bit! Stephanie Kenseth is going to require that someone other than her take the fall for all this. Sure, she's the one that's guilty. Guilty as hell! In all of these situations, she and Bill were the ones who were guilty. But she's not going to jail. The Kenseth's don't go to jail. Royalty doesn't go to jail, you know this. Someone will go to jail, or worse, for her crimes. You have to know this to be true!"

Tedie let his words sit for a moment while he kept his eye contact fixed on Jeffrey. "Let me do you a small favor now and ask you a couple questions that your paid attorney, the attorney you are going to have to pay for I should say, is going to ask you. But I'm going to ask you for free."

"Jeffrey Saint, at any time, did Stephanie Kenseth send you an email which contained potentially incriminating information? At any time? If yes, then you can be incriminated."

"At any time were you in a conversation where Stephanie Kenseth was present, and illegal activities or potential illegal activities were discussed? If yes, then you can be incriminated."

"Did you at any time have knowledge of foreign money coming into Stephanie Kenseth's campaign coffers, and fail to report it?"

Tedie now leaned forward against the table again, more animated than before.

"I could go on and on, but it would be pointless. I've not seen your emails, and I haven't been in the meetings or had the conversations you've had. But here is something I know for certain. Stephanie Kenseth is corrupt. And no one, not you, me, anybody, can be in the company of corrupt people and not have the filth get on you. It is the nature of the beast and you cannot prevent it. You can try like hell to avoid it, but you cannot prevent it."

Again, Tedie paused to let his words sink in.

"And here is one other thing you need to consider. And I am sure your paid attorney is going to tell you the same thing. Don't think for a second that Stephanie does not have a file containing notes, details of conversations, and copies of emails that she will use to sacrifice others in order to save her skin. Jeffrey Saint's name is in that file. Mark my words. You don't escape the noose as many times as Stephanie has without being good at this. She's damn good, and knows exactly what she is doing."

For a moment, Jeffrey searched his memory for anything incriminating he might have been associated with, even loosely. Nothing came to mind other than the campaign contributions. He had built firewalls for himself, shielding himself from their handling, but now he wondered how firm those protections were. He did not question that Stephanie was dirty and he was intimately close to many of her endeavors. He honestly believed he had never willfully done anything illegal in Stephanie's service. But he also knew innocent people get framed in this town and in this business, all the time.

Suddenly, he felt a jolt in his chest. He remembered the recent meeting he had with Stephanie, Amuh, and that strange character named Truman. The nature of that conversation clearly included discussion of activities which would constitute election fraud. He also remembered Stephanie had said nothing during the part of the conversation where they were discussing the finer details of how Truman would perpetuate the crime.

Colton Tedie continued to talk, but Jeffrey was no longer hearing him. He immediately felt ill. He felt flush, and he felt cold sweat forming on his forehead and back. He felt like he was about to throw up.

"Excuse me, Mr. Tedie. I drank a lot of water before coming here and I need to use the restroom. Do you mind?"

"Of course."

Hurriedly, Jeffrey located the restroom down the hall before getting sick. He was thankful there was no one else there as he involuntarily emptied the contents of his stomach into the toilet bowl. He was also thankful he managed to avoid getting any of it on his tie or his shoes. He flushed the commode, then turned and stood for several seconds. He leaned on the vanity, and stared deeply into the reflection of his own eyes in the mirror. He could never remember being this scared. He knew the future scenario that Tedie had just described was entirely possible. Breaking his gaze after several seconds, he hurriedly rinsed his mouth and made sure his appearance was unsullied. Satisfied, he headed back to the conference room.

Bequeeta was still at her station, perched outside the conference room. This time though, after opening the door to let him back into the room, she followed him in. She stood at attention as Jeffrey returned to his seat.

Tedie looked at him as if he knew exactly what had just happened. This made Jeffrey even more uncomfortable. He prided himself on never giving his emotions away to his opponents, or even his colleagues.

"Feel better?"

As nonchalantly as he could, Jeffrey responded, "Sure. Yeah, better."

"Good. Because what we have to talk about next is very important, and it must stay in this room. That assumes, Jeffrey, that you wish for our conversation to continue."

"Of course, yes I do."

"The nature of what I want to talk to you about next is sensitive. I asked Bequeeta to join us so she can pat you down for a wire. I hope you understand and are okay with that. In my position, I cannot be too careful. If you're game, go ahead and stand up and Bequeeta will quickly do a non-invasive, painless pat down to ensure its just us in this room."

Jeffrey thought for a moment. He didn't think he'd ever been patted down in all his time working in Washington. He was certain, however, that he'd never been patted down by a six-foot-tall black woman. He was frightened, but a little excited at the same time. But, mostly he was frightened. Slowly, he rose from his chair. As Bequeeta performed her duty, Jeffrey assumed that his quick exit and return from the restroom led Tedie to believe he had been handed a recording device. He thought of the scene from the Godfather when Michael went to the restroom to obtain the weapon he would use to kill two people.

Bequeeta acknowledged she was finished by taking a step back from Jeffrey and nodding to Tedie.

"Jeffrey, now if you don't mind, please also give your phone to Bequeeta. She will sit with it outside the door, and give it back to you when you leave. I apologize, but this action is also completely necessary."

Jeffrey complied and handed Bequeeta his phone. Tedie waited for the door to close behind her before continuing.

"When we began this conversation, I mentioned there is a great opportunity available right now that will soon be gone. This opportunity has the potential to make us both a lot of money, as well as greatly diminish the likelihood that you end up in jail."

"Or worse?" Jeffrey said with a faint chuckle.

"Or worse," responded Tedie. "Would you like for me to continue, for me to describe the opportunity I see for the two of us?"

"By all means."

"Jeffrey, you are familiar I am sure with the story of Robin Hood?" Jeffrey nodded his head in affirmation. "As the legend of Robin Hood has made its way through time, a very important element of it has been changed. Robin Hood did not rob the rich to help the poor. It's not that simple. Robin Hood robbed the greedy royalty of the time period and returned the money to those it had been confiscated from at the tip of a sword."

"Jeffrey, your boss is sitting on a big pile of dirty money at the Foundation. I think I know a way we can relieve her of some of it. She has it in a vault, so to speak. I have part of the combination to unlock that vault. I suspect you have another part of the combination to open that vault. Together, I think we can crack that vault open and liberate a lot of money from her greedy royal hands."

Jeffrey swallowed hard. He had never once considered taking any money from anyone. But Tedie was making it sound like the easiest thing, and the most obvious thing, to do. It sounded like something he had potentially done before.

"Stephanie Kenseth is powerful because of her title and her money. If I deny her from owning the POTUS title in this presidential race, and we deprive her of her stay-out-of-jail money, she is essentially defenseless against the FBI, which keeps you and other innocent people out of harm's way for just being associated with her."

It was still hard for Jeffrey to accept that he would be an active participant in a scandal. It was something he worked hard to avoid in his vocation, which in the political capital of the free world was easier said than done.

"Mr. Tedie, let's just say I like the sound of all of this. You're assuming one thing that I think you might be mistaken on: I don't have access to any of the ICSJ Foundation cash or accounts."

Tedie looked at Jeffrey as if studying him. "Do you know who does, or who might have that information?"

Amuh's name popped into Jeffrey's mind. "Yes, I might."

"Is that person also at risk of suffering from Stephanie's trouble with the FBI? Is this person exposed in the same manner that you are?"

"Maybe. Probably."

"Do you think this person wants to go to jail?"

"Or worse?" asked Jeffrey again.

"Or worse?"

"No, I'm sure she doesn't. I think she might potentially cooperate if she understood the stakes."

"Let's continue this conversation assuming you can get your friend to cooperate, and that she has the information that we need." Jeffrey nodded. "Do you know what ACH stands for?" Jeffrey shook his head. "ACH stands for Automated Clearing House. It's a banking term. It's how money electronically gets from one account at one bank to another account in another bank."

"Like a wire?" asked Jeffrey.

"Not exactly. With a wire, the bank initiates the send and another bank acknowledges the receipt of the money. There are tons of protocols and safeguards in sending a wire. An ACH transaction by contrast, is much more automated, and the bank is much less likely to notice the transaction unless it is unusual in some way. There are literally millions of ACH transactions that occur on a daily basis, with millions and millions of dollars moving from one account into another."

He continued, "I have a hunch that a lot of the dirty money in the Kenseth Foundation account got there via ACH transfer. If my hunch is correct, and the account can receive ACH transfers in, it must also allow ACH transfers out. The ACH functionality of an account is either on or off. If it is on, money can move both ways, in and out. Jeffrey, you have no idea, most people have no idea how easy it is to take money from an account via ACH. All you need is the account number and the bank routing number where the account is housed, an internet connection, and a bank account to receive the funds."

Jeffrey was now a little perplexed. "I told you, I'm not sure I have access to the account number and routing number."

Tedie smiled. "But I do. When Stephanie handed me checks numbered one and two out of that account, she handed me the account number and routing number."

Jeffrey thought for a moment. "So, why do you need my help?"

Tedie smiled again. He had Jeffrey thinking hard about the scheme, which is right where he needed him.

"Excellent question. In order for this plan to have the greatest likelihood of success, I need to know which banks have sent money into the Foundation's account. If we initiate money flowing out of the ICSJ Foundation account, most likely, someone at First National Bank of the Everglades is going to notice. If money flows out of the account back to a bank that sent money in, that transaction is most likely not going to be looked at twice by an observant banker. Money moving out of the account to a totally new location is more likely to draw suspicion. Suspicion is the number one enemy of this plan."

Jeffrey was finally emerging from the fog which had clouded his brain since recalling the election fraud conversation he was party to. His senses were beginning to sharpen. "Let me make sure I understand. You already have the information necessary to pull this heist off. What you don't have is enough information to pull it off with a low probability of being detected."

"That is correct, Jeffrey. Now you are catching on."

"You indicated one of the necessary elements to make this happen is a bank account to receive money into. I'm assuming that is something you will handle?"

"That also is correct. My suspicion is at least some of this money came from overseas. I already have account relationships overseas with multiple banks. Setting up additional accounts at those banks is easy for my far-reaching organization to do without raising suspicion."

Jeffrey continued to think. "I don't know any other way to ask this question, Mr. Tedie. How do you not get caught? How does the money trail not lead straight to the recipient?"

"Great question, Jeffrey. Something tells me you are a natural born bank robber." Jeffrey didn't know whether he liked the sound of that. "The initial movement of money out of the Foundation account is absolutely traceable. What is not traceable is the next path the money takes. The account we move the money to is opened, funded by the money received, and then that money is moved out by another ACH transfer. The destination of the subsequent ACH is a protected piece of information at the bank. And, even if someone comes looking for that subsequent destination, whether they're looking legally or illegally, by that time the money has been moved multiple times and has vanished." Tedie paused to make sure Jeffrey was following him.

Jeffrey was increasingly gaining the sense Mr. Tedie was speaking from past experiences. He continued, "But here is the bigger reason you don't get caught. You are stealing money from a thief. It's not like the thief can go to the police and ask for help. The public is unaware of the amount of money in the Foundation account. It is also unaware of how the money was obtained. If the public knew, Stephanie would be done politically. If it were brought to light how she came into possession of the sums of money I suspect are in that account, she would never again garner public support for any type of political position. The only people who are going to be aware of this heist are the people who successfully pull it off... and Stephanie Kenseth."

"Like in the movie *The Bank Job*."

"Exactly like the movie *The Bank Job*. When you steal something that has itself been stolen or is not supposed to exist in the first place, you don't have to worry about the police."

Jeffrey was warming significantly to the plan. The embarrassment of throwing up just a few minutes before in the men's room was quickly fading. It was being replaced with the exhilaration the plan might actually work, and he would be in possession of an enormous amount of money. He and Amuh estimated there might be as much as a billion dollars in the account.

"And all you need from me are the names of banks from which ACH transactions have been originated into the Foundation account?"

"That is correct. And especially for the foreign banks, I need the exact name."

"And without this information, the plan does not work."

Tedie was realizing he had Jeffrey on board. He knew Jeffrey had just transitioned from education to negotiation.

"Actually, the plan can work without that information. Like you said before, having the bank names increases the likelihood of success, and it increases the likelihood of creating a larger payoff, rather than a smaller one."

Jeffrey now asked the most important question, "What kind of split are you proposing?"

"I think 55/45 is fair. It's actually very generous on my part. We are essentially 50/50 partners. I just get an extra 5 percent for administering the account set ups and movement of the money to safe and anonymous places."

Jeffrey had his response ready before Tedie finished speaking. He waited several seconds to respond, feigning contemplation. "No can do. There are three people in this deal. If I split my 45% with someone else, I only get 22.5%. It needs to be thirds, equal thirds. You can pay the thirds after paying for the expenses of the account set ups and the transfers."

Tedie was impressed. He had not expected push back. He now wished he had started at 75/25. However, his surprise did not diminish his desire to make as much as he possibly could on the deal. After all, it was his idea, and his reputation that was on the line.

"Jeffrey, what you do with your 45% cut is up to you. I am certain you can obtain the information I need by offering your informant far less than half of your take. And remember, I don't have to have this information. I can make the deal happen without it."

Jeffrey responded, "Without the information, you run a much greater risk of getting caught. Don't try to make me believe it is not valuable to you. If it were not valuable, you would not have asked me here. And with the information, the payday will be much larger. I heard you say so. Equal thirds is fair and reasonable."

Tedie closed his eyes, leaned his head to the right and shrugged his shoulders as if to communicate a reluctant acceptance of what Jeffrey had just said. "Deal," he declared as he extended his right hand toward Jeffrey. Jeffrey smiled, firmly shook Tedie's hand, and responded in kind. "Deal."

Tedie rose to his feet and Jeffrey followed suit. "Jeffrey, I need this information quickly. Stephanie is under tremendous pressure. Desperate people do desperate things. We need to get to that money before she potentially sends it out to someone else in an attempt to save her skin."

"I should be able to get it within 48 hours." Jeffrey now turned toward the door.

"Wait. Take this." He reached into the briefcase situated in the chair next to him and handed Jeffrey a small black phone. "I will text you with information on the accounts my people will set up for you and your accomplice. It is through those accounts you will receive your take. My phone number is saved in this phone. I've also taken the liberty of installing an encryption app. Only communicate with me though this app. It's the only way we both can ensure our messages are secured. You're the only person who has my number, and it will only be activated during this brief period we are doing business together. Do you understand?" Jeffrey nodded, sliding the phone into his pocket. "Oh, and don't forget to grab your other phone from Bequeeta.

I'm sure she has enjoyed using it to call her family in Jamaica." They both laughed. It felt good to laugh. As Jeffrey opened the door, he found Bequeeta standing dutifully outside. She was smiling and had his phone in her outstretched hand. Jeffrey thanked her as he took it from her. He walked down the hall, regularly checking his six to confirm Bequeeta was not walking out with him. After several seconds of walking and making sure he wasn't being followed or escorted, he checked his phone's recent call history. He was relieved to find no calls to Jamaica.

Accomplice

We need to talk asap. When is a good time to call you?

Amuh saw Jeffrey's text and smiled. She always enjoyed Jeffrey's company, even if they were just talking on the phone. She sensed a curious urgency to his request.

1:00 today. Looking forward to it, doll.

Amuh wondered why Jeffrey would need to speak with her urgently. She assumed it pertained to Stephanie's recent issues with the FBI. Like everyone else, Amuh had learned of Stephanie's summons to the White House via the media.

Exactly at 1:00pm, Amuh's phone rang.

"Jeffrey, how are you?"

"I'm good, Amuh. I hope you are the same. Hey, where are you right now?"

Amuh could sense an uncharacteristic tension in Jeffrey's voice. This made her uneasy. "I'm actually in DC with Stephanie. She wanted me to spend the night here to help her prepare for her meeting today. She wanted me with her, although to be honest, I'm not really sure why."

Jeffrey was pleasantly surprised Amuh was in town. He preferred to have this conversation in person. He was glad he thought to ask for her location before starting the conversation.

"Wow. That is great!" Amuh immediately noticed Jeffrey sounded more at ease. "So where are you right now, exactly?" he asked.

"I'm in Georgetown, at Baked and Wired. I had to get my hands on some Hippie Crack."

As distracted as Jeffrey was after his conversation with Tedie, he could not ignore a comment like that. "Your what?!"

"Hippie Crack. It's the best granola in the world. They make it right here in DC. You've never had it?! I'll bring you some."

Jeffrey rolled his eyes. "Great. Bring me some. You know where my office is right? I'm just across the river from where you are, in Arlington. Meet me here was soon as you can."

"Of course. What's with the urgency, Jeffrey? It sounds like something is wrong."

"I'll tell you when I see you."

The lack of playfulness in his response caused alarm bells to go off in her head. Jeffrey was always cool and possessed a quick wit. Neither of these had been apparent during their short call. He had not denied something was wrong when she asked. He was definitely nervous, which made her nervous.

Jeffrey sat in his office waiting for Amuh. He was looking out of his window over Arlington, contemplating how to structure his conversation with her. Should he appeal to her greed first and talk about the money? Should he appeal to her fears, and talk about the potential danger they were both in? Should he shield her from the fact Colton Tedie was directly involved and fail to mention that he had met with him earlier in the day? These thoughts were still racing through his mind as the door to his office opened and Amuh walked in.

"Oh my god, Jeffrey! I cannot believe how beautiful the view is from your office!"

"This is your first time here isn't it? Yes, it is pretty stunning. Soothing as well, when needed."

Jeffrey had a short coffee table in his office surrounded by four chairs. At Amuh's insistence, they moved the coffee table next to the window. They each sat in a chair facing the window, with their shoeless feet propped on the coffee table. They placed the bag of Hippie Crack on the table between them. Jeffrey was grateful for the opportunity to say what he had to say in a more relaxed atmosphere. He was still coming off the anxiety high of being patted down by a six-foot Jamaican woman, propositioned for a federal crime, and handed a burner phone, all in the same morning. This was all new and surreal to him.

Despite thinking about his approach for over a half an hour, Jeffrey had still not decided on a road map for their conversation. He sat there in silence, struggling to know how to start. Amuh was admiring the view. She detested silence, so, she just started talking.

"You have an incredible view of the Iwo Jima memorial."

Jeffrey, ever the perfectionist, responded, "It's actually the Marines Memorial. And yes, it is stunning."

Amuh smiled and shook her head slightly. "Whatever." A pause ensued before Amuh began again.

"Do you ever stop to think about how bad ass those guys were? I mean, they were eighteen, nineteen years old, running up hills to face machine guns and an enemy who preferred death to surrender. Crazy."

Jeffrey responded, "Semper Fi."

"Do or die."

In unison they both started chanting, "Gung ho, gung ho, gung ho!" Now they were both laughing.

Still laughing, Amuh asked, "What is that even from?"

"I don't know. Some war movie I guess that we both saw when we were young, innocent, and impressionable. Maybe *Full Metal Jacket*," Jeffrey said while still laughing.

"Maybe."

Jeffrey knew it was time. He still not have a roadmap in his head. So he just started. "Amuh, when you told me about how the money got into Stephanie's Foundation account, you mentioned that you would receive a text or an email letting you know about the transaction. Is that right?"

"Yes. Different banks preferred different methods for documenting it. Some were in a text, some were through email. Stephanie set it up so that I would receive the notifications, and then I would tell her when money would come in so she wouldn't have to call the bank or check her balance online."

"What information would the text or email contain?"

"The name of the sending bank, the amount sent, and a code name, like Felix or Charlie, or something like that. The code name meant nothing to me, but Stephanie knew who they were."

"Were any of the sending banks foreign?"

"Yes, I'd say half of them, or more. The foreign bank deposits were more prolific."

Jeffrey was now satisfied that Amuh had the information that Tedie needed. She had the names of the sending banks. Her information validated what Tedie had conjectured. This gave Jeffrey confidence to move forward with his proposition. A nervous smile now spread across Jeffrey's face.

"Amuh, let's play a fun little pretend game. I bet you liked pretend games when you were a kid." He reached into the open bag between them and picked up a handful of Hippie Crack.

Amuh suddenly felt more at ease. This sounded much more like the Jeffrey she knew. "Actually, I hated them. But I'll play along if you like." A smirk came over Jeffrey's face as they both continued looking out of the window over Arlington.

"In our pretend game, which you love, you are walking along a path with someone you care about."

"That's weird, cause I hate walking."

"Shut up and listen already," came Jeffrey's quick reply as he pelted the side of Amuh's face with small pieces of granola. Jeffrey continued on, "You are walking along and you come to a fork in the path. You must choose which way to go. One route is a little risky. There is a chance you could go to jail. But this route likely leads to great riches… you will just have to betray a trust of someone close to you if you take this route."

"The other route is also risky. If you take this route, you might end up in jail, or possibly even worse. There are no riches along this route. In fact, there is likely tremendous personal and financial cost to taking this route. You do not, however, have to betray anyone's trust to take this route. But beware, someone you trust may in fact betray you along this route."

Amuh thought for a moment with her hands folded in front of her and her index fingers pressing against her chin. "So, either route may lead to prison. One route I might get rich, the other route I might go broke. The rich route I betray someone. The go broke route I get betrayed. Sounds pretty simple to me. I take the first route."

Jeffrey nodded his head slowly. "Let me ask you another question. This is a new scenario. You're at a bar sitting next to a person who puts $100,000 down on the bar and walks away. No one sees the money but you. You get the sense the person worked hard for that money, and you know he truly needs it. But, you also know you can take it and probably not get caught. Do you take it?"

"No, that would clearly be wrong."

"Okay. Now let's change one dynamic. What if you knew the guy came into possession of that money by illegal or unethical means. Now do you take it?"

"How do I know the money is ill-gotten?"

Jeffrey responded in exasperation, "It doesn't matter how you know, you just do. You didn't do anything wrong to get this information. You just have trustworthy information that states this as fact."

Amuh hesitated momentarily. "Probably I would take the money," she slowly said.

Jeffrey again nodded his head. "Second to last question. Stephanie Kenseth is faced with either going to prison for a short time, or selling me out, which means I would go to prison for an even longer time. Who ends up going to prison?"

Amuh now turned her gaze away from the window and looked at Jeffrey. Smiling she said, "Aw, don't worry Jeffrey, I'll come visit you in jail!" He now threw another small handful of Hippie Crack at her face.

"Now, my last question. Same scenario, but it's *you* or Stephanie going to jail. Who's taking the fall?"

Amuh now took Jeffrey's question much more seriously than she had when it was about him. She suddenly felt a hollow pain in her stomach. She chose to answer his question with a question of her own.

"Jeffrey, what exactly are you getting at? You are scaring me."

Jeffrey turned his body to face her. "You should be scared, Amuh. I should be scared. I *am* scared. Stephanie is in deep shit with the FBI. I think someone is going to prison. And we both know that William and Stephanie made careers out of having others take the fall for them."

Amuh bristled at the thought. "Don't talk like that, Jeffrey. I mean it, now you are really scaring me. And besides, I haven't done anything wrong. And I'm sure you haven't either."

"There are two things that you and I each need to realize. One, it's people like you and me who take the fall for people like Stephanie Kenseth. Whether we've done anything wrong or not is immaterial. Two, can you honestly say, while employed by Stephanie, can you beyond the shadow of a doubt honestly say you have not been party to an email or conversation or written correspondence in which something kinda sorta illegal was being discussed or proposed? Whether it was your idea or not?" He paused. "Amuh, whether you were the one who made it happen or not, you are complicit if you knew of any wrongdoing and didn't report it. That is where she will hang you."

The hollow place in Amuh's stomach now grew. She knew Jeffrey was right, but she did not want to believe it. "Stephanie would not do that to me, and I don't think she'd do that to you either."

Jeffrey could not control the laugh that erupted from deep within. "Ha! Amuh, that is bullshit, and if you don't know it, you are not nearly as smart as I give you credit for. Michael Griffey ate a bullet for the Kenseths. Cindy Thomas went to prison for the Kenseths. I bet they and a dozen others we don't even know about weren't nearly as close to Stephanie as you or me. I respect her. Don't get me wrong, I respect her and I choose to come and do this job every day. But if it comes down to my ass or hers, my ass is grass. Yours too. You need to wise up, girlfriend."

Amuh sat there silently, looking deep into Jeffrey's eyes. He could tell she was still not convinced; still did not want to believe what he was saying. He leaned in a little closer. "Amuh, do you remember that guy Truman you put in front of Stephanie recently? Think back to how that conversation evolved as he talked about how he would pull off the voter fraud. Stephanie did not say a word. It was you and me doing the talking."

"Yeah, but we told the guy to get lost."

"You and I told him to get lost. Stephanie didn't tell him to get lost. Stephanie took his card. Do you remember that? Stephanie's campaign is tail spinning right now due to her scandals. Don't you think it's possible that Stephanie is going to contact him? We know she has the money to pay for the guy's services. Right this minute, she could be planning on committing blatant election fraud, and you and I were in the room doing the talking when the plan was laid out. And that is exactly what the guy will testify to at the Congressional hearings that will follow the elections. Who do you think is going to jail for that? After all, it was you who introduced him to Stephanie."

Amuh could now feel her heart beating in her chest. Her mouth was dry and her mind was racing. She'd been associated with politics long enough to know the scenario described by Jeffrey was entirely possible. The fact that Stephanie was in the middle of it actually made it all the more likely. And despite her devotion to Stephanie, she knew if it came down to a decision of who got burned at the stake, it wasn't going to be Stephanie.

Her eyes communicated the anxiety that had come over her. She reached out with her left hand and grasped Jeffrey's right forearm. "Jeffrey, we're in deep shit."

"Yeah, I know we are."

Amuh now stood up, but she had no intentions of leaving. "Well, what are we going to do? How can you sit there and be calm? We have to do something to protect ourselves!"

A thin smile slowly spread across Jeffrey's face, partly because he'd successfully sold his message to Amuh, and partly because he found it humorous that Amuh, this person he had great professional respect for, was unraveling before his very eyes while he was holding the antidote. But he was quickly humbled when he remembered his own unraveling in the men's room at the Jefferson earlier in the day.

Calmly, Jeffrey said, "We are."
"We are what?"

"We are going to do something. And the first thing we're both going to do is we are both going to sit down and get our shit together."

Amuh was honestly unaware of the fact she was standing. It had been more of a reflex reaction than a conscious decision. She shook her head slightly as if having been shaken out of a daydream, and sat down again.

"Okay, the next thing we are going to do is take away the lioness's teeth, then steal the lioness's treasure. And we're both going to get stinking filthy rich in the process."

Amuh's head was still clouded the by same fog that had engulfed Jeffrey while he sat across from Tedie in that hotel conference room. She made a half-hearted attempt to decipher the message behind Jeffrey's words. Feeling overwhelmed and dizzy, she stood back up, looking angrily at Jeffrey.

"What the fuck are you talking about with lions and teeth and treasure? This is serious business! We're going to jail and you're talking about this like it's a fucking Disney movie!"

Jeffrey successfully suppressed the gut laugh that threatened to escape. In his most empathetic voice, he said, "Amuh let's try this thing again. First, we're both going to sit down." Again, Amuh was unaware she was standing. She retook her seat. She also reached out to take both of Jeffrey's hands, which he had extended toward her.

"Second, we're going to think this through, and then we're going to act." Amuh was comforted by the feeling of his hands holding hers.

Jeffrey continued, doing his best to speak slowly and calmly for her, "What is it that gives Stephanie Kenseth power? I'll tell you. It's her money and her title. We're going to take away her money, and the voters are going to deny her the title she craves. At that point, she will be defenseless against her vast enemies, a list which starts with the FBI."

Amuh looked as if she was in total agreement so far. Jeffrey continued, going for the close, "How'd you like to stay out of jail while at the same time get your hands on the money at the Foundation?"

Amuh's focus sharpened noticeably when Jeffrey brought up the Foundation's money. Amuh had received so many messages regarding the large sums of money coming into the Foundation that it was almost surreal to her. The aggregate amount of money she assumed was in the Foundation account was fantastical.

"Well I'd love to stay out of jail, and I'd love to have even ten percent of what is in the Foundation account. But you're going to have to explain to me how we accomplish that. What are you now, a bank robber?"

"I'll do you even better than ten percent, I'll get you thirty-three percent. And no, I'm not a bank robber yet, but I've got an experienced partner."

Amuh's jaw visibly dropped. The fact that someone besides Jeffrey was helping to hatch this plan made it even more plausible to her. She couldn't get her brain and her mouth to work together to form a response, so she simply raised her eyebrows at Jeffrey until he had no choice but to continue.

"You're not going to believe me when I tell you."

She snorted involuntarily. "Jeffrey! I can't fucking believe we're having the conversation that we *are*. So, at this moment, I'm apt to believe just about anything."

"I had a meeting earlier today with Colton Tedie."

"What?!"

Jeffrey continued, "Yes, with Colton Tedie. He has half the information needed in order to electronically steal the contents of the Foundation account. You have the other half. He doesn't know you exist, which is probably a good thing. He has the account number and bank routing number. You know the banks from which those deposits were made from. With that information, he is able to electronically, and apparently inconspicuously, move money out of the Foundation account. A small amount at first. If that is successful, then large amounts. Potentially very large amounts. Then, we all split the take in thirds."

Amuh was still not sure whether to believe what she was hearing. Again, she said nothing, so Jeffrey continued.

"You and I will have separate accounts in a Cayman Islands bank to which the money from the Foundation account will be deposited. The bank accounts will have account numbers only, no names. Only you and I will have the numbers. It's completely anonymous and non-traceable. What we do with the money from there is up to us."

"If everything goes as planned, you and I get rich, and Stephanie loses her ability to hire Truman to help her win. Stephanie will have no idea where the money went, and neither will anyone else. She can't cry foul, because most of that Foundation money is extortion money or bribes. She's powerless to use law enforcement to try and track down the money. And she's doubly powerless because her war chest is gone and she can't buy people off."

Amuh continued to process what Jeffrey had said for several seconds before speaking. "Just like that? It's as easy as that? No. It can't be that easy, Jeffrey."

Jeffrey's face was dead serious. "What's our choice, love? I get the feeling Tedie has done this before. And even if he hasn't, and even if it's a long shot, what's our other option?"

Amuh thought for a minute before speaking again. "How do we know Tedie won't screw us? How do we know he will give us our thirds?"

"Well, frankly we don't. We have to trust him. With his banking contacts all over the world, he has the network already established to pull this off. We don't."

She looked worried.

"Let me say this though Amuh, I think we can trust him. He's pompous and loud and arrogant and exaggerates wildly at times, but I do not believe he is, at his core, a liar. I hope I don't find out I'm wrong. But I think we can trust him. And I don't see that we have much choice."

Amuh concurred. "You're right about that. We don't. So… tell me what you need from me."

"I need the names of the banks from which deposits came into the Foundation account."

"I have those right here on my phone. You write them down while I call them out."

A Little, Then a Lot

With Amuh's help, Jeffrey was able to deliver the names of thirty banks to Tedie within just a few hours of their meeting. These were the banks that the deposits to the Foundation had originated from over the course of several years.

Early the next morning, Tedie sent Jeffrey a text from his burn phone. He confirmed that his organization had at some point done business with all but three of the banks, and setting up accounts at the banks he knew could happen fairly quickly. Tedie's organization was so large and did business under so many names, it was not difficult to open accounts using existing yet obscure corporate structures which were many levels removed from Colton Tedie.

The accounts that would be created at the twenty-seven banks would only be open for a few days. The purpose of these accounts was strictly to receive funds which were taken from the Foundation, and then to quickly disperse those funds out. After that, the accounts were useless. Closing them quickly would help obscure the money trail, should anyone try to trace where the money went. Like Tedie had said in the meeting, tracing the first movement wouldn't be too difficult. Tracing the subsequent moves would be nearly impossible.

On the 13th, Tedie again sent a message to Jeffrey from his secret phone line. He indicated that all the accounts had been successfully set up. He also provided two bank account numbers from the First International Caribbean Bank of the Cayman Islands. Neither of the accounts had a name associated with them. The could only be accessed by phone or in person, and the only identification required was the account number.

Jeffrey immediately called Amuh after receiving the account numbers.

"What's your favorite number?"

Amuh thought for a moment. "A million. As in dollars wanted."

"Cute. I need a smaller number," was Jeffrey's response.

Amuh thought again. "My dad was a big Mickey Mantle fan. He was number seven. I'll go with seven."

Jeffrey looked at the two account numbers. One of them had two sevens in it, the other only had one. He gave her the account number with two sevens.

Amuh repeated the number he gave her back to him. She had it right.

"The initial password for your account is Thunder Bolt. You can change it, but you'll need that the first time you call."

Amuh now asked, "So what happens next?"

"Um, I'm not totally sure. I'll find out and let you know."

Jeffrey called the number Tedie had given him, but there was no answer. Jeffrey then sent a text:

WHAT HAPPENS NEXT?

Ten minutes later, Jeffrey received a response.

CHECK YOUR EMAIL. LOOK IN YOUR SPAM.
SUBJECT LINE: WHAT HAPPENS NEXT. USE
DECRYPT TO READ.

Jeffrey went to his spam folder and saw a
message with the matching subject line. He did not
recognize the email address it was sent from. The
body of the message was encrypted, resulting in
completely unreadable text. Jeffrey was grateful that
Tedie was being ultra-careful to cover their tracks.
After running the email through the decrypting
function of the program he had been instructed to
install earlier by Tedie, he was able to read it. The
message said, "Making first withdrawals tomorrow in
small amount. If successful, will follow up daily with
larger amounts. In two days, check your balance."
        Jeffrey assumed he should be just as cautious
as Tedie. He decided to call rather than electronically
communicate with Amuh. He assumed he could trust
Amuh, in the same way she was trusting him.
        "Hello, Jeffrey."
        "How are you doing?"
        "Sitting here kind of nervous, you know?"
        "I understand. He says we should check the
bank balance in two days. First withdrawals are
tomorrow. Then the money is moved into our
accounts."
        "Do you think this is going to work?"
        "I do. I really do. Since my conversation with
him, I've read a dozen articles on the Internet written
by business owners who got robbed in the same
manner we are using to share in Stephanie's
Foundation money. It's actually very common. If she
does not have ACH blocks or protections on that

account, it is absolutely vulnerable to us or somebody else."

He paused, then answered the question he knew would be coming next. "If she does have blocks on the account, then our efforts will be immediately thwarted, and you are I are back to modeling orange jump suits."

"Well… then let's hope she doesn't have the account blocked. Thanks for the call."

"Talk to you in two days, Amuh."

On Monday, Jeffrey was distracted. He had banking transactions on his mind. Even while he was on his morning run, which was normally a welcomed diversion from reality, he could not stop thinking about what was supposed to happen that day. Not to mention the risks he and Amuh were taking, especially the risks he was exposed to if the plan did not work. His morning run time was nearly three minutes faster than his normal pace. He attributed this to the adrenaline in his system from the soon to be initiated sequence of events. Events that would, either way, shape the rest of his life.

Throughout the day, while working in his office, he caught himself constantly scanning the three televisions for a Breaking News headline that indicated something was up with Tedie (or anyone else) in relation to Stephanie Kenseth's money. He was relieved as the hours passed that he did not see anything related to their scheme come across the screen.

Through fits and starts, Jeffrey managed to make it through the day. His typical leave time was 6:00pm. He had no plans for the night, and this worried him. He knew he was going to have trouble sleeping. In the midst of this thought, his phone rang. It was Amuh. He smiled as he reached for the phone.

"How's your day been?"

Amuh responded, "I'm going nuts. How about you?"

"Same here. I've been unproductive as hell. And I'm not looking forward to tonight. Hoping my buddy Jack Daniels can help me sleep."

"Well, how about a different buddy to take your mind off your day and help you sleep?" Jeffrey smiled. Amuh was as subtle as ever.

"Well, that certainly is… a thought." was the wittiest thing he could think of to say.

Amuh continued, "I seem to recall we had a pretty awesome time the first time. And I definitely recall you saying it was so good you might be talked into it again."

Jeffrey decided to play hard to get. "Do you really think it's good idea? I mean, I think we're about to be business partners, even if only for a few days."

Amuh didn't pick up on Jeffrey's lame joke about workplace relations. Her tone switched to one of desperation.

"Jeffrey, I'm really nervous. And super scared. I've already had two glasses of wine in the hour I've been home, and they've had no effect. This whole thing is happening because I chose to share the Foundation information with you, so you owe me this. Besides, have you ever had sex when you are scared and nervous?"

Jeffrey disagreed that the wine she had consumed was not having an effect, but he thought better of arguing that point with her. Instead, he answered her question honestly, "No, I can't say that I have."

"It's really, really powerful sex. It's like your senses are more alive and you feel less inhibited."

Jeffrey could think of nothing to say in response. It was clear he was going to have to follow her orders tonight.

"Meet me at my apartment in an hour. I need this and so do you. You'll thank me later."

"Alright, I'll see you then."

"Oh, and Jeffrey, in addition to loving sex when I'm nervous, I'm also an emotional eater. Be a dear and pick up a large Forest Shroomin' pie from We The Pizza on your way here. You'll thank me later for that as well."

Jeffrey loved pizza. But he hated the smell of it in his car. He was reminded of this as he drove down Pennsylvania Avenue with Amuh's pie of choice in his passenger seat. "There's a reason people pay for delivery" he thought as we wound his way through DC traffic.

Jeffrey was meticulous about the look and cleanliness of his Mercedes, both inside and out. He knew from experience it would take several days to get the pizza smell out of his car. Even though rain was falling hard and his wipers were on high, he cracked his windows in an effort to get fresh air circulating. As soon as he did, copious amounts of rain water began to run down the leather door's interior. He quickly returned the windows to their closed position. "Great. Pizza smell today, mold tomorrow."

After driving two more blocks, Jeffrey found his route blocked by a multi-car accident. This only served to increase his frustration level. As he fumbled with his phone to engage navigation to find an alternate route, he dropped it between the seats. "Fuck!" Jeffrey could now visibly feel his anger rising. He looked in the rearview mirror and took note that his ears were red, his personal tale tell sign that he was not in control of himself. He grabbed the steering wheel with both hands, pulled himself up in his seat and yelled, "Why am I doing this?" His actions were so dramatic and his voice so loud the passenger in the car to his left turned her head quickly to look at him. The speed of her movement caused Jeffrey to notice her. He hadn't even realized anyone was beside him in traffic. This lack of spatial awareness was yet another clue that he was spiraling out of control, and fast.

He was soon motioned by a police officer to move forward through the lane which had been created to recommence traffic flow. He quickly found a parking lot, pulled in, and shut his car off. He looked at himself in the mirror again, this time to try to center his emotions. He found himself repeating, this time in a much calmer tone, "Why are you doing this?"

For many years, Jeffrey had been at peace with his sexuality. He was confident he was 100% gay, always had been. So why was he questioning it more and more lately? It wasn't just because he was on his way to Amuh's house to have sex with her for a second time. Since the tragic death of his mother and sister in a car wreck two years ago, he had begun asking himself why, and most recently if, he actually was gay.

As a young boy, Jeffrey's sister had made fun of him for having a penis. When he was five, she made him pull his pants down in her room while all her friends were over. They all laughed at the peculiar member between his legs. Though he had since forgiven her for this and many other childhood offenses, since her death he had begun to wonder what affect this treatment might have had.

As if this weren't enough to make him timid around girls, his mother, who was ever present, discouraged him from having any type of a romantic relationship, even throughout high school. He remembered how angry she got that one day when she picked him up from school and saw him having an innocent conversation with a female friend his freshman year.

Every morning when he was in the shower, his mother would make his bed and lay out his clothes for the day. When he finally objected in his junior year of high school, she took him to the store so he could pick out some of his own clothes, but she never stopped laying out his clothes, no matter how much he protested.

His father had disappeared from the family picture when he was very young. He had very few memories of him, or what he had looked like. Jeffrey had no idea where he was or if he was even alive. He was sure part of what his mom was doing was just trying to make everything normal, predictable for her family. And for herself.

He had been devastated for weeks after their passing. But as he had emerged from mourning their deaths, he had found himself questioning for the first time since college whether he was the way he was by choice or by circumstance.

His first lover was in college, and was the RA of his freshman dorm. He was known for using his position of authority to seduce insecure freshman who were away from home for the first time. Jeffrey was pretty sure he was the RA's first conquest of his incoming group. He enjoyed the sex, and the two carried on secretly, then publicly, for his entire freshman year.

Over the years he had tried sleeping with women, usually when he was drunk, and never in the context of a relationship. He had found those encounters unfulfilling, and he never felt at ease when he was naked in front of a woman. He assumed he had his sister to thank for this. He was now on his way to have sex with a woman for the second time, which up to this point had never happened. Sitting in the car with the rain hitting the windshield, it occurred to him that he had not had sex since his last encounter with Amuh several months ago. Was that possible? Was he truly that busy with the campaign? Or had he lost interest in men? He was pretty sure he had not lost interest in sex. At least, he hoped not.

He had begrudgingly agreed to have sex with Amuh the first time. And though he went to their rendezvous anticipating they might end up in bed together, it was not something he necessarily wanted to happen. She had information he wanted, and sex was the cost to get it. To him it had been a business decision. Much to his surprise, he had enjoyed his one night with Amuh. She was a beautiful and skilled lover. But when he reflected on it later, he realized his enjoyment stemmed as much from how easy it had felt to lie with her as the act itself. He didn't regret that. Real human connection was something he didn't get to experience too often these days.

He looked in the mirror one last time. Darkness had fallen quickly and he needed the interior light in order to look into his own eyes. He liked what he saw. He saw the Jeffrey he wanted others to see: he was confident and in control once more. He turned the light off and began looking around to get his bearings. He was shocked to realize he had turned into Amuh's parking lot when he was frantically looking for a place to calm himself. He chuckled, realizing just how out of it he must have been just a few moments prior.

He checked his watch. It was later than he thought. Time flies when you're examining your life all the way back to childhood. His phone, which had eluded his search previously, was now easily found. As he pulled it from between the seat and console, a text came in from Amuh as if on cue.

ARE YOU COMING OR NOT??!?!?!

WELL I'M NOT EVEN BREATHING HARD YET LOVE. BUT IF YOU'LL LET ME IN, I'M SURE YOU CAN HELP FIX THAT.

It took only a second to see her reply.

HUH?!?! ARE YOU HERE?

Jeffrey's phone chirped to signal the message at almost the exact same time he was knocking on her door, holding a wet pizza box. The storm had gotten worse as he had sat in the parking lot, so he had sprinted to her building. His fine clothes and shoes were drenched. As he waited for her to open the door he thought he'd never been so thankful for an awning.

Since it was Amuh who had called him for their liaison, Jeffrey had anticipated the apartment would be dimly lit, and even expected there might be candles involved. To his surprise, when Amuh opened the door his eyes were pierced by the level of light escaping the doorway. Without so much as a 'hello' or 'come in from the rain, you poor soul', Amuh simply grabbed the pizza with her right hand. In her left hand, she held the nearly empty remains of a wine glass. "Thank goodness you are finally here!" she chided as she turned and began walking toward the kitchen.

Though the ambiance of her apartment did not reflect the purpose of his visit, Amuh's garments most certainly did. She was wearing a black bustier with garters that supported thigh high black stockings. Below the bustier she wore a turquoise cheeky panty. When she opened the door, she had made no attempt to veil herself. Did women really dress like this? Jeffrey didn't know, but he felt as if it was a lot of wasted effort.

Jeffrey followed behind her as she walked into the kitchen, her initial bounty in hand. He was surprised to find himself checking out her ass as she walked. During their first encounter there had been no opportunity for sightseeing. At Jeffrey's request the act was done almost completely in the dark.

Watching Amuh walk away, he was quite certain he had never seen a better ass. Amuh was tall. Jeffrey estimated five feet ten inches. She had long, shapely legs which led up to her wide hips and tiny waist. Jeffrey was certain her curves were sculpted through a lot of hard work in the gym. Like a young boy who had discovered his father's stash of Playboy, he was temporarily mesmerized.

He paused to hang his coat up on back of the dining room chair. As he rounded the corner to follow her into the kitchen, he was greeted with even more blatant, yet confusing, sexiness. Amuh was bent over at the waist, her face only inches from the pie, deeply inhaling the savory scent of her mushroom pizza. When she noticed he had entered the kitchen, she looked over her shoulder and winked, then wiggled her ass to tease him. Jeffrey could not resist. He walked up behind Amuh, placed his hands on her hips and squeezed hard. Her faint moan signaled approval, and he began slowly tracing his fingers along her hip bones, up and across her lower back, and along the curve of each muscular—yet soft—cheek.

Suddenly, a flash of light lit up the sky right outside Amuh's kitchen window, followed by a loud clap of thunder. It was so close it shook the house. All the lights in the apartment extinguished and they were enveloped in silence. No television noise, no hum of the appliances, just the steady patter of the rain pouring down.

Without saying a word, Amuh turned and faced Jeffrey. She began softly kissing his lips and unbuttoning his shirt. When his shirt hit the floor, she placed her hands on his hips and moved forward, pressing her body to his. This move caught Jeffrey by surprise, and caused him to take a step back until he found himself pressed up against the oven behind him.

He now began kissing Amuh more aggressively, probing his tongue deep into her mouth. His hands were again on her ass, pulling her eagerly into him. He heard a strange, staccato ticking noise, followed by the sound of combustion coming from behind him. A blue flame illuminated the previously dark room. Jeffrey jumped and looked at Amuh with wide eyes.

"What was that?" he exclaimed, making no effort to hide his alarm.

Amuh was laughing. "That's my gas stove, silly. Your butt lit the eye. It's got a battery backup so it works when the electricity is out."

Slightly embarrassed, Jeffrey responded as coyly as he knew how. "Well that's appropriate because your butt was lighting me up."

Amuh grinned. "Move over."

Jeffrey complied, shifting to the side to let Amuh access the stove. To his surprise, she turned the burner down, but not off. She liked the blue light given off by the flame.

Turning her attention back to Jeffrey, she slowly lowered herself to her knees in front of him and began unbuckling his belt. Then, she carefully hooked her fingers through the first two beltloops and slid his slacks down to the floor. She ran her hands up his muscular legs and up over the front of his boxer briefs, sending a shiver throughout his entire body. She slid her fingers into the waistband and grabbed a nice handful of his ass before sliding his boxers down his thighs.

She repositioned herself slightly before grasping him with both hands. He was fully erect, and Amuh sensed he was more confident, more at ease than during their first time together. This increased her level of arousal as well. She took him into her mouth and began to slowly caress him with her lips and tongue. She slid one hand down to his testicles and with her other hand she grasped the back of his thigh to help her leverage.

This continued for several minutes and Amuh could tell Jeffrey was enjoying it. He had one hand in her thick black hair, and with his other hand he was caressing her shoulder. To her surprise, Jeffrey asked her to stop. He pulled her up gently and gave her a deep, intense kiss. Again, to her surprise, it was Jeffrey who now lowered down to his knees. The oral sex in their first encounter had only gone one way. Amuh had expected that would also be the case tonight. Her arousal increased further with the anticipation of this unexpected turn.

Jeffrey began pressing his nose against Amuh's panties. He had his hands on her ass again, this time more aggressively squeezing her and pulling her toward his face. His intent was to keep this up just long enough to make Amuh wonder if this was a tease or something more. When her breathing reached the pace he was waiting for, he brought his hands to her thighs to unclasp the garter attached to her bustier. He had no intention of removing her stockings. He just wanted to be able to free her panties from her body. He liked this whole naughty librarian getup.

Once her panties were removed, he began intensely kissing the inside of her thighs, occasionally flicking his tongue against her soft skin. As he inched closer to her clitoris, he could feel her tensing up. The angle was not ideal, but the length of Amuh's legs compensated for this. He didn't want to dilute the moment by changing positions, and he was fairly certain he was currently in a position which Amuh had not anticipated. He liked this.

While he was in college, Jeffrey had a close female friend who was lesbian. One night while sharing a joint and watching a lesbian sex scene in a movie they rented, she described to Jeffrey in great detail how to give head to a woman properly. For reasons he had never understood, her instructions had embedded in his memory. Prior to this moment, he had never planned to put those instructions into practice.

Jeffrey proceeded to try and please Amuh in the same way she had just pleased him. He tried to keep his head still. He applied pressure alternately with his lips and his tongue. Judging from Amuh's audible reaction, he thought he was getting it right.

After several minutes, Amuh grabbed Jeffrey by the wet hairs on his head, indicating it was time for him to stand. She greeted him with a long, deep kiss. She now took him by the hand and led him to the bedroom. Jeffrey noticed the sheets had already been turned down.

Amuh laid down on the bed first, on her stomach. She placed her head on the pillow and stuck her ass up in the air. Jeffrey let out a near growl, and quickly entered her from behind. He did not know if he had ever been this aroused. As a result, his thrusts were quick and deep. He wanted to prolong the moment, but he was so consumed with desire his instincts took over. His only goal was to reach orgasm without regard to technique. Amuh sensed this and approved. She encouraged his efforts with intense moans. In this environment, it did not take long to achieve his release. As he orgasmed his entire body shivered. He could not recall the last time he climaxed this intensely.

While still on his knees, he leaned forward and lowered his body onto Amuh's warm back. He then wrapped his arms around her torso. He enjoyed hearing and feeling her breathing. Her heart was still beating rapidly. After holding this position for over a minute he collapsed on the bed next to her.

Rather than linger in the moment, Amuh quickly got up. This caused Jeffrey to be slightly disappointed, and surprised him.

"Where are you going?"

Amuh answered as she exited the room. "To get some pizza! You jumped me before I had a chance to eat any of it and I'm starving! Stay there and I will bring you a piece."

Jeffrey smiled. "A piece of what?"

"Oh, shut up!"

Jeffrey was not sure what woke him first; the heartburn or the light coming in through the window. As his mind came into focus, he determined it was the heartburn. He tried to recall the last time he'd eaten pizza at 11:00pm. He prided himself on his discipline and healthy habits. He wasn't sure he'd ever eaten pizza at 11:00pm. At this moment, despite an uninhibited, memorable night, he was certain he never wanted to again.

He sat up in the bed and noticed Amuh was not there. He checked the time. It was 7:27. He also could not recall the last time he'd slept this late. He attributed this to the fact he and Amuh had had sex for several hours with only limited pauses to drink more wine and catch their breath. Amuh was certainly right he thought, about having sex when you are nervous. He's had some late-night sex in the past, but none of it had ever been as intense as what he'd enjoyed last night.

Amuh walked into the room with two cups of coffee and sat on the bed next to him. He noticed she was wearing his blue striped button-down shirt and nothing underneath.

"Oh, hi there little miss sunshine. Nice shirt."

"Good morning yourself." Amuh leaned over to give him a light kiss on the cheek. "You sleep good?"

Jeffrey returned her smile as he looked at her and asked, "*Did* we sleep?"

Amuh's smile grew as she looked down at the sheets before looking back up at Jeffrey. "I told you sex was so much better when you're scared. And I bet you didn't think about politics or money or jail once during those several hours last night, did you?"

Jeffrey sat up to take a sip of coffee. "You would be correct on both counts, my dear."

Jeffrey noticed Amuh's phone on the night stand. For the first time, it occurred to him that today was the day they could call to confirm whether the first deposit had been successful. Still looking at her phone, he asked, "Have you called the bank yet?"

"I did." His stomach flipped. "I found out the First International Caribbean Bank of the Cayman Islands does not open until 9:00am."

He chuckled. "Well that's a bugger."

"That depends on your perspective." As she spoke, Amuh shifted from sitting cross legged on the bed to straddling Jeffrey's torso. "Have you ever had sex in the shower while you're nervously waiting for time to pass?"

At 8:59, Amuh and Jeffrey were sitting at the kitchen table. They had each cleared their calendars for the entire morning. They had already entered the phone number for the bank on their phones, and they were waiting for the minute hand to tick over to hit "send."

When the clock finally changed to 9:00, they both hurriedly hit the green button to dial the number. They looked at each other anxiously as the signal traveled several hundred miles to a Caribbean island neither had ever been to.

Amuh's call got there first. "It's ringing!"

A pleasant voice on the other end said, "It's a beautiful day at First International Caribbean Bank of the Cayman Islands. How may I assist you?"

Amuh did her best to hide her nervousness. She cleared her throat and tried to sound professional. "I'd like to check my balance, please."

"I can assist you with that. Please go ahead and provide me with your account number."
Amuh read the digits, and the banker repeated them back to her.

"Now please provide me with the password."

"The password is Thunder Bolt." Amuh noticed Jeffrey had ended his call and was focused intently on her conversation.

"Thank you. The balance in your account is $158,333.33. Is there anything else I can do for you today?"

"No, you've been most helpful. Thank you." She ended the call.

Amuh sat in silence, starring at Jeffrey, who was also silent. From the look on her face, Jeffrey could tell she liked what she had heard. He couldn't take it any longer. "Well?!" he demanded.

"Jeffrey, there is a hundred fifty thousand dollars in my account."

Jeffrey eyes widened to match Amuh's. "Really?"

"Yes, really!" Amuh sprang from her chair and wrapped her arms around Jeffrey's neck. Just as abruptly, she broke off the embrace and returned to her seat, still giddy.

"A hundred fifty thousand dollars! Can you believe that?!" Amuh noticed Jeffrey was not saying anything about his account. Then she remembered his call did not last nearly as long as hers. "What did you find out? Do you have the same thing? Or more? I'm going to be mad at you if you have more than me, Jeffrey!"

"What I found out is the First International Caribbean Bank of the Cayman Islands only has one customer service line, and you got through to it before I did. All I got was a recording."

Amuh started laughing uncontrollably. She was laughing so hard tears began running down her face. Jeffrey was laughing too, but not with the same enthusiasm as Amuh.

Finally, Jeffrey asked, "Okay, why do you find that so funny?"

After a few more seconds of unbridled laughter, Amuh managed to speak. "I'm sorry. For a minute there, you looked like Charlie Brown when all he got was a rock while trick or treating."

Eventually, Jeffrey got through to a customer service representative, and confirmed his balance was the same as Amuh's. As happy as he was to be one hundred fifty thousand dollars richer, Jeffrey was surprised the number was not larger. When he was back at his apartment he sent a text to Tedie's burn phone.

> THANKS FOR THE DEPOSIT LAST NIGHT. GRATEFUL, BUT THOUGHT THE NUMBER WOULD BE HIGHER.

A few minutes later a response came back.

INTERNATIONAL MOVEMENT TAKES DAY
LONGER. ONLY DOMESTIC RECEIVED LAST
NIGHT. 5@100 LESS 5% MGMT EXP.

Jeffrey interpreted the message to mean that only five of the one hundred thousand dollar transactions came out of the Foundation account, and that Tedie had deducted five percent of the take to cover management expenses. He ran the math on his phone and it worked out to the identical amounts he and Amuh had received. He anticipated the number would be larger tomorrow.

Payouts and Payback

Lee Roy Butcher was having a bad day. He'd been awarded another speeding ticket coming into work. It was the third one he'd received in less than a year after realizing a lifelong dream of owning a Corvette. Unfortunately, the state trooper who'd written him the ticket did not have an account at The First National Bank of the Everglades, nor was he impressed that Lee Roy was the bank's president.

His bad luck continued through his first two meetings of the day. In the first meeting with the Asset Quality Committee, he'd learned that two of the bank's largest loan clients were frequently making their payments substantially late, and a restructure of their loans would be required. This would likely result in regulators requiring his bank to classify the loans, which would have a material negative impact on bank earnings.

In the second meeting, this one with the Personnel Committee, he learned the bank was substantially out of compliance with President Ingle's healthcare regulations, and this information had only been discovered due to an unexpected audit. The bank could easily fix the issues, which were due to an innocent misunderstanding the law's complex requirements. But there would likely be fines required, as well as negative press.

So, when his phone rang at 11:00am and showed Teresa Edwards' name on the caller ID, he was in no mood to take the call. Teresa was the Operations Manager for the bank. He knew that anytime Teresa called him, which usually happened around 11:00am, it meant that she thought she had found an incidence of fraud that rose to the level of requiring his attention. He hated these calls. Once, and only once, Teresa had been right and that had been several years ago. After that incident, the frequency of her calls to him had increased to at least one per week. Apparently today was the day for this week's call.

He picked up the phone and quickly said, "Teresa I've just come out of a couple of meetings and have more planned this afternoon. Tell me quickly what you've got."

"I certainly understand Mr. Butcher, and I will make this as brief as I can. It involves the ICSJ Foundation account."

Butcher sat up a little straighter in his chair, and momentarily stopped reading the emails he had pulled up on his screen.

"There is a $100 million check trying to clear the account. But that's not all. There are twenty-seven ACH transactions which sent funds out of the account yesterday. I've never seen that much ACH activity with the account, and I know you pay special attention to this client."

Butcher recalled the recent conversation he'd had with Mrs. Kenseth, in which she indicated there would be large sums leaving the account.

"When was the check dated?"

"October 12th. It is signed by Mrs. Kenseth and appears to be written in her hand. Butcher checked his calendar. He had notes from the 12th and that *was* the day she called him.

"Is there anything unusual about the ACH transactions?"

"They were all the same amount; $100,000. Each went to a bank which had previously sent funds into the Kenseth account. We of course don't know which accounts, just the bank."

Like everyone else in her home state of Florida, Butcher was aware of Mrs. Kenseth's issues with the FBI. The fact the funds left her account and went back to banks where money had come from made sense to him. He suspected she might be temporarily returning money to the original donors, as a means of hiding it, with plans to call it back later.

"Teresa, you are correct, I do pay special attention to this account. It's part of my responsibility as bank president. Something you would not be aware of is a conversation I had very recently with Mrs. Kenseth. She let me know to expect to see large amounts of money leaving the account, and not to be alarmed."

Teresa asked, "So you don't think you need to make Mrs. Kenseth aware?"

Butcher checked the time. "No. I told you she and I had a previous conversation, and the account activity you describe is consistent with what she told me to expect."

"Okay, Mr. Butcher, I'll make a note of that."

Butcher knew that was Teresa's way of saying she would be sending him a cover-her-ass email in just a few minutes.

"Fine. Oh, and Teresa, something else you should be aware of. I am leaving this afternoon for a banking conference in Washington. I'm going to be the keynote speaker at the Community Bank break out session, as well as a panel member for the Strength in Diversity panel discussion. It will likely be very difficult to reach me by phone. Therefore, there's no need to try to call me on any further activity on the ICSJ account. Understand?"

"Understood, Mr. Butcher. Enjoy your trip."

Five minutes later, Lee Roy received the email from Teresa. It read, "Per our conversation, I am confirming that you are comfortable with the recent activity in the Kenseth Foundation account. And that due to your upcoming travel schedule, I am not to contact you with similar activity on said account." As was his routine, he moved the email into a folder he had simply named "Teresa."

■■

Jeffrey got the recording again. "Dammit, Amuh!" he yelled into the phone. He wasn't actually mad, just disappointed that she'd beaten him again. It was 9:00am on Wednesday the 19th. He was much more excited about today's balance check than yesterday's. He assumed there would be many more deposits today. At this very moment, he could be a multi-millionaire. He counted to thirty slowly, then dialed the number again.

As the phone was ringing, he got an incoming call. He looked to confirm his suspicion. Amuh was calling him. He decided she could wait.

A voice on the other end of the line picked up. "It's a beautiful day at First International Caribbean Bank of the Cayman Islands. How may I assist you?"

Jeffrey provided his account number, and the new password he'd chosen: 175.

"Your balance today is $2,438,333.33. Deposits in the amount of $2,280,000 were made last night. Is there anything else I may assist you with?"

"No, that will be all. Thank you."

Jeffrey immediately hit the Facetime button on his phone. When the call connected with Amuh, he instantly saw her eyes were bugging out and her mouth was hanging open. He opened his mouth to speak, but was quickly drowned out by a primal scream coming from the speaker.
Jeffrey, swept up in the moment, responded in kind. Their collective screaming went on for a full ten seconds. There was nothing else to say. She winked at him and disconnected from the video call.

Several minutes later, Jeffrey sent a message to Tedie's secret number. It was unusually brief.

WOW.

The response came quick.

TODAY WE GO LARGE. PREPARE FOR YOUR MIND TO BE BLOWN.

On Saturday, Teresa Edwards came into the office. Saturday was not a normal work day for her, but she did not want to wait until Monday check the Suspicious Activity log from the processing activity Friday night. She specifically wanted to check the activity on the ICSJ Foundation account. She was not particularly surprised with what she found. For the third straight day, two hundred seventy million had left the account overnight. ACH withdrawals of ten million each had gone to twenty-seven different banks. The same twenty-seven banks which had been receiving funds out of the account for five straight days. The balance in the account was down to forty million dollars, its lowest in many years.

In spite of Mr. Butcher's comments, she was wary of the activity. She had a sense the account was being robbed by sophisticated thieves. She felt helpless, but she knew if there were an audit, she was covered by Mr. Butcher's decision not to notify Mrs. Kenseth. After all, she had a copy of the follow-up email she had sent him. She always made multiple copies of those emails, and she made sure to place one copy in the safe deposit box she maintained for herself at another bank.

She had her own reasons for not particularly caring if Stephanie Kenseth was indeed being wiped out financially. Teresa Edwards was the niece of Amanda Jones. Amanda Jones had publicly accused William Kenseth of sexual harassment while he was governor of Florida. Through private and public sources, Amanda Jones's life and reputation had been completely destroyed as a result of the allegation she made, which ultimately could not be proven. Teresa Edwards had always believed her aunt had been sincere. She also believed Stephanie Kenseth was behind much of the effort to destroy her aunt, in order to protect her philandering husband. "Paybacks are hell," she thought as she logged out of her computer.

As Jeffrey picked up his phone to call the bank, he noticed a text on his burner phone.

WE ARE DONE. THIRD STRAIGHT PAY DAY AT THE RACE TRACK; NO NEED TO GET GREEDY. GREED GETS CAUGHT. ENJOY.

When he attempted to respond to the text, an error message came back indicating it was a non-operating number.

It was now 9:01 on Saturday, and he called the bank. He was surprised to hear a voice pick up, as he assumed Amuh would beat him to it again. For the third straight day, a deposit of $85.5 million had been placed into his account. His five-day total was just over $259 million.

Even though it was Saturday, he was at the office preparing for the election which was quickly approaching. His phone lay in his lap, and he was slouched in his office chair, looking out over Arlington. He was in disbelief. He spun in his chair and faced his desk. He found his notepad and wrote the number $259,000,000. He was smiling as he stared at it. He then tuned to his computer screen, changed the font to 36 and typed out $259,000,000. Deciding that font was not large enough he changed it to 48 and typed it again. He leaned back in his chair, clasped his hands on top of his head while looking at his screen and slowly said "Ho-ly shit."

Hell to Pay

On Monday October 24th, Barry Ingle was on his way to deliver his final speech as President of the United States to the United Nations.

After the speech, he would be meeting privately with several key UN leaders to discuss the logistics of being named Secretary General of the United Nations immediately upon leaving the White House. He had decided merely holding the title of the US Ambassador to the UN was not enough. The Secretary General's seat was not a cheap one to obtain. During his meetings today, he would be making gifts to several UN Council members who would soon cast their vote on the next Secretary General. The source of his funds for these gifts was the $250 million he was receiving from Stephanie Kenseth. He knew the Secretary General's seat was the best position in the world from which to proselytize climate change and his other pet projects. From this position, he could be expected to raise millions for his soon-to-be-created Center for Climate Change.

Just before arriving at the UN, he received an unexpected and unwanted phone call from his banker.

"President Ingle, I am so sorry to inconvenience you, but I thought this matter required your attention. The $50 million check you deposited

Friday evening is trying to clear your account, and it is being returned insufficient funds. It is written from the same account that $100 million successfully posted from last week."

President Ingle's lips curled in and he cursed under his breath. The checks he was carrying as tribute would be no good if a total of $150 million was not in his account when they posted. This unforeseen issue had the potential to change everything he had planned.

"Thank you, Jimmy. Hold the check and reapply it tomorrow. I'm sure there is just a misunderstanding."

Ingle immediately called Stephanie Kenseth, who was traveling between campaign stops in New York. She saw his name on the caller ID and hesitated before answering. Despite her new-found hatred of her extortioner, she was wary of the damage Ingle could do to her before she became president, and potentially even after. She forced a smile and took the call. "Hello, Mr. President. What can I do for you today?"

Ingle made no attempt to hide his anger. "Kenseth I told you not to fuck with me."

So much for pleasantries, she thought. "What are you talking about?"

"I'm talking about your check not being good, that's what I'm talking about! My bank just called. The check you wrote bounced."

"I'm sure there is a simple explanation. I can assure you there are plenty of funds in that account to cover the check, many times over. Let me call my bank, and I will call you back."

She immediately called Lee Roy, who was at that very moment sitting in his office contemplating how to break the news to Stephanie that a check was trying to clear her account without sufficient funds.

"Hello, this is Lee Roy Butcher."

"Lee Roy, this is Stephanie. How are you today?"

"I am great Mrs. Kenseth, and I hope you are the same. I'm glad you called."

That caught her attention. "Really, why is that?"

"There is a $50 million check trying to clear your account, and your balance is just under $40 million. I need you to make a $10 million deposit to make the check good."

Though a chill went down her spine, Stephanie maintained her calm composure, assuming there was a logical explanation why $850 million was missing from her account.

"Lee Roy, I'm sure there is some kind of error here. There is over $850 million in that account. You need to double check and allow that $50 million check to clear. Change that, first I want you to clear the check, then work on finding your error. I've made commitments to very important people with that $50 million check, and I need to let those people know immediately, as in right now, that the check is good. Tell me you are going to honor that check."

"Do you plan to make a deposit soon, Mrs. Kenseth?"

"Lee Roy, if that is what you need me to say, then yes I am making a deposit soon. I'll make it just as soon as you call me and tell me the account has the money in it that it should have in it."

"Well Mrs. Kenseth, in checking your account activity, there have been several hundred million dollars in withdrawals in the past several days. Over a hundred withdrawals, totaling over $800 million."

Stephanie Kenseth was speechless. She could not believe what she had just heard. She was disarmed. After several seconds of silence, Lee Roy probed her for a response. "Mrs. Kenseth, did you hear me?"

His words helped snap her back to reality. She began yelling. "Lee Roy what the FUCK are you fucking talking about? There should have only been two recent withdrawals, totaling $150 million. What the fuck do you mean $800 million is gone? How the hell is $800 million just all of a sudden gone? Why was I not called and told there was this kind of suspicious activity on my fucking account!?"

"Mrs. Kenseth, you called me several days ago and told me to expect to see money coming out of the account. And that is what we saw. We saw activity consistent with what you told us to expect, so we did not call you."

Stephanie was shaking. Her eyes were closed and her teeth were clenched so hard her jaw was throbbing. She was only able to take quick, shallow breaths. It took her several seconds to compose herself well enough to speak. When she did, she spoke slowly and firmly, with her eyes still closed tightly.

"Lee Roy, here is what you are going to do. First, you are going to cover that check. Second, you are going to find my money and get it back. All of it. You are going to get all of it back, Lee Roy or there is going to be hell to pay. I think you know what I am capable of. Are we clear, Lee Roy?"

Lee Roy Butcher's stomach now felt as deep and bottomless as the ocean. His voice quivered as he spoke.

"We will cover the check, Mrs. Kenseth. And I'll see what I can do about the other issue." He expected a response, but there was none. Stephanie had ended the call as soon as she heard the check was good.

With trembling fingers, she immediately texted President Ingle.

MISTAKE FOUND, SIMPLE BANK ERROR, CHECK IS NOW GOOD.

The response came quickly.

NO MORE SCREW UPS. FBI IS EAGER.

The following day, Lee Roy Butcher received his typical the-sky-is-falling call from Teresa Edwards earlier than normal. It was only 8:30am.

"Yes, Teresa?"

"Good morning, Mr. Butcher." He could tell by the sound quality she was using the speaker phone.

He interrupted, "Teresa who is in the room with you?"

"Well, sir, I was just about to say I'm sitting here with Tammy Scruggs, Head of Deposit Operations. She came upstairs to let me know there is a $50 million check trying to clear the Kenseth Foundation account."

Butcher responded, "That was yesterday, we already cleared that up."

"No, sir. This is an *additional* $50 million check. The payee is either a person or a company called Truman. One word only. The $50 million check you approved yesterday placed the account in a $10 million deficit." She paused for a moment. "Did Mrs. Kenseth tell you when she would be making a deposit to cover that overdraft?"

"No. Tell me what more you have found out about the withdrawals from her account."

"There is nothing additional to add. That $850 million is gone and we cannot retrieve it. The banks it went to won't share any information, and they are not obligated to. They did say some of the accounts have already been closed. The receiving banks will not disclose who owned those accounts without that information being subpoenaed."

Tammy Scruggs enthusiastically took the opportunity to interject. "Many of the receiving banks are foreign. Good luck getting information from them! Has Mrs. Kenseth indicated that she wants to open a criminal probe?"

"No. And don't cover today's $50 million check unless I call you back with other instructions." He ended the call.

Butcher decided to text rather than call Stephanie Kenseth.

> ADDITIONAL $50 MILLION TRYING TO CLEAR
> YOUR ACCOUNT TODAY. ACCOUNT IS
> OVERDRAWN $10 MILLION. NEED DEFICIT
> MADE WHOLE BEFORE ANY ADDITIONAL
> CHECKS CAN BE COVERED.

Within minutes his phone was ringing, and Stephanie Kenseth's name was flashing on the caller ID. He stared at it, and choose to let it keep ringing. Ten minutes and ten unanswered calls later, he turned the phone off. He walked out of his office with his suit jacket still hanging on the back of his door. He didn't speak to anyone as he headed to his car to drive off. He suspected the $10 million overdraft would never be covered, which would cost him his job as CEO. His greater fear, however, was the wrath of Stephanie Kenseth.

Lee Roy Butcher resigned as President of First National Bank of the Everglades two days later. Two days after that, he was seen enjoying a drink at his favorite bar, the White Water Tavern. He left with a woman no one recalled ever seeing there before. The next day, his car was identified at a nearby hotel. His body was found in a room registered to a Mrs. Smith. Based on the needle marks in his arm, the immediate cause of death was presumed to be drug overdose. Whether the drugs were voluntarily or involuntarily taken was never determined.

On October 26th, Stephanie Kenseth received a text from a number she did not recognize. She opened it and determined it's source was Truman. The text read:

> YOUR CHECK BOUNCED. DEAL IS OFF. I HAVE LIQUIDATED THE ORIGINAL $50 MILLION DEPOSIT FOR LACK OF PERFORMANCE ON YOUR PART AND EXPENSES INCURRED TO DATE. GOOD FUCKING LUCK IN THE ELECTION.

That same day, when the final $50 million check bounced, President Ingle held a news conference indicating he was formally allowing the FBI to re-engage their criminal investigation of Stephanie Kenseth. He indicated new evidence had come to light which clearly indicated the investigation must continue, even in the face of criticism that the effort was politically motivated. He used the press conference as an opportunity to indicate he was looking forward to Director Smith resuming the helm at the FBI.

Last Card

"Where's Stephanie?"

"What?"

Amuh leaned in closer to Jeffrey's ear. Though the mood at the New Yorker Hotel was subdued by the incoming election night results, the noise level wasn't. "I said where is Stephanie? I've not seen her in several hours."

"Ah. She's in her room. I'm on my way to go see her in just a minute."

"Do you want company?"

"I'd love some, but I think it's best to not surprise her right now. She texted me a few minutes ago, asked me to come see her. I think it's a business visit. Her text said she wanted to ask me a question."

Amuh gave Jeffrey a look of concern. She had been very uneasy since their successful heist of millions of dollars from the ICSJ account. He returned her look with a flash of his eyes. Though Jeffrey seemed at ease, his unspoken communication did not allay her anxiety. Just as she began to lean in again to continue the conversation, she felt someone's hand on her waist. It was Margaret Kurtz, a longtime donor and friend of Stephanie. Though she was smiling, her eyes were red and the area around them were still moist from fresh tears. They exchanged a long embrace. When they separated and Amuh opened her eyes, Jeffrey was gone.

As the elevator began its ascent, Jeffrey assumed this would be his last meeting with Stephanie for some time, possibly ever. To the extent possible in the last days of a campaign he was responsible for managing, he had been avoiding direct contact with her. For at least a week, the outcome of the election had been a fait accompli, and no amount of orchestration on his part was going to change that. This, coupled with his newfound wealth, had caused him to mentally and emotionally check out of the lost cause, and begin plans for the next phase of his life. This last meeting with Stephanie would be the punctuation on the end of a great partnership.

The bell of the elevator brought Jeffrey back into the moment. He resolutely stepped out and began the walk down the hall. He immediately noticed two unfamiliar Secret Service men seated outside Stephanie's door. He did not recognize them at all. In fact, he wondered if they were actually Secret Service. They were both conspicuously large men. Their suits, which were more expensive than those typically worn by Secret Service, could not hide the fact these men were more than just fit underneath. They were big.

They kept their eyes on him as he approached the room, and he responded in kind. He noticed one of them look at a picture on his phone as he approached. Neither rose to open the door to Stephanie's room, which further caused him to question whether they were Secret Service. Jeffrey offered a curt "Good evening" as he reached for the door handle. One of the men touched two fingers to his forehead and nodded as if to give a salute.

It took a moment for Jeffrey's eyes to adjust to the dim lights inside the large room. Stephanie was standing with her back to him, looking at the city skyline through the large window. The light from the city highlighted the periphery of the white dress she was wearing, giving the impression of an aura around her. Her hands were clasped behind her. In the many years they had worked together, Jeffrey had never thought of Stephanie as elegant. In this moment, seeing only her back against the backdrop of the skyline, elegant seemed inadequate.

As he walked toward the living area, he noted a partially consumed bottle of Scotch on the bar, and two empty glasses on the coffee table between the couch and two chairs in the living area. The presence of a second glass caught his attention. He noted the door to the bedroom was closed, however he saw light escaping from underneath. Has she left the light on or was someone in there? He suddenly became very aware of the lack of control he currently had in this environment. He was uneasy, to the point of being slightly afraid. He stopped shy of entering the living area and decided to force Stephanie to speak first. In the moment, this was the only defensive maneuver he could think of.

Though she never acknowledged Jeffrey's presence in the room, it did not take long for Stephanie to speak. With her face still pointed at the clear barrier between her and the city, she asked "How's the mood?" She paused briefly. "Downstairs. How's the mood?"

She now turned to face Jeffrey. The look of elegance quickly evaporated. Even in the dim light and from several feet away he could see the puffiness around her eyes. Light from the city reflected off the moisture surrounding her eyes. She wore no makeup that he could ascertain. She was barefoot, which made her appear small and almost poor, despite the $4,000 dress she was wearing. In all the years they had worked together, he'd never seen her in a state like this.

Without speaking, she walked toward Jeffrey and sat down on the couch. She motioned with her hand for Jeffrey to take the seat opposite her. As she did this, he noticed her cell phone in her hand. The screen was lit and appeared to be displaying a sent text. He yearned to see who the text was to, but he was too far away.

Stephanie's question and appearance caused him to no longer be aware of the fear he had felt a moment ago. The emotion had been replaced by a sense of guilt. He rarely felt guilt. He felt guilty for having made a bad call on picking Tedie as the loser. Guilt for having checked out emotionally several days before the election when the outcome was inevitable. Guilt for…

No guilt for the money. The money was guaranteed guilt free. The exchange rate at the Bank of Jeffrey Saint was so heavily tilted toward the value of money, no negative sight or emotion stood any chance of counter balance. He had long since reasoned that the money was dirty to begin with and therefore amoral. He would not allow himself to feel any guilt for being clever enough to steal it. As he took the seat across from her, his feelings of guilt were replaced by righteousness.

He took note that the seat was cool; there was no residual body heat, just as there was probably no one in that bedroom. But just as he became comfortable in this thought, he noted a second chair to his left, which was also opposite the couch. He fought the urge to examine it to see if there was a recently created impression in the seat cushion. He determined his best course of action was to simply address Stephanie's question.

"Somber. Melancholy. Everyone is eager to hear from you." His tone was encouraging.

Jeffrey heard Stephanie sigh. Barely audible, he interpreted its meaning to be a whistful "as if..." Stephanie broke eye contact with Jeffrey and turned her face again toward the window. Her chin was resting on the heel of her right hand and her fingers were curled, hiding her mouth.

Jeffrey leaned forward. "Everyone downstairs is very proud of you. With this campaign, you accomplished things no woman in this country ever has before. The people downstairs are hurting, as you are now. They will rally to you, regardless of the election result."

Stephanie turned her face back toward Jeffrey. But the look it contained was now different. The sadness was gone. It had been replaced with anger. "Are you hurting, Jeffrey?"

Jeffrey paused and pulled back slightly. He had not anticipated this question. And now he feared that his reflexive pause would belie his answer. He needed to be crafty. He furled his brow intentionally as if to appear hurt. He locked eye contact for one... two... three seconds before responding. "Stephanie, I cannot believe that you ask me this question. Of course I am hurting. It was my job to run the campaign that successfully placed you in the White House, and we came up short. We are all hurting."

Stephanie was certain that Jeffrey had no clue he had just made this discussion about himself. This emboldened her. She repositioned herself slightly on the couch to square her body toward his. Crossing her legs, she leaned back and placed her clasped hands in her lap. "Jeffrey I just need to know, is there anything you need to tell me?"

Another question Jeffrey had not expected. If it had not been made clear by her body language, he was now certain the conversation had taken a turn, and not in his favor. The fear he had felt entering the room now returned. His mouth was suddenly dry and he could feel his heart beat in his neck. He hoped he could respond in a way that masked the emotions running through his body.

He gathered himself. "No." He allowed his voice to lilt upward when he spoke, intending to indicate the question confused him. "Should I?"

Stephanie now looked more agitated than before. He could feel the distance between them widening. Did she know? How could she know? Tedie had indicated this would all be anonymous. Had they been discovered? Did Amuh make a terrible mistake? His mind was racing as the pit in his stomach grew.

"Jeffrey, you and I have worked together a long time. You are brilliant, valued, and precious to me. And that is the only reason we are having this conversation. I'm going to ask one last time, is there anything you need to tell me?"

He felt alone and exposed. He wondered if he had been betrayed. By who? Was she bluffing? He wasn't sure, but he feared the consequences for him were terrible if she were not. He could not afford to answer that question incorrectly.

In all the time he had known Stephanie Kenseth, he had never fully revealed himself to her. Though a subordinate to one of the most influential women in national politics, he was a master puppeteer. There was a ruse, a subterfuge necessary to have Stephanie think of him as he intended. In order to have her expose her vulnerabilities, he had always acted in a way that would cause her to underestimate him. Like a pistol fighter needing an edge, he knew someday he might need that margin, some small advantage, to escape the clutches of this powerful woman. He felt trapped. So he drew, and fired.

"There is one thing."

Stephanie's face bore a sense of upright satisfaction.

"I have an insurance policy." The look on Stephanie's face changed quickly. "I have in my possession, actually in a safe deposit box, several things which are very valuable."

He paused. He didn't want to go further. He'd never rehearsed this conversation. He hadn't thought it would ever be necessary. Though true, he wondered if it were even believable.

Momentarily dumbfounded, she asked, "What are you talking about? And what the hell does that have to do with this conversation?"

Jeffrey continued awkwardly. He could not look at Stephanie. He looked at the table between them as he spoke deliberately. "Many years ago, a friend of mine was stationed at the Naval Observatory. He was there when William was killed. He called one day and said that as Stephanie Kenseth's campaign director, he had something I should see. So I did. It was a phone that contained pictures of William lying on the floor inside a building, with what looked like two bullet wounds in his chest. He was actually laying on top of a turned over plant, his body was contorted. In one picture, his right hand was reaching up, probably toward the person taking the picture. There was this horrible look of fear and pleading on his face. In other pictures, he looks… dead."

He paused and looked at Stephanie. Her face was void of emotion but her eyes were burgeoning.

He continued, "My friend gave me the phone, and the names of the personnel with you the night William died. Leveraging my friend's credibility, and acting in the capacity as your campaign director, I separately talked with each of them over the course of several months. I pretended to know what had happened, so they spoke to me freely. They were not aware that I was recording the conversations with my phone. It didn't take long to completely put the puzzle together. Two of them gave me Louisa Jenkins' name, the White House maid living in Columbia Heights who you had call the police with a fraudulent account of how William was shot. I recorded my conversation with her, too."

He now looked directly at Stephanie. Her face remained emotionless. It concealed the anger inside of her, anger she was directing at herself. The activity at the Naval Observatory had been very intense in the days following William's death. She had even moved out briefly, and took many of their personal belongings with her when she did. She had not seen the Japanese ambassador's phone since that move. She had assumed (incorrectly, now it seems) the phone was in one of several boxes at her New York home, boxes which she had never opened after William's death.

Jeffrey now went for the close. "Stephanie Kenseth's political identity was inseparable from William's career, until his untimely and unfortunate death. The false narrative surrounding his death was rocket fuel for you as you successfully emerged from his shadows and launched your own political career. I fear it would be devastating to your credibility and any future public or private career you seek to create, should this information become public."

He now stood. "You of all people know how intensely deep and wide my network is, including many members of the press. I have never brought this up to you, because I am loyal to you. But know this, there are two keys to the safe deposit box containing the phones and pictures and recordings. They are held by two different dear friends who are well placed in the media community. Neither knows there is an additional key. Either key will open the box. Both of these individuals have standing instructions that should I mysteriously disappear, or upon my natural or unnatural death, they may have the contents of the box."

Stephanie remained silent and emotionless as Jeffrey turned and walked to the door. In the midst of her greatest disappointment, Jeffrey's words had caused the pain of William's death to be fresh again. She closed her eyes hard, in an unsuccessful attempt to prevent the tears from escaping.

Jeffrey's heart was racing as he tried to maintain a steady pace down the hall toward the elevator. He had just played his last card. He would not consider the play a win until he was on the elevator and out of the building. Once there, he would call Amuh.

As he approached the elevator, he heard its bell ding. Fortuitous timing, he thought. To his great surprise, Ahuh stepped out and began walking toward him. Not knowing how much Stephanie actually knew, and working under the assumption they were being watched, he thought it prudent that he and Amuh keep up appearances and simply pass in the hall.

However, as they got closer to each other, Amuh raised her left hand to reveal her phone and its screen. It looked like the text message screen. What was she trying to communicate? That she too had been summoned to Stephanie's room? Was it Amuh that Stephanie had messaged just a few moments ago? Or was Amuh simply asking Jeffrey to send her a text about what had happened?

As they passed in the hall, they made direct eye contact. Amuh looked afraid. Jeffrey tried to convey calm, and raised his left hand as if to return a 'wave' she had just given him. But with his right hand, he was quickly reaching for his phone. He knew he only had a few seconds to text her before she reached Stephanie's door.

Standing outside the open elevator door, he frantically searched for his last text to her. Relieved, he found it quickly and typed:

I TOLD HER NOTHING

He hit send and looked to his right, watching as Amuh got closer and closer to Stephanie's door. Why wasn't she looking at her phone? As he stood there watching and waiting for Amuh to receive his text, he heard the elevator door begin to close. He was aware one member of the security detail was looking at him with a puzzled look. He had to make a decision. Why was Amuh not checking her phone? He stepped onto the elevator just before it closed.

Where Did You Hide?

One of President Tedie's first calls after the inauguration was to Jeffrey. It was the first time they had communicated since their successful liberation of the Foundation's money, and the first time they had spoken on-record in months. Jeffrey took the call immediately.

"Hello, and congratulations, Mr. President."

"Thank you, Jeffrey you are very kind. I guess I do owe all of this to you and your brilliance with the PTL Committee."

Jeffrey laughed. "Angry White Man did quite well for himself."

"Indeed, he did. In more ways than one. I guess I really did make sure Stephanie got scholnged. Anyway, Jeffrey, I'm in need of a highly professional and competent Chief of Staff, and I can't think of anyone I'd rather have in the role than you. Will answer the call and serve your President and your country? I'll be honest; the pay isn't great, but for a man in your position that should not be an issue. Will you agree to be the first openly gay Presidential Chief of Staff?"

Jeffrey was stunned. It took him a moment to respond. "Mr. President, I am truly honored and humbled by your gracious offer. But alas, I must pass.

I think I'm going to exit politics for a while. I may even go buy myself an island."

"I can't say as I blame you. You let me know when you need a hotel on that island. I will make you a very good deal."

"I'm sure you will, Mr. Tedie. Watch out for yourself as president. Lots of danger in Camelot."

"Indeed Jeffrey, indeed."

"One last comment Mr. Tedie, if I may. There are rumors that you will pardon Stephanie, pending the outcomes of the hearings and potential trial. I hope you will."

Jeffrey could not see Colton Tedie nodding his head. "So noted Jeffrey. And I admire your concern for your former boss."

Stephanie Kenseth made what was assumed to be her final appearance before the congressional commission on Monday April 3rd, 2017. They were investigating the millions of dollars of conflict of interest payments made into the ICSJ Foundation. Having lost the election, and now without any political cover to protect her, many individuals, groups, and even governments had come forward to admit they had provided what were essentially bribes in exchange for Mrs. Kenseth's favor when she became president. This was presumed to be her last appearance, because the FBI was expected to formally charge Mrs. Kenseth with many crimes, even potentially treason, the following day.

Mrs. Kenseth knew this was probably her last chance to be in control of the stage, to be the one molding her current public image and future legacy. She had spent weeks preparing for this opportunity. She had notes on each and every donation made to her Foundation. She would rely on the Foundation's Charter, which was to do good in the world, as her shield from attack. She would use her gender, age, and defeat in the election as her shield. She was prepared for any question about the Foundation, or at least she thought she was. Just as Tedie had used his speech at the Republican Convention to alter fate, she hoped to use her testimony today to alter hers and avoid incarceration.

Chairman Tripp Downey of South Carolina called the hearing to order. Before formal comments and questions could commence, the ranking Democrat on the committee demanded the right to make a defense of Mrs. Kenseth and impugn the inquiry as a political witch hunt. Mr. Downey acknowledged the ranking Democrat and indicated his time would come. But as chairman, it was his privilege to ask the first question and he planned to exercise that privilege.

Turning to Mrs. Kenseth he said, "Mrs. Kenseth I only have one prepared question to ask you today."

Realizing that she who asks the questions controls the conversation, and forgetting that it was in her best interest in this moment to appear humble, Stephanie Kenseth responded, "Lay it on me. What is that question, Mr. Chairman?" Her hands were clasped in front of her, and her forearms were resting on the table.

Mr. Downey showed no reaction to her flippancy. He continued, "Ms. Kenseth, where in the hell did you hide $800 million? Scores of forensic accountants have identified how many donations were made to the ICSJ Foundation, and the parties who made the donations, as well as the amounts of the donations. But none of those forensic accountants have been able to determine where you hid that money. So, please tell us, where did you hide $800 million?"

For all the hours she had spent preparing, Stephanie Kenseth had not anticipated this question. Momentarily, her vision blurred and she lost sight of the committee sitting only a few feet in front of her. Like two animals fighting over the same carcass, the desire to laugh and cry welled up in her simultaneously. She was at a loss for words, a place she rarely found herself in. Her entire career raced through her mind. The early excitement of being married to William. They had both been so idealistic in the early days. Then there was the rush of being the Governor's wife. The power. The affairs. The pain. The separate careers. The riches. And now the agony. She longed for William.

She was unaware of how long she was absorbed in that fog. She was pulled from her reflection by the Chairman's stern voice.

"Ms. Kenseth, are you going to keep us in suspense all day? I want to know, the American public *deserves* to know, where is all that money?"

Outwardly, she wore the smile of a person who knows a secret. She *did* know a secret, just not the one the chairman cared about.

Opening her mouth to speak, she was aware she was about to do something she had never done as one being pursued. She was about to give a straight and truthful answer. She chuckled slightly, which caused the right corner of her mouth to rise and form a slight smile despite the lone tear rolling down toward it. She slowly raised her gaze from the table in front of her to look Mr. Downey square in the eye.

"I wish I knew, Mr. Chairman. I wish I knew."

■■

Amuh watched the drama of the hearing unfold on satellite television. She was saddened to the point of tears. She bore no ill will toward her former boss, and she felt no small measure of guilt for having stolen from her. Just then, she heard Jeffrey's voice calling out from beyond the sailboat's cabin door.

"I'm taking the dingy to the marina, love. You want anything?"

She paused before answering. "Yes, yes I do. We need to talk."

About the Author

Jerrell Deaver is a native and current resident of North Carolina, and is a decades-long student of the political environment in the United States. He sincerely hopes you find your time and monetary investment in this book to be worthwhile.

He is also the author of *I Didn't Know THAT Was in the Bible.*

Reviews of this book are always appreciated. Please share your thoughts at www.facebook.com/ahugedirtypileofmoney